"SIT BACK AND ENJOY.
An outrageously wild and disparate cast . . .
range over the Holy Land and other parts, and
somehow seem to connect in their highly original
ways. . . . Sophisticated, surreal fun with
a cutting edge."
Publishers Weekly

"WHITTEMORE IS A MASTER
of deadpan, fanciful falsifications—rewriting
history and populating it with a brigade of
unequivocally odd, oddly endearing movers and
shakers . . . cosmic coincidences, and only the
driest comic touches propel Whittemore's
dervishes round and round in a whirl that's as
blessedly straightforward in style as it is subtly
provocative in its inventions."
Kirkus Reviews

"OLYMPIAN IMAGINATION . . .
Whittemore is to Vonnegut what a
tapestry is to a cat's cradle."
Rhoda Lerman

Sinai Tapestry

Edward Whittemore

AVON
PUBLISHERS OF BARD, CAMELOT AND DISCUS BOOKS

AVON BOOKS
A division of
The Hearst Corporation
959 Eighth Avenue
New York, New York 10019

First Avon Printing, July, 1978

AVON TRADEMARK REG. U.S. PAT. OFF. AND IN
OTHER COUNTRIES, MARCA REGISTRADA,
HECHO EN U.S.A.

Printed in Canada

For Cat

Contents

PART ONE

1.	Strongbow	3
2.	Wallenstein	25
3.	Cairo 1840	44
4.	Sinai 1836–1843	56
5.	The Haj	65
6.	YHWH	93
7.	The Tiberias Telegrams	102

PART TWO

8.	O'Sullivan Beare	121
9.	Haj Harun	136
10.	The Scarab	155
11.	Maud	171
12.	Aqaba	180
13.	Jericho	185

PART THREE

14.	Stern	193
15.	The Jordan	209
16.	Jerusalem 700 B.C.–1932	234

Contents

17. *The Bosporus*   244
18. *Melchizedek 2200 B.C.–1933*   265
19. *Athens*   269
20. *Smyrna 1922*   279
21. *Cairo 1942*   302

PART ONE

I

Strongbow

Standing straight out in front of him, thick and menacing, was a medieval lance twelve feet long.

The Arabic Jew, or Jewish Arab, who owned the entire Middle East at the turn of the century passed his early life exactly as had his English forebears for six hundred and fifty years.

At the family estate in southern England he was taught to care for flowers, especially roses. His parents died while he was young and his aunts and uncles moved into the manor to raise him. In due time he would receive his title and become the twenty-ninth Plantagenet Strongbow to bear it, merely one more Duke of Dorset.

For it seemed that destiny had found a resting place among the Strongbows. At one time, thought to be about 1170, one of their line had helped subdue eastern Ireland and been given a title because of it. Since then the family had lapsed into patterns. Confusion had been lost or forgotten. Instead there was repetition and order.

The oldest son in each generation always married on the day he assumed his majority and became the new lord. His wife matched him in wealth and shared his concern for flowers. Children appeared at regular intervals until five or six had been born, more or less equally divided between males and females. By that time the duke and his duchess were thirty, or nearly thirty, and both abruptly died by accident.

The accidents were routinely silly. After drinking an excess of mead late at night they might fall asleep and fall into the fireplace. Or they might doze off in a trout stream and drown in a foot of water.

Following the flight of a butterfly after breakfast, they would wander off a parapet. Or they would absentmindedly swallow a mutton joint whole, causing suffocation. Or a mild sexual diversion such as dressing up in medieval armor would lead to fatal hemorrhaging in the pelvic region.

In any case both husband and wife died at the same time, at about the age of thirty, and it was then the duty of the deceased lord's younger brothers and sisters to return to the manor to rear their five or six nieces and nephews.

It was a family custom that these younger brothers and sisters never married, but being close in age they had no difficulty resettling in the manor of their childhood and enjoying one another's company. At the beginning of the Christmas season they gathered together in the large banquet hall for twelve days of festivities that had come to be called the family game, a traditional sport in which the hall was cleared of furniture and opposing teams were formed with the goal of running a satin pillow from one end of the hall to the other.

During the first hour of play each day intensive grappling was permitted. But thereafter a firm grip on the genitals of an opposing player was sufficient to stop the advance of the pillow and bring on a new scrimmage for its possession.

Under these conditions, despite their wealth and genuine concern for flowers, it was unlikely the Dukes of Dorset would ever have distinguished themselves in the world even if they had lived beyond the age of thirty, and in fact none ever did.

From the end of the twelfth century until the beginning of the nineteenth century, successive Plantagenet Strongbows grew up with a sound knowledge of roses and a vague memory of their parents, learned the family game by watching their aunts and uncles, passed into manhood and sired an heir and a new brood of aunts and uncles before succumbing to another silly accident, thereby perpetuating a random family scheme which was their sole contribution to God and man and England.

Until in 1819, the year of Queen Victoria's birth, a different sort of infant was born in the Dorset manor, different either because of a mutation in genes or because of the terrible disease he suffered at the age of eleven. In any case this slight boy would one day end six hundred and fifty years of placid Strongbow routine by becoming the most awesome explorer his country ever produced.

And coincidently the most scandalous scholar of his era. For whereas other famous theoreticians of the nineteenth century formulated vast, but separate, concepts of the mind and body and society, Strongbow insisted on dealing with all three.

That is, with sex in its entirety.

Not sex as necessity or diversion or in the role of precursor and memory, not even sex as an immediate cause or a vague effect. And certainly not in terms of natural history or inevitable law.

Sex neither as habit nor suggestion but simply sex by itself, unplanned and chaotic and concomitant with nothing, beyond all hope of conspiracy, previously indistinguishable and now seen in infinity.

Sex as practiced. Sex as it was.

At the time, an inconceivable proposition.

* * *

In addition to the family game in Strongbow Hall there was also a family mystery. In a manor so old it was only to be expected that some arcane relationship must exist between the structure and its inhabitants, its source secret, probably a hidden sliding panel that opened onto dark passageways leading down into the past.

In fact the huge manor was said to include in its foundations the ruins of a major medieval monastery, unnamed, thought to have been desecrated when its monks were discovered practicing certain unmentionable acts. And close beside those ruins were the ruins of an underground Arthurian chamber, vaulted and impregnable, which had also been desecrated when its knights were discovered practicing other unmentionable acts.

Even deeper in the ground, according to legend, there were the ruins of a spacious sulphur bath only fitfully dormant, built during the age of the Romans.

Next to these baths was a small but impressive sacrificial circle of stones from the even more distant era of the druids.

While lastly, surrounding all these subterranean relics, was an immense erratic design of upright monoliths, astronomical in nature, erected in antiquity by a mighty people.

No one had ever discovered the secret passageways that led to these buried remnants beneath the manor, even though they had always been hunted. For centuries Strongbow aunts and uncles, on rainy afternoons, had armed themselves with torches and organized search parties to try to find them.

Of course minor discoveries had been made. In any given decade a group might come across a cozy unused tower cubicle heaped with furry rugs or a small snug cellar hideaway just big enough for three people.

But the family mystery remained. Tradition claimed

the secret sliding panel might well be found in the dark library of the manor, yet strangely Strongbow aunts and uncles never led their search parties there. When a rainy afternoon came they invariably went in other directions.

Thus the aunts and uncles who became the overseers of the manor early in the nineteenth century might have sensed irrevocable changes afoot when they saw the eldest of their wards, the future lord, spending his afternoons in the deserted library.

The awful truth became clear when the boy was eleven, on the winter night set aside each year for the family's heritage to be recounted by the older generation to the younger. On that night everyone gathered in front of the great fireplace after dinner, the aunts and uncles with their snifters of brandy, sitting solemnly in large chairs, the boys and girls absolutely still on cushions on the floor. Outside the wind howled. Inside the little children stared wide-eyed at the crackling logs as the ancient lore of the place was recounted.

A shadowy medieval monastery, began an aunt or an uncle. Hooded figures thrusting yellow tapers aloft. Chants in archaic syllables, incense and bats, rites at the foot of a black altar.

Underground chambers from the age of King Arthur, whispered another. Masked knights riding through the mists in eternal pursuit of invisible combat.

Roman legions fresh from the land of the pharaohs, hinted a third. Barbaric foreign gods and pagan battle standards. Luxurious baths wreathed in steam behind the walls of sumptuous palaces.

Druidical rituals, suggested a fourth. Naked priests painted blue clinging to mistletoe, a single towering oak in a lost grove, apparitions in the gloom on the moors. From the deeper recesses of the forest, eerie birdlike cries.

And long before that, whispered another, massive

7

stones placed on the plains in a mystical pattern. The stones so gigantic no ordinary people could have transported them. Who were these unknown people and what was the purpose of their abstract designs? Yes truly we must ponder these enigmas for they are the secrets of our ancestors, to be recalled tonight as so often over the centuries.

Indeed, murmured an uncle. So it has always been and so it must be. These undying marvels are hidden in the ancient library of our manor, reared by the first Duke of Dorset, and there lies the secret within all of us, the impenetrable Strongbow Mystery.

A rustle passed around the fireplace. The children shivered and huddled closer together as the wind whined. No one dared think of the maze of lost passageways spiraling down into the earth beneath them.

A thin voice broke the silence, the voice of the future lord.

No.

Sitting erect, farther from the fire than anyone else, the boy gazed gravely at the heavy swords suspended above the mantle.

No, he repeated, that's not quite correct. In the last year I've read all the books in the library and there's nothing like that there. The first Plantagenet Strongbow was a simple man who went to Ireland and had the usual success slaughtering unarmed peasants, then retired here to polish his armor and do some farming. The early books he collected were about armor, later there were a few dealing with barnyard matters. So it seems the family mystery is simply that no one has ever read a book from the family library.

The disease that felled him the following day was meningitis, which killed his younger brothers and sisters. Thus there would be no aunts and uncles in the next generation and a comfortable routine dating from the reign of Henry II was suddenly shattered.

In its place lay a sickly wasted boy, dying, who made up his mind to do what no Strongbow had ever done, to enter confusion and not let destiny rest. His first decision was to live and as a result he became totally deaf. His second decision was to become the world's leading authority on plants, since at that early age he wasn't fond of people.

Before the attack of meningitis his height had been average. But the revelations that came with the approach of death, and his subsequent bargaining with fate, brought other changes. By the time he was fourteen he would be well over six feet tall, and by the age of sixteen he would have reached his full height of seven feet and seven inches.

Naturally his aunts and uncles were utterly bewildered by these strange events in his twelfth year, yet they tried to go on living as the Strongbows had always lived. Therefore while he lay recovering in bed, it being the Christmas season, they gathered in the great banquet hall for the customary pillow match. And although fearful and disturbed they bravely carried on as usual, resolutely polishing family tradition just as the first duke had once polished his armor.

While the furniture was being cleared away they picked their teams and playfully jostled one another, smiling and nodding and politely guffawing and lightly patting a bottom or two, patiently forming queues and just as patiently reforming them a moment later, stolidly standing one behind the other as they commented on the rain and tittered hopelessly in agreement.

The hour closed to a few minutes before midnight on Christmas Eve, what should have been the beginning of twelve companionable days of nuzzling and scrimmaging. But when the playing field was cleared, precisely when the satin pillow was ceremoniously

placed in the middle of the floor and the fun was
ready to begin, a dreadful silence swept through the
hall.

They turned. In the doorway stood their gaunt
nephew, already an inch or two taller than they
remembered him. Standing straight out in front of
him, thick and menacing, was a medieval lance twelve
feet long.

The boy went directly to the middle of the room,
skewered the satin pillow and hurled it into the fireplace, where it burst and blazed briefly. Then in words
alternately booming and inaudible, for he hadn't yet
learned to modulate his voice without hearing it, he
announced they were all dismissed from his house
and lands forever. Any aunt or uncle found on the
premises when the clock struck midnight, he shouted,
would receive the same punishment as the pillow.

There were shrieks and a rush to the door as the
future Duke of Dorset, twenty-ninth in his line, calmly
ordered the furniture returned to its place and assumed control of his life.

Young Strongbow's first act was to make an in-
ventory of the artifacts in the manor. With his
botanist's interest in cataloguing he wanted to know
exactly what he had inherited, so with a ledger in one
hand and a pen in the other he went from room to
room noting everything.

What he found appalled him. The manor was an
immense mausoleum containing no less than five
hundred thousand separate objects acquired by his
family in the course of six hundred and fifty years of
doing nothing.

There and then he decided never to encumber his
life with material goods, which was the real reason,
not vanity, that when the time came for him to disappear into the desert at the age of twenty-one, he

did so carrying only his magnifying glass and portable sundial.

But such extreme simplicity was for the future. Now he had to master his profession. Methodically he sealed off the rest of the manor and moved into the central hall, which he equipped as a long botanical laboratory. Here he lived austerely for six years, at the age of sixteen writing to the Rector of Trinity College stating that he was prepared to take up residence at Cambridge to receive a degree in botany.

The letter was brief, attached to it was a summary of his qualifications.

Fluent ability in Early and Middle Persian, hieroglyphics and cuneiform and Aramaic, classical and modern Arabic, the usual knowledge of Greek and Hebrew and Latin and the European tongues, Hindi where relevant and all sciences where necessary for his work.

Lastly, as an example of some research already undertaken, he enclosed a short monograph on the ferns to be found on his estate. The Rector of Trinity had the paper examined by an expert, who declared it the most definitive study on ferns ever written in Britain. The monograph was published by the Royal Society as a special bulletin and thus Strongbow's name, one day to be synonymous with rank depravity, made its first quiet appearance in print.

Almost at once three sensational incidents made Strongbow a legend at Cambridge. The first occurred on Halloween, the second over a two-week period prior to the Christmas holiday, the third on the night of the winter solstice.

The Halloween incident was a fistfight with the most vicious brawlers in the university. After drinking quantities of stout these notorious young men had adjourned to an alley to pummel each other in the autumn moonlight. A crowd gathered and bets were taken while the sweating fighters stripped to the waist.

The alley was narrow. Strongbow happened to enter it just as the brawlers went into a crouch. Having spent a long day in the countryside collecting specimens, the wild flowers he now carried in his hand, he was too exhausted to turn back. Politely he asked the mass of fighters to stand aside and let him pass. There was a brief silence in the alley, then a round of raucous laughter. Strongbow's bouquet of flowers was knocked to the ground.

Wearily he knelt in the moonlight and retrieved his specimens from the chinks in the cobblestones. When he had them all he moved forward, flowers in one hand and the other arm flailing.

Because of his extraordinary reach not a blow fell on him. In seconds a dozen men lay crumpled on the pavement, all with broken bones and several with concussions. The stunned onlookers pressed against the walls as Strongbow carefully dusted off his flowers, rearranged his bouquet and continued down the alley to his rooms.

The second incident involved England's national fencing tournament, which was to be held at Cambridge that year. Although unknown as a fencer Strongbow applied to enter the preliminaries to the tournament, a kind of exhibition for amateurs, on the basis of letters of recommendation from two Italian masters with international reputations. When asked which event he wished to enter he said all three, foil and épée and sabre as well.

The proposal would have been ridiculous even if he had studied privately under two masters. But in the end he was allowed to enter all three classes because the letters from the Italians, as he pointed out, failed to mention which event was his specialty.

Actually none of them was, nor had he ever studied under the two Italians or anyone else. A year earlier, aware that his rapid growth might render him awkward, he had decided to improve his balance. Fencing seemed as useful as any exercise for that, so he read the classical manuals on fencing and dueled with himself in front of a mirror an hour each day.

The time came for him to go up to Cambridge. While passing through London he learned that two famous Italian masters were in the city instructing members of the royal family. Curious about several techniques he was using that didn't seem to be in any of the manuals, he offered the Italians a large sum of money to pass some judgment on his moves.

An hour was duly arranged. The masters watched him do his exercises in front of a mirror and wrote the letters of praise he carried on to Cambridge.

But secretly the two men were less enthusiastic than alarmed by what they had witnessed. Both realized Strongbow's unorthodox style of fighting was revolutionary and perhaps unbeatable. Therefore they canceled their engagements and left London that same night to return home in the hope of eventually mastering his techniques themselves.

At Cambridge, meanwhile, the national tournament opened early in December. Refusing to wear a mask because he wasn't used to one and refusing to reveal his methods, Strongbow won straight matches in the foil and épée and sabre and advanced from the preliminaries into the main competition. There he continued to fight maskless and continued to win with as much ease as ever.

At the end of two busy weeks he had reached the finals in all three events, itself an unprecedented accomplishment. The finals were meant to occupy most of a weekend but Strongbow insisted they be held one after another. All together they took less then fifteen minutes. In that fierce span of time Strongbow consecutively disarmed his three masked opponents while himself receiving only one slight prod in the neck.

Furthermore, two of the champions he defeated had dislocated wrists by the end of their matches.

In less than fifteen minutes Strongbow had proved himself the greatest swordsman in English history.

Having done so, he never entered a fencing contest again. The cause for this was assumed to be his extreme arrogance, already unbearable to many. But the truth was simply that Strongbow had stopped growing. He no longer needed a special exercise and had given up the tiresome practice of parrying with himself in front of a mirror.

He never lost his style as a swordsman, however, and decades later it was still distinct enough to betray his true identity, as nearly happened in a tiny oasis in Arabia more than forty years after he left Cambridge.

Strongbow was then over sixty and living as the poorest sort of bedouin. The oasis was on the haj route from Damascus and one day Strongbow had to move quickly to turn aside a murderer's sword, which he did, causing the murderer to wound himself. Then he squatted on the ground and began to bind the man's wound.

Traveling in the caravan that year was Numa Numantius, the German erotic scholar and defender of homosexuality, who happened to witness the performance and was astounded by it. At once he led his Arab dragoman over to Strongbow.

Who are you really? asked the German, his interpreter repeating the words in Arabic. Strongbow replied meekly in an ignorant bedouin dialect that he was what he appeared to be, a starving man of the desert whose only cloak was the arm of Allah.

Numantius, the leading Latinist of the day and an exceedingly gentle man, said he knew for a fact only two European fencing masters had ever been able to execute that particular technique, both Italians now dead, and that although no one else in the Levant might be able to recognize the wizardry it implied, he certainly was. For emphasis he even gave the maneuver its official Latin designation. The interpreter repeated all this to Strongbow, who merely shrugged and went on binding the wound. Numantius was growing more curious.

But master, whispered the interpreter, how can such a one be expected to answer? Look at his filth and his rags. He's a wretch and a dog and that was a lucky blow, nothing more. Surely there can be no learning of any kind in such a brute.

But there is, said Numantius. How it can be I don't know and it's making me dizzy just to think of it. So please tell him if he swears by his God he has never heard of these two Italians, I'll give him a Maria Theresa crown.

The words were repeated in Arabic and a large crowd gathered. The money offered was a fortune in the desert and there was no way a poor bedouin could be expected to refuse it. But Strongbow had never sworn falsely in his life. Thus there was a more lengthy exchange between him and the interpreter.

What does he say? asked Numantius in awe. Does he swear?

No, he doesn't swear. In fact he says he once knew these two men in his youth.

What?

Yes, in a dream. In this dream he went to a large city from a large estate he owned. In that large city he hired these two men to watch him use a sword, and that was when they learned the secret of this particular maneuver as well as others. And he adds that since it was truly his secret in the beginning, what you saw him do here a few minutes ago was original and real, whereas what you saw those two Europeans do years

15

ago was imitation and unreal. And all this he says in a language so barbaric it is almost impossible to understand him.

Numantius staggered.

Original and real? Imitation and unreal? What gibberish is this? What madness?

Just that, whispered the interpreter hurriedly as he and the frightened crowd fell back. Now quickly, master, we must leave. His eyes, don't you see it?

And indeed Strongbow's eyes were rolling in his head, his head was swaying on his shoulders and his whole body had begun to shake uncontrollably. He was sending himself into a dervish trance, a trick he had learned long ago when he first came to the desert and the impenetrability of his disguises might have been in danger. As he knew, no Arab would remain close to a dervish suddenly possessed by spirits.

The crowd withdrew muttering charms and a dazed Numantius retreated with them fearing he might be a victim of brain fever, rejoining the caravan and leaving behind the only opportunity there would ever be to discover what had really happened to the young Duke of Dorset after his shockingly obscene disappearance in Cairo on the eve of Queen Victoria's twenty-first birthday.

But it was the third incident at Cambridge that was most significant to Strongbow in the end because it involved the Secret Seven, or the Immortals as they were also known.

This undergraduate society had been founded in 1327 to mourn the passing of Edward II after a hot poker had been thrust up the king's anus. Through legacies the society had gradually grown in wealth until its endowments surpassed those of any other private institution in Britain. It supported numerous orphanages and hospitals and commissioned portraits of its members for the National Gallery.

The protection it provided its members was absolute and perpetual. If a member happened to die in a remote corner of the Empire his body was immediately pickled in the finest cognac and brought home at the society's expense.

Among its alumni were kings and prime ministers, scores of bishops and battalions of admirals and generals, as well as many country gentlemen who had never been known for anything other than certain eccentric dealings with their valets. The alumni of the Secret Seven, in short, constituted the richest and most influential old-boy network in the land.

Of all the masturbation societies in the public schools and universities of England, none could match its enduring prestige.

As indicated by its name, only seven undergraduates were members at any one time, their term running from midnight on a winter solstice to midnight on the following winter solstice, when a new group of seven was chosen. During their year as members the reigning Seven, other than engaging in masturbation, spent their time discussing the merits of their potential successors.

The Christmas holidays began well before election night but all Cambridge undergraduates in Britain, by secret agreement according to tradition, sneaked back to their university rooms by devious routes on the day of the winter solstice. There every gate and door was left unlocked and no one stirred in the wild hope of a miracle. The Seven were known to begin their visits at eleven o'clock at night under cover of darkness and end an hour later, the last man chosen being the most illustrious of the new group and its future leader.

Thus Strongbow, who hadn't bothered to interrupt

his research with the Christmas holidays, was sitting
in his rooms one winter night perusing a botanical
treatise in Arabic when seven loud knocks struck his
door. The handle then turned but nothing happened.
Strongbow's door was locked. He had just emerged
from a bath and, still warm, hadn't bothered to dress
yet.

Of course he didn't hear the knocks but he did
notice the handle turning ineffectually. He went over
to investigate and immediately seven young men filed
into the room and drew themselves up in a row. They
didn't seem surprised by his nakedness but the leader
of the group spoke his classical Greek in a confused
tone of voice.

Your door was locked.

That's right.

But it's midnight on the winter solstice.

Correct. And so?

But don't you know what happens on this special
night?

I know we have more night than any other night,
but who are you anyway? Amateur astronomers?

You mean you don't *know* who we are?

No.

The Secret Seven, announced the leader in a hushed
voice.

My God man, thundered Strongbow, I can see you're
seven but what's your infernal secret?

You mean you've never even heard of us?

No.

But we're the most ancient and honored secret
society in England.

Well what's your secret? What kind of a society is it?

A masturbation society, said the leader with dignity.

Strongbow roared with laughter.

Masturbation? Is that all? What's so secret about
that? And why in God's name are we speaking Greek?

18

You are elected, intoned the seven young men in unison.

I am? To what?

Our society. The Seven Immortals.

Immortal you say? Because you masturbate?

The Seven were stunned. There had never been any question of explaining their society to anyone, let alone justifying its purpose. They stood in line speechless. Strongbow smiled.

The Seven Sages of Greece, are you? How often do you meet to exchange your wisdom?

Two evenings a week.

Not enough, said Strongbow. Am I to confine myself to masturbating only two evenings a week? Ridiculous.

No one's confined. That's just when we meet formally.

But why be formal about it at all? A ludicrous notion.

The leader began talking about charity and fraternity. He even mentioned kings and archbishops and famous statesmen who had been members of the society, but all these impressive names Strongbow waved aside with a long sweep of his arm.

Listen, o wise men. Masturbation is certainly relaxing, but why have a society for it and one that is secret at that? Nonsense. Pure farce.

You don't mean you're refusing election, stammered the leader.

Of course that's what I mean. What an absurdity.

But no one has refused election in five hundred years.

Distinctly odd. Now I've cooled down from my bath and I think I should dress and get along with my duties. The chapter I'm reading has to do with *Solanum nigrum*, probably known to you as deadly nightshade, composed in Cordoba in 756, learned but not quite right. Shall I explain the irregularities to you? We'll have to switch from Greek to Arabic but of course you can carry on with your usual activities.

The door opened. The seven young men slinked away into the longest night of 1836. Midnight had come and gone and in refusing to accept immortality Strongbow had insufferably effronted over three hundred of the most powerful Englishmen of his day, not to mention the memories of another three thousand dead heroes of his race, an insult that would be well remembered nearly half a century later when he published his monumental thirty-three-volume study entitled *Levantine Sex.*

Nor was it merely his intellectual ferocity, his savage fighting skills or his insolent disregard for tradition that caused him to be viewed as dangerous at Cambridge. There was also his unfathomable manner.

For of course no one realized Strongbow was deaf and that he could only understand others by reading their lips. Therefore anyone outside his field of vision was ignored as if nonexistent, just as any event occurring behind his back was ignored as if nonexistent.

There was the disturbing occasion in the spring, for example, when a heavy downpour caused half the botanical laboratory at Cambridge to collapse at dawn. The laboratory was thought to be empty but the thunderous crash was so great the entire university rushed to the spot within minutes.

What they saw standing on what had once been the third floor, the precipice only a few inches behind his feet, was Strongbow bent over a microscope studying the lines of a new spring leaf, oblivious to the destruction that had jolted everyone from their beds.

Strongbow's concentration, in sum, was frighteningly aloof and apart. Because of his unnatural height he bore only a distorted resemblance to a man and the only voices he seemed to hear were those of plants.

In other eras he might have been burned at the stake as the Antichrist, and undoubtedly it was only because his nineteenth-century world was so rational that he was merely regarded as exceptionally perverse, maniacal and un-English.

But significantly, it was this very rationality that Strongbow would one day assault with such devastating results.

His career at Cambridge culminated in an episode both brilliant and typical, yet so extravagant it was considered intolerable by many, including the Archbishop of Canterbury and possibly the new monarch then awaiting her coronation, Queen Victoria.

Strongbow stood for his tripos examinations at the end of one year rather than the customary three, and his achievement was such that he had to be awarded a triple first, the only time that ever happened in an English university. As a parting gift to English scholarship he proceeded to announce he had discovered a new species of rose on the banks of the Cam.

Even if proposed quietly the discovery would have been shocking. In a land devoted to roses it seemed unthinkable that six centuries of British scholars could have gone punting on the Cam and entirely overlooked a species.

But the proposal wasn't made quietly. Instead Strongbow noisily nailed it to the chapel door one Sunday morning just as the service ended and the faculty began to appear.

The uproar throughout the nation was immediate. An official board of experts was convened, to be chaired by the Archbishop of Canterbury, who would cast a deciding vote should that ultimate resort to fair play become necessary.

Strongbow's evidence, arranged in ninety-five theses, was removed from the chapel door and studied in full by the board. The Latin was impeccable and to their dismay they found there was nothing to consider or vote on. The discovery was genuine. There was simply no way to assign the rose to any of the existing species.

And as its discoverer Strongbow had the inalienable right to name it.

The archbishop led a select delegation to Strongbow's rooms. After congratulating him warmly the archbishop eased into a persuasive discourse. A new rose had been found for England, a new monarch was soon to be crowned from the House of Hanover. How magnanimous it was of God, working through a brilliant young scholar and nobleman, to bless the land and Her Britannic Majesty at this time, in this manner.

While the archbishop spoke Strongbow remained bent over his workbench examining a blade of grass with his enormous magnifying glass. When the archbishop finished Strongbow straightened to his full height, still holding the glass in place, and stared down at the delegation.

Behind the powerful lens of the magnifying glass his unblinking eye was two inches wide.

During his year at Cambridge Strongbow's disgust with his family's history had fully matured. He could no longer abide the memory of the silly accidents that had killed twenty-eight successive Dukes of Dorset, the silly aunts and uncles who had been returning to the manor for centuries to raise its orphans, the silly family mystery which was just another name for illiteracy, above all the silly sexuality that had gone by the name of the family game.

At the same time he had grown increasingly contemptuous toward England, which he found too small and prim and petty for his needs. And being still young, he preferred to believe his country was more to blame than his family for six hundred and fifty years of Strongbow silliness.

So his enormous eye rested on the archbishop and his speech was short.

Your Grace has made reference to the House of Hanover, Germans who arrived here some five hundred and forty years after my own dukedom was established. It is certainly true the Plantagenet Strongbows did nothing for England in six and a half centuries, but at least they had the decency to do it on English soil. Therefore we will honor that soil and Victoria of Hanover by naming this discovery the *rosa exultata plantagenetiana.* Thank you for coming, and thank you for recognizing the inevitable existence of this rare flower.

Nothing more was said on either side of the workbench. The huge eye continued to hover near the ceiling as the shrunken delegates crept out the door.

Strongbow immediately disappeared from England, his first journeys allusive and unrecorded. From time to time a detailed monograph on the flora of western Sudan or eastern Persia appeared in some European capital, posted from Damascus or Tunis and privately printed according to his instructions.

And at least once a year a dozen new species of desert flowers would be described, the discoveries invariably genuine. So although he continued to be feared and disliked even when far from home, the English botanical community had no choice but to admire his accumulated research.

Yet in fact Strongbow was spending very little time on botany. Instead, unexpectedly, he had turned his vast powers of concentration to the study of sex, an endeavor that eventually would bring about the fall of the British Empire.

But that was of no concern to Strongbow. What was important to him was the startling discovery he made in a Sinai cave after only a few years in the Middle

East, that the lost original of the Bible actually existed, a secret he would share with only one other man in his century.

With that discovery began Strongbow's forty-year search for the Sinai Bible and his lifelong speculations about what the mysterious lost original might contain, of all his legacies to the twentieth century the one that would most intrigue and baffle his sole child and heir, the idealistic boy one day to become a gunrunner named Stern.

2

Wallenstein

*Men tend to become fables and
fables tend to become men.*

❊

Before being killed at the order of the Habsburgs, a
former Czech orphan named Wallenstein had twice
risen to become the all-powerful Generalissimo of the
Holy Roman Empire during the religious slaughter
known as the Thirty Years War.

A variety of enemies had hunted the fugitive through
the mists of northern Bohemia, but when finally
trapped the halberd driven through his chest was held
by an English captain commanded by an Irish general.
The year was 1634 and that killing, followed by the
specter of an eagle, which in Arab lore traditionally
lives a thousand years, brought to the Mediterranean
the apparent ancestor of the man who would one day
undertake the most spectacular forgery in history.

While he lived and scavenged, Generalissimo Wallenstein had immersed himself so excessively in
astrology that everyone in his family detested stars—
with one exception, an indolent nephew who believed
in nothing else. Therefore the morning the nephew
learned of his famous uncle's death he immediately
rushed to consult his local wizard.

The wizard had been up all night nodding in his
observatory. He was on his way to bed but he couldn't
turn away his most important client. Wearily he laid

out his charts and tried to come to some conclusion. By the time he did he was falling asleep.

Bribes, screamed the nephew. Can they save me? Should I flee?

Eagles, muttered the wizard.

The Wallenstein nephew leapt from his chair.

Flight. Of course. But where to?

I'm sorry, all else is unclear.

Wallenstein shook the wizard by his beard but the old man was already snoring. He galloped back to his castle above the Danube where his confessor, a Jesuit in the habit of dropping by for a glass of wine at noon, was waiting. He saw that the nephew's left eyelid was drooping, a sure sign of profound agitation. Having traveled widely for his order, he suggested Wallenstein unburden himself. As the nephew talked the priest calmly emptied their bottle of wine.

Shqiperi, he murmured at length. An excellent vintage, my son.

What's that? asked Wallenstein, peering out from under his drooping eyelid.

I said this is a remarkably fine vintage.

No, that other word you used.

You mean the ancient name the Albanians used for their country? Thought to have meant *eagle* originally? Certainly an old race, the Albanians, who have survived because their land is mountainous and inaccessible. Probably they once identified themselves with the eagles of the place.

The Jesuit seemed unsurprised as Wallenstein dropped to his knees and confessed he had never believed in stars. There was a further exchange, after which the priest praised the young man for not falling victim to his uncle's astral follies.

He then absolved him of various sins, suggested a number of Hail Marys and wished him success in the south, if he should ever travel south, meanwhile accepting responsibility for the wine cellar beneath the castle if its owner were ever absent.

The first Wallenstein in Albania considered himself a temporary exile from Germany. The country was barbarous and he intended to leave as soon as possible. Nevertheless he had to live so he moved into a castle and took a local wife.

When a son was born he allowed the baby to be named after Albania's national hero, a fifteenth-century Christian turned Moslem turned Christian who had been given the name by which history knew him while a hostage to the Turks, Lord Alexander or Iskander Bey, or Skanderbeg as his countrymen pronounced it when he finally returned to his native land and became its most famous warrior, tirelessly storming Christian fortresses for the Turks during the first half of his life, then tirelessly defending those same fortresses against the Turks for the second half of his life.

After several decades of exile Wallenstein learned that his dead uncle was no longer considered a threat to the Holy Roman Empire. It was now safe for him to return to his home above the Danube. Elated, he drank a quantity of arak one evening and climbed his tower to see what the stars of an Albanian night might say of his future.

Unfortunately a condition that was to afflict his male heirs for generations came over him. His drooping left eyelid slipped lower and lower until it closed.

Unable to gauge distances with one eye, he stepped off the tower and landed on his head in a fountain one hundred feet below, instantly dead and never able to reveal that the stars had told him it was his destiny to found a powerful Albanian dynasty, and that a pardon from Germany resulting in his immediate death was the surest way for this to happen.

Thereafter the drooping left eyelid was apparent in all Skanderbegs soon after birth. As with the progenitor of the clan, the eyelid tended to droop more severely under the pressure of alcohol or when death was near.

With it went other unmistakable traits inherited from the original Albanian Wallenstein, who had always suspected his uncle's Holy Roman enemies were sending spies down from the north to assassinate him.

As a result the Skanderbeg Wallensteins were deeply suspicious men. They moved furtively and never dared look anyone in the eye. When guests were in the castle the master disappeared frequently, being seen now slinking along the far side of the garden, next in the kitchen behind a cupboard sneaking a quick glass of arak, a moment later peeking out of a tower with a spyglass.

What the family malady amounted to, in short, was an unshakable conviction that the entire universe was ordered with the sole purpose of endangering Skanderbeg Wallensteins. The plots they imagined were vague yet pervasive and thereby explained all events on earth.

By tradition they received no education. War was their vocation and they left home at an early age to pursue it, fighting fiercely against either the Turks or the Christians as had their contradictory namesake, the national hero. Yet curiously not one of them was ever killed in battle. Although always campaigning they somehow managed to survive the massacres perpetrated by their enemies and return to their castle to become extremely alert shrunken old men.

Thus in almost every way the Wallenstein men were the exact opposites of the Strongbows, who died young never suspecting anything. In their dark damp castle perched gloomily on a wild Albanian crag, a windy and insecure Balkan outpost, these aging illiterates were forever given to rampant instabilities and extravagant reversals of character.

Then too, the Skanderbeg Wallensteins had never been father and son. Combining love with sensual pleasure was beyond them and they were impotent with their wives. Sexually they could only be aroused by very young girls of eight or nine.

When a new bride was brought to the castle this situation was delicately explained to her by the resident mother-in-law. There was nothing to worry about, however, since the castle had a large staff of loyal retainers. Matters could be easily arranged, as indeed they had been for nearly two hundred years.

The resident matriarchs were always quick to claim that the Wallenstein men loved their women well. Yet the fact was that successive Skanderbegs were never related, perhaps the real reason why these masters of the castle so violently distrusted everyone at home and spent most of their lives away in wars.

Generally their fathers were stolid Albanian butlers or gamekeepers whose interests were limited to the confines of a pantry or a nest of grouse. But in 1802 the new wife of a Skanderbeg happened to take to her bed a young Swiss with a passion for details, a highly gifted linguist who was on a walking tour to the Levant. Later that year a Wallenstein heir was born for the first time in history without a drooping left eyelid.

The boy was unusual in other ways, being both shy and ascetic. At an age when other Skanderbegs would have been glancing lasciviously at girls of four or five, preparing for their adult sex life with girls of eight or nine, he seemed to notice no one at all. Nothing interested him but the Bible, which he read incessantly. In fact this Skanderbeg passed his entire youth without leaving the castle, all his time spent in the private conservatory he had built for himself in its tallest tower.

From the conservatory he had superb views that stretched all the way to the Adriatic. The walls of the room were lined with Bibles and there was an organ at which he sat playing Bach's Mass in B Minor long into the night. Before he was twenty it was said he had memorized the Bible in all the tongues current in the Holy Land during the Biblical era. So of course no one was surprised when he paused at the gate one morning, there to cross the moat into the outside world for the first time, to announce he was on his way to Rome to enter the Trappist monastic order.

When Wallenstein professed his vows he did so as Brother Anthony, in honor of the fourth-century hermit and founder of monasticism who had died in an Egyptian desert at the age of one hundred and four. As a monk he continued to live much as he always had until he was sent to Jerusalem and ordered to make a religious retreat to St Catherine's monastery.

This lonely enclosure of gray granite walls at the foot of Mt Sinai, fortified by Justinian in the sixth century, was supported by a curious tribe called the Jebeliyeh, bedouin in appearance, who had been forcibly converted to Islam a thousand years earlier. But actually the Jebeliyeh were descendants of Bosnian and Wallachian serfs, and therefore not very distant neighbors of the Wallenstein castle, whom Justinian had forcibly converted to Christianity three hundred years before that, then sent to the Sinai so the monks could tend to their prayers while others tended their sheep.

When a Trappist first arrived in the Holy Land it was common practice for him to be sent to St

Catherine's to consider these and other wonders concerning time and emperors, prophets and the desert.

As part of his working day at the monastery Brother Anthony was directed to clear away the debris in the dry cellar of a storeroom long in disuse. He uncovered a mound of hard earth, and in keeping with God's plan for regularity in the universe he began chipping away the mound to level the floor.

His tool struck the edge of a cloth. A few minutes later a large bundle lay in his lap. Carefully he unwound the lengths of stiff swaddling and found a thick stack of parchment. He lifted the cover, read the first line of Aramaic in the first of the four columns on the page, closed his eyes and began to pray.

After some minutes he opened his eyes and gazed at the flowing mixture of Aramaic and Old Hebrew, knowing that no Biblical texts survived in those dead tongues, suspecting, therefore, that here before him was one of the oldest Old Testaments in existence.

The lost original perhaps?

Once more Brother Anthony closed his eyes to pray, this time for deliverance from vanity. Then he opened the manuscript again and it struck him as a blow. The New Testament as well? Centuries before Christ had lived?

His hands trembled as he turned the pages, recalling the various Bibles he had memorized. It was absolutely impossible, but by the end of the afternoon two facts had enveloped his mind in darkness.

First, this Bible was complete and without question the oldest Bible in the world.

Second, it denied every religious truth ever held by anyone.

The stories it told distorted every event that had

taken place over three millennia in the Eastern Mediterranean, in the Holy Land and more particularly in
Jerusalem, legendary home of Melchizedek, King of
Salem which also meant King of Peace, the fabled
priest of antiquity who had blessed the future patriarch
of all three faiths when first the shepherd Abraham
journeyed forth from the dawn of the east with his
flock.

Melchizedek's very existence was in doubt and so
was that of Jerusalem, which since Melchizedek's
reign had always been the ultimate destination of all
sons and prophets of God toiling up from the desert,
stern with their messages of salvation for the eternally
queasy souls of that city.

Possibly, the pages implied, Melchizedek had lived
elsewhere or been someone else. And just possibly,
there had never been a Jerusalem.

To Brother Anthony the words before him were
terrifying. What would happen if the world suddenly
suspected that Mohammed might well have lived six
centuries before Christ rather than six centuries after
him?

Or again, that Christ had been a minor prophet in
the age of Elijah or a secret messiah in the age of
Isaiah, who alone knew his true identity and rigorously
followed his instructions?

Or that Mohammed and Isaiah were contemporaries,
brethren in a common cause who comforted one another in moments of trial?

Or that idols were indeed God when made in the
shape of Hector or David, Alexander or Caesar, if the
worshipper was living in the same era as one of these
worthies?

Or more or less in the same era.

Or at least thought he was.

Or that the virtures of Mary and Fatima and Ruth
had been confused in the minds of later chroniclers

and freely interchanged among them? That the virtues ascribed to Fatima more properly were those of Ruth? That the song of Ruth had been sung by Mary? That the virgin birth called Mary's belonged to Fatima?

Or that it was true from time to time that innumerable Gods held court in all the high and low places? That these legions of Gods were variously sleek and fat or gnarled and lean, as vicious as crazed brigands or as gentle as doting grandfathers?

That they passed whole epochs vaguely preoccupied with the slit necks of bulls, ambrosia, broken pottery, war, peace, gold rings and purple robes and incense, or even gurgling vacantly while sniffing and sucking their forefingers?

Although at other times there were no Gods anywhere? Not even one? The rivers wending their ways and the lambs bleating with mindless inconsistency?

Or that the carpenter who had gone down to the Jordan to be cleansed by his cousin was either the son of Fatima or the father of Ruth? That Joshua had gained his wisdom from the fifth Abbasid Caliph of Baghdad, who might himself have been Judas or Christ if only he had foreseen a painful future as clearly as he recalled a blissful past?

That David and Julius Caesar had been secret card-playing cronies? That Alexander the Great had challenged them both to a primitive sort of backgammon for nominal stakes, winning easily, yet had gone on to lose his earnings to a chattering barber whose only other distinction in history was that he had cut Mohammed's hair?

That Abraham had passed on his legacy to the Jews through his first son, Ishmael the wanderer, and his legacy to the Arabs through his sedentary second son, Isaac? And since he had no more sons, that he rejected outright the paternity claims of the Gentiles and refused to take any responsibility whatsoever for them?

33

Or that the trumpet beneath the walls of Jericho had been blown by Harun al-Rashid, not stridently but sensuously as was his manner, as he seductively circled the oasis seven times and brought his people into a happy land?

In order that Joshua might take a promised bath in the Jordan and Christ might retire to a sumptuous court on the banks of the Tigris to spin forth a cycle of tales encompassing the dreams of a thousand and one nights?

And so on in the windblown footsteps that fled across the pages of this desert manuscript where an entire fabric of history was woven in magical confusion, threaded in unexpected knots and colored in reverse patterns, the sacred shadows of belief now lengthened or shortened by a constantly revolving sun and shifting moon.

For in this oldest of Bibles paradise lay everywhere on the wrong side of the river, sought by the wrong people, preached by a prophet different from the one who had been heard, an impossible history where all events occurred before or after they were said to have occurred, or instead, occurred simultaneously.

Numbing in its disorder and perplexing to the edge of madness. Circular and unchronicled and calmly contradictory, suggesting infinity.

But the worst shock of all came on the final pages, where the compiler of the Bible had added an autobiographical footnote.

He was blind, he said, and had been blind since birth. His early life had been spent sitting beside dusty waysides in Canaan with a bowl in his lap crying out for alms, always close to starvation.

In time he learned a few more coins always came his way if he chanted imaginary histories and the like, for there was nothing poor toilers on the road loved more than a description of wondrous events, their own lives being both dreary and hard. And perhaps not surprisingly after so many years spent gathering gossip, he had no difficulty making up tales.

Before long an old couple had come to him with their son, an imbecile. The boy couldn't tell night from day or summer from winter, but while he was still young his parents had discovered he drew shapes in the sand very well. An idea had come to them. Why not see if the boy could memorize the alphabet? Very few people could write. If the boy learned to do so he could become a scribe and copy down the documents others dictated to him. The advantage, of course, was that he wouldn't have to understand what he was writing.

It took many years and all their money but the task was accomplished. Their son could write beautifully, his teachers said so. When a reed was placed in his hand he wrote down exactly what was said, no more and no less.

The problem was that the other difficulties still remained. Now the parents were both ill and wanted to make some provision for their son's future. They thought of the blind storyteller. What if the boy accompanied the blind man on his travels and wrote down his words, in exchange for which the blind man could show their son when to sleep and eat and wear more or fewer clothes? Wouldn't it be a fair and useful partnership?

Well it had seemed a good arrangement, said the blind man, and from that day forward they had proceeded from dusty wayside to dusty wayside making a meager living. Affection had grown into love and they had become like father and son. All had worked out for the best in the dusty waysides of Canaan.

But here the blind man had to make a confession.

The histories his adopted son had faithfully copied down weren't histories at all, for several reasons.

For one, because the blind man only knew what he heard, having no eyes to verify anything.

For another, because his position in life was lowly and he knew little about great events, having never heard more than bits and pieces of rumors.

Thirdly, because the din beside a dusty wayside was often deafening, and how could one old man be expected to extract a coherent theme from so much noise?

And lastly, perhaps because he felt the truth could be rendered more accurately anyway when dealing with the open spaces of the future rather than the murky depths of the past. In the future anything might happen, so he could be flawlessly correct in reporting it. Whereas in the past, although some events were known and others suspected, many more were neither known nor suspected.

Furthermore, why belabor his poor listeners with the past? These wretches longed for new worlds, not old. Between them they had only a few coppers to hear hopefully where they might be going, knowing full well where they had already miserably been.

In any case, the blind man humbly noted, men tend to become fables and fables tend to become men, so in the end it probably didn't matter whether he was dealing with the past or the future. In the end it must all be the same.

And wasn't it also possible that all prophecies were really histories misplaced by tricks of time? Memories in disguise? Pains and torments spilled out in weariness when memory no longer could bear its heavy burdens? When it lightened itself by taking a part of the past and putting it in the future?

He thought so, but even if he was confused he had still taken care not to cheat his listeners, by varying his accounts so there would always be new matters for them to consider. Occasionally he chanted about mighty wars and migrations and who begat whom, and although he sometimes presented the solemn side of life he also included the sensuous and sacrificing, all the while enlivening his chants with anecdotes and sayings and reports, curious inventions, every manner of adventure and experience that might come to mind.

And so the entertainment had gone on for years in dusty waysides, the blind man giving his recitals and his imbecile son recording them word for word.

Until with increasing age a time had come when they had both grown stiff in the joints. Then they had sought a warm place to assuage their aches and gone south into the desert, to the foot of a mountain called Sinai, where they were sitting at the very moment this last chapter was being dictated.

Having already been in the desert for some time, the blind man could not be sure what era was current in Canaan. But not too long ago a traveler had passed their way and he had asked him what news there was in Canaan, and the man had replied that a great temple was being built on a great mountain by a great king called Solomon, which of course meant little enough to the blind man since as long as he could remember great temples were always being built in Canaan on great mountains by great kings who all had one name or another.

So here the dictation was coming to an end. Unfortunately he couldn't add his own name to these recitations because in his blindness and poverty, being no one of importance, he quite simply had never had a name.

And finally, in conclusion, he advised that the verses had their best effect when chanted to the accompaniment of a lyre and a flute and a ram's horn, these pleasing sounds tending to alert passersby that something of interest was taking place beside the road.

But gentle blind man doth not will not shalt not knowing [*it was written after that, the lines indented to set them apart from the previous text, the words formed in a particularly proud and elegant script*], saith imbecile of imbeciles adding few some several own thoughts first Abraham last Jesus last Isaiah first Mohammed thought of thoughts adding over years of years saith wanting hoping hope of hopes here Matthew Mark Luke John sharing work here Prophet love of loves here Lord never adding much Gabriel doth not will not shalt not adding much adding little Ruth little Mary little Fatima here Elijah there Kings here Judges there Melchizedek word of words Lord of Lords saith soon doth not will not shalt not winter summer day night ending imbecile of imbeciles ending desert end gentle end blind end no name man end doth not will not shalt not too cold too hot too hungry tired saith sleepless saith starving saith holding hands ending father of fathers son of sons no name ending kingdom come ending amen ending be with you ending saith end ending of endings end.

Brother Anthony closed the book and groaned. He had read the last pages in horror. The mere thought of it paralyzed him.

A nameless blind beggar chanting whatever came into his head? His mutterings recorded by an imbecile who saw fit to insert a few shadowy thoughts of his own? The two of them moving their shabby act from wayside to wayside with no other purpose than to make a meager living?

Drifting away to the desert while Solomon was building his temple? Coming to rest at the foot of Moses' mountain for no other reason than to ease their arthritis? Lunatic prophecy and moronic fancy collaborating to produce original Holy Scripture fully seven hundred years before the first appearance of the Old Testament? More than eleven hundred years before the first tiny fragments of the New Testament?

Chants by dusty waysides varied to vary the entertainment? Lyres and flutes and ram's horns squeaking and rumbling to attract attention? Roadside gossip overheard and repeated? Men begatting in Canaan? Curious inventions in Canaan? These and other odd bits of rumors twisted and retold for a copper coin?

Then on to another dusty wayside? Eventually to retirement in a warm place good for the joints? The divine source of inspired religion, these whimsies concocted by two rambling anonymous tramps in 930 B.C.?

Brother Anthony went down on his knees and prayed for enlightenment.

Night came. He wrapped the manuscript in its swaddling cloth and reburied it in the storeroom cellar. On the way to his cell he made signs that God had instructed him to remain in seclusion until he found the solution to a personal problem.

For the next week he fasted in his cell, drinking one small cup of water at sunrise and another at sunset, and at the end of those seven days he decided what had to be done.

Melchizedek must have his City of Peace, men must have their Jerusalem. There had to be faith in the world and if the cause for it wasn't there, he would provide it. If the Father of the real Bible was an aging blind beggar and the Son was an imbecilic

39

scribe, then Wallenstein would become the Holy Ghost and rewrite Scripture the way it ought to be written.

The decision he had made in his cell was to forge the original Bible.

Of course he couldn't place his forgery in the tenth century B.C., when the imbecile had recorded the blind man's recitations. His Bible had to be a genuine work of revealed history, not a jumble of capricious tales assembled by two stray tramps. Thus it had to come sometime well after Christ, which meant writing it in Greek.

But when?

In prayer he turned to his namesake for guidance and at once the question was answered. The great St Anthony had gone into the desert in the fourth century, so that would be the date of his forgery. Time enough after Christ for all the truths to have been gathered, yet still earlier than any complete Bible in existence.

Secretly he revisited the storeroom cellar and buried the real Sinai Bible more deeply in the clay so that it would not be discovered in his absence. Then without warning he left the monastery and returned to Jerusalem, to the quarters of his order, where his unauthorized arrival during the morning meal caused worried looks from his brothers.

Immediately he shattered the silence by announcing he had learned something at St Catherine's that transcended his vows of obedience, silence and poverty. He must be allowed to go his own way for a number of years or he would be forced to abandon the Trappists.

The monks in the refectory were stupefied. When his shocked superior warned in a quavering voice that merely suggesting such blasphemy constituted a fatal nakedness before God, the former Brother Anthony at once removed not only his cassock but his loincloth, exposing even his genitals, and left the room without an explanation of any kind. Behind him his weeping former brothers stayed on their knees for hours praying beside their bowls of gruel.

Wallenstein meanwhile, penniless and naked and shivering violently in the cold winter wind, limped through the narrow alleys of Jerusalem abjectly begging coins. And although soon starving and frostbitten, his first coins went not for a crust of bread or a loincloth but for a stamp and an envelope. In this letter to Albania he directed that a huge sum of family money, his by right as the Skanderbeg of his generation, be sent to him.

While waiting for the money he continued to beg in the streets but also found time to begin his special studies, the cumbersome process of teaching himself the secrets of ink, more specifically the techniques of making ancient inks from dyes and crude chemicals. He also began teaching himself to analyze ancient parchments by feel and taste and smell in order to determine their exact age. Lastly he applied himself to the eccentricities of writing styles.

Throughout this period of second initiation he wore only a loincloth and lived in a miserable basement hole in the Armenian Quarter, supporting himself by begging.

When the money finally arrived Wallenstein equipped himself as a wealthy and erudite Armenian dealer in antiquities and journeyed to Egypt seeking a large supply of blank parchment produced in the fourth century, neither weathered nor well cared for during its fifteen hundred years, parchment that had been quietly resting in some dry dark grave for all that time.

In Egypt he was unsuccessful and returned to Jerusalem nearly insane with despair only to discover the parchment he sought was already there in the Old City, apparently buried at the bottom of an antique Turkish safe in a cluttered shop owned by an obscure antiquities dealer named Haj Harun, an Arab so destitute and bewildered he readily parted with the treasure as if unaware of its immense value.

Wallenstein rejoiced. Undoubtedly a man less fanatical could never even have conceived of such a forgery, for the task he had set for himself was no less than to deceive all scholars and chemists and holy men in his own era and also forever.

But Wallenstein was fixed in his love for God, and in the end he did succeed.

It took him seven years to assemble his materials. Another five years were spent in the basement hole mastering the precise style of writing he would need for the forgery. During this time he assumed many disguises so that every step of his work would always remain untraceable. And he had to spend the entire Wallenstein fortune, selling off farms and villages in Albania, to maintain his disguises and buy what he needed.

At last when all was ready he traveled once more to St Catherine's and presented himself as a ragged lay pilgrim of the Armenian church, requesting and being given a tiny cell in which to meditate. That night, as planned, while the moon waned to nothing Wallenstein crept into the storeroom cellar he remembered and stole the real Sinai Bible from its hiding place.

The next morning the shabby Armenian confessed he needed an even more lonely retreat and said he would seek a cave near the summit of the mountain. The Greek monks tried to deter him, knowing him to be mad, but when they saw he couldn't be swayed they blessed him and prayed he would find relief in the examination of his soul.

Once in the cave Wallenstein unpacked the supplies he had cached there, the chemicals and stacks of precious fourth-century parchment. Then he knelt and embraced the sensuous gloom of his martyrdom.

3

Cairo 1840

*Dropping from sight with a
whoop precisely as the clocks
chimed midnight and announced
the arrival of the Queen's
birthday.*

❊

When last seen and recognized as himself, in Cairo at
the age of twenty-one, Strongbow was described as a
thin broad-shouldered man with straight Arab features
and an enormous black moustache. Summer and
winter, no matter how hot the weather, he wore a
massive greasy black turban and a shaggy short black
coat made from unwashed and uncombed goats' hair,
these barbaric garments said to be gifts from some
wild mountain tribe in outer Persia. His face was
proud and fierce and melancholy, and when he smiled
it was as if the smile hurt him.

In the streets of Cairo, even in the most elegant
European districts, he carried a thick heavy club under
his arm as if on guard, some kind of polished twisted
root. But by far his most striking characteristic was his
piercing stare, which seemed to look through a man
and see something beyond.

It was said he slept only two hours a day beginning
at noon. One of his pleasures in those days was floating
down rivers on his back, naked, at night. In this

solitary nocturnal manner he had explored all the great rivers of the Middle East and he was fond of repeating that no single experience could compare to arriving in Baghdad under the stars after long hours drifting on the dark languid waters of the Tigris.

His professional work, which was still assumed to be botany, occupied only three hours of his day. Specimens were examined and catalogued from eight to nine-thirty in the morning and again from ten-thirty until noon, the rest of his time being given to thinking and walking or floating.

He seldom spoke to Europeans and if one of them said something irrelevant to his needs he either turned his back or menacingly raised his polished twisted club. Yet he would tarry for hours in the bazaars with the poorest beggars and charlatans if he thought they had something interesting to tell him.

It was claimed he ate almost nothing, restricting himself to a small raw salad at sunset.

His drinking habits were even more abstemious. Alcohol in any form was out of the question, as were Bovril and dandelion brews, milk, coffee and orange presses and mild malt mixtures. But what was most disgusting to his countrymen, he absolutely refused to drink tea.

Instead, at teatime, he sipped mare's milk warm from the animal, a cup then and another at sunrise.

When last seen and recognized as himself, Strongbow had also begun to acquire scars from his travels.

A javelin thrown by a tribesman in the Yemen transfixed his jaw, destroying four back teeth and part of his palate. With the weapon still in his head Strongbow fought off the tribesmen with his club and spent the rest of the night walking to a coastal village where there was an Arab with sufficient understanding of anatomy to remove the javelin without taking his jaw with it.

The work was done but the jagged mark down the side of his face remained.

While swimming across the Red Sea under a full moon he fell victim to a fever that blistered his tongue with ulcers and made it impossible for him to speak for a month.

Near Aden, after secretly penetrating the holy sites of both Medina and Mecca disguised as an Arab, only the second European to have done so, he was stricken with another fever that he treated with opium. While largely unconscious he barely escaped being bled to death by a local midwife who solicitously shaved his body and plastered his groin with a thick mass of leeches.

Groin and palate and tongue, Strongbow early acquired scar tissue from his strenuous explorations. But it wasn't these Levantine wounds that were to determine his future course in the Middle East. Rather it was certain unsuspected conversations he had on both love and a haj in Timbuktu, and not long after that, love itself in Persia.

Strongbow first learned of the man known as the White Monk of the Sahara in Tripoli, where the former peasant priest from Normandy had been an insignificant White Father missionary for some years before abruptly deciding one evening, after a long lonely afternoon spent lying in the dust under a palm tree, that the Christian dictum to love thy neighbor meant what it said. Abandoning his order and traveling south, he eventually crossed the wastes to Timbuktu.

There Father Yakouba, as the renegade peasant priest now called himself, became a nefarious legend throughout the desert because of his heretical message that love should be all-encompassing, so complete as to include sexual relations between large numbers of people all at once, strangers and families and whole neighborhoods tumbling together whenever they chanced to meet.

When many bodies are pressed together, preached the White Monk, the need for vanity vanishes. The alpha and the omega are one, coming and going are one, the spirit is triumphant and all souls enter holy communion. So God is best served when as many people as possible are making love day and night.

It is especially important, preached the White Monk, that no one should ever find himself alone and unoccupied and feeling excluded on a hot afternoon, gazing longingly at passing groups of people. Nor should passing groups of people stare defiantly at a solitary outsider. Instead both sides should mix at once in the love of God.

Even though Timbuktu was strictly a Moslem city, Father Yakouba's Christian message was well-received from the beginning, perhaps because that caravan outpost was far from nowhere, perhaps as well because so many of its inhabitants were displaced villagers accustomed to knowing everyone they met.

In any case Father Yakouba was increasingly surrounded by enthusiastic converts of all ages and colors ranging from light brown to deep black, who in time produced a growing community of children until his polysexual commune accounted for fully half the population of Timbuktu, surpassing in size all but the largest towns between central Africa and the Mediterranean.

The story fascinated Strongbow the evening he heard it in an Arab coffee house. Before midnight he was out in the desert beyond Tripoli, magnifying glass in hand should any rare specimens appear in the moonlight, tramping south along the ancient Carthaginian trade route that led through Mizda and Murzuk to Lake Chad, a distance of thirteen hundred miles.

There he paused to soak his feet at dusk and dawn before turning west to Timbuktu, a distance of twelve hundred miles.

As one of the first six or seven Europeans to arrive in the city since the Roman era, Strongbow expected at least some kind of welcome or demonstration when he appeared in its streets. But to his surprise no one took any notice of him, the place apparently so remote all events were equally plausible to its inhabitants. Although disappointed, Strongbow recorded this fact for future use and began asking directions to the White Monk.

The replies he received were useless. A man pointed backward and forward, a woman nodded to the right and left. Wearily he sat down in a dusty square holding the flowers he had picked that morning in the desert. There was nothing else to do so he examined them through his magnifying glass.

They're very pretty, said a soft voice.

Strongbow peered under his magnifying glass at what appeared to be an elderly Arab dwarf. The tiny creature was smiling up at him. Some fifty or sixty children suddenly arrived to play in the square.

I'm an English botanist, said Strongbow.

Then you're new here and you're probably lonely.

At the moment I'm just tired.

Well won't you come play with the little children then? That always helps.

With his magnifying glass Strongbow adjusted the dwarf to life-size.

Little man, I've just walked two and a half thousand miles to meet someone called the White Monk of the Sahara, and now that I'm here I can't find him. So you see I don't exactly feel like playing with little children.

L'appétit, said the dwarf, vient en mangeant.

Strongbow dropped his magnifying glass and the flowers slipped through his fingers as the tiny old man merrily wagged his head.

Didn't they tell you I was a dwarf somewhat advanced in years?

No.

And so you pictured quite a different man?

Yes.

The dwarf laughed.

Well of course you're still very young. Would you care to come to my house for some banana beer?

Strongbow smiled.

Which is your house, Father? No one was able to tell me.

Oh they told you all right, you must have been distracted by your walk. In this part of town all the houses are mine.

Father Yakouba guessed almost at once that Strongbow was deaf, the first person ever to do so. But when Strongbow asked him how he had known, the elderly man only nodded happily and poured more banana beer.

Just then two or three hundred children ran by the bench where they were sitting in a courtyard, the dust rising high in their wake and settling slowly as they swept away.

My birds of the desert, said Father Yakouba, passing from one hour of life to another. Prettily they come with their chirpings, lightly they go on their wings. And who is to chart their course but me? And where would they alight if not in my heart? Now and then I may miss a rainy day in Normandy, but down here a rainy day is a memory that belongs to another man. You walked over two thousand miles to get here but do you know I've often made such journeys in an afternoon following the flights of my children? Yes, their footprints in the sky. You haven't begun it yet?

What's that, Father?

Your haj.

No. I haven't even considered one.

But you will of course, out here we all make one eventually. And when you do remember there are many holy places, and remember as well that a haj isn't measured in miles no more than a man is measured by his shadow. And your destination? Jerusalem? Mecca? Perhaps, but it may also be a simpler place you're looking for, a mud courtyard such as this or even a hillside where a few trees give shade in the heat of the day. It's the haj itself that's important, so what you want is a long and unhurried journey. A flight of birds just passed us, going from where to where in the desert? I don't know, but when they alight I'll have arrived at my holy place.

Father Yakouba leaned back against the mud wall, his face wrinkled into a thousand lines by the desert sun.

Will you go from plant to plant? he asked.

No, Father, I'm beginning to think not.

Good, from people to people then and a rich and varied journey is what you want, so pray you are slow in arriving. And when you meet someone along the way stop at once to talk and answer questions and ask your own as well, as many as you can. Curious habits and conflicting truths? Mirages as well? Embrace them all as you would your own soul, for they are your soul, especially the mirages. And never question the strange ways of others because you are as strange as they are. Just give them God's gift, listen to them. Then you'll have no regrets at the end because you'll have traced the journey in your heart.

A haj, mused Strongbow, I hadn't thought of it that way.

Father Yakouba smiled shyly.

It's time for my afternoon nap now. Tell me, do you think you could do me a small favor when you return to Tripoli?

Anything at all, Father.

Do you think you could send me a bottle of
Calvados? Would that be too much? It's true we
change our lives and banana beer is fine, but now and
again I do recall a rainy day in Normandy.

They laughed together on that hot afternoon in a
dusty courtyard in Timbuktu, laughed and parted and
talked for several more weeks before Strongbow left
to cross the Sahara once more, pausing again at Lake
Chad to soak his feet at dusk and dawn.

In Tripoli, Strongbow arranged for the first of many
shipments of Calvados to his new friend and also
began that enthusiastic exchange of letters, later assumed to have been lost during the First World War,
that was to become the most voluminous correspondence of the nineteenth century.

The following spring in Persia, during a cholera
epidemic that killed seventy thousand people, Strongbow contracted a temporary and partial blindness that
made it impossible for him to read books, but not lips.
He made use of his time by having the Koran read to
him so that he could memorize it. While convalescing
he fasted and prayed and was subsequently ordained
a Master Sufi when his eyesight returned.

But more important, at the beginning of that epidemic he had fallen in love with the mysterious Persian
girl whose death was to haunt him for years. He only
knew her for a few weeks, no more, before the
epidemic carried her off, yet the memory of their
tender love never left him. And it was while memorizing the Koran in his sorrow that he decided he would
make a haj as Father Yakouba had suggested, when
the time came, and that because of the gentle Persian
girl it would be a sexual exploration into the nature
and meaning of love.

Thus for many reasons Strongbow was considered
morbidly vain and pedantic by Englishmen in the

Levant. The opinion was general and even universal, although it also had to be admitted that no one knew Strongbow at all.

Nor wanted to, as was made apparent at the lavish diplomatic reception given in Cairo in 1840 to honor Queen Victoria's twenty-first birthday. The highest-ranking officials were there as well as the most important European residents in Egypt. Because of his imposing lineage Strongbow had to be invited, but of course no one imagined he would attend. A formal evening lawn party with reverent toasts to the queen was exactly what he could be expected to detest.

Yet Strongbow did appear, entirely naked.

Or rather, naked of clothes. As so often he wore his portable sundial strapped to his hip, a monstrously heavy bronze piece cast in Baghdad during the fifth Abbasid caliphate. But the huge sundial hung well to the side and its leather strap crossed his hips well above the groin, thereby concealing nothing.

Strongbow's entrance was dignified, his step measured and even ponderous. He presented himself to the reception line and bowed his way gravely down it, then chose to position himself at the end of the garden in front of the orchestra, as conspicuous a spot as could be found.

There, alone and erect, he stood displaying his full figure of seven feet and seven inches without saying a word or moving a muscle, in one hand a bulging leather pouch, in the other his familiar and gigantic magnifying glass, which he kept close to his eye while gazing down on the waltzers.

For perhaps an hour he stood studying the dancers until he was evidently satisfied with his performance. Then he broke into a smile, laughed loudly and strode straight across the dance floor to the far side of the garden, where the wall was highest.

One leap carried him to the top of the wall. He shouted that he had once loved well in Persia and they could all go to hell, swung the sundial behind him and lingered a moment longer, dropping from sight with a whoop precisely as the clocks chimed midnight and announced the arrival of the queen's birthday.

But so commanding was Strongbow's presence and so bizarre his reputation, not one of the guests had seen his nakedness. All the comments made later had to do with his unpardonable rudeness in leaving at the moment he had, his raucous laughter and unseemly yelp upon doing so, his equally blatant reference to some obscene experience in Persia, his defiant exit over the wall instead of through a gate, the heavy bronze sundial he had once more insisted on wearing and tossing back and forth to impress people with his strength, and especially the great discomfort everyone had felt having that grotesquely large eye, two inches in diameter, staring down at them from its unnatural height.

Insofar as his attire or lack of it was concerned, it was assumed he had ignored propriety as usual and come in his normally outrageous costume, the massive greasy black turban and the shaggy short black coat made from unwashed and uncombed goats' hair.

Outrageous behavior as usual, but that night in 1840 when he climbed over a garden wall wickedly flashing a smile and shaking his sundial and shouting about love, his nakedness unrecognized, was the last time anyone would ever see the giant in his guise as Strongbow.

The sundial and the gigantic magnifying glass were both remembered from that night but not the other article he had with him, the bulging leather pouch. In fact he had to walk many blocks to a poor section of the city before he met a blind beggar who could relieve him of it.

Or rather a miserable old man sitting in a squalid alley with a cup in his lap pretending to be blind.

When Strongbow's shadow approached the beggar began his whining chant, but when the apparition was closer the old man's eyes jumped even though he had trained himself for years never to let them register a thing.

By Allah, whispered the astonished man.

Yes? said Strongbow.

The beggar gasped and turned his eyes away. Foolishly he held up his cup and struggled to find the cringing words of his profession.

God give thee long life, he mumbled at last, for as truly as I come hither, by Allah I am naked.

The voice trailed off hopelessly, the cup wavered in the air. Strongbow nodded and intoned the stately words used to turn away a beggar.

In God's name go then with such a one for He will surely give thee garments.

Then he squatted and smiled and put his hands on the beggar's shoulders. He drew close and winked.

Now that we have that out of the way, my friend, what is it you were about to say?

The beggar also smiled.

For forty years, master, I've sat on this very spot in a stinking loincloth repeating those same words to thousands and thousands of passersby. And now.

Yes?

And now I face a man who really *is* naked.

Strongbow laughed. He opened the leather pouch and a shower of Maria Theresa crowns poured into the beggar's lap. The man gazed at the thick gold pieces in awe.

Bite one, said Strongbow. Timidly the beggar picked up a coin and bit it. His eyes widened. His hand was shaking so badly the coin clattered against his teeth.

They're real?

Quite so.

A fortune. A man could retire and live like a king for the rest of his days.

And I prophesy you will.

They're not to be mine?

Every last one.

But why, master?

Because I've been carrying them all night to give to someone blind enough to see the world as it is. Now on your way, beggar. Allah gives the blind man garments in abundance when he sees well.

Strongbow turned and marched down the alley laughing, the bronze sundial clinking against the stone walls. It was over. He was ready to begin his haj in earnest. Behind him a triumphant yell rose in the air.

A miracle, o sleeping Cairenes. God is great and Mohammed is His prophet.

4
Sinai
1836-1843

*And the building of the wall it
was of jasper, and the city was
pure gold.*

It took Wallenstein seven years, working entirely from
memory, to forge the original Bible. He also added
two noncanonical books to his New Testament, the
Epistle of Barnabas and the Shepherd of Hermas,
spurious texts that would serve to assure experts his
codex had indeed been written during the early
unformed days of Christianity, before bishops had
agreed which books were Holy Scripture and which
belonged to the Pseudepigrapha.

In the summer Wallenstein's cave blazed with a
merciless heat. In the winter ice hung in the air and
torrential rains crashed down the mountain. Fevers
blurred his brain and rigid pains crippled his fingers.

When he lost the use of one hand he switched his
reed pen to the other and went on writing, letting the
warped hand heal, something else he had taught himself in Jerusalem because he knew the work in the
cave would surpass any man's endurance unless he
could write with both hands.

From the wandering Jebeliyeh he received a little
food and water as the Greek monks had ordered,

placed in a small pot at the foot of the mountain where he could retrieve it every third day or so, unobserved in darkness. For although the monks honored the crazed Armenian's desire to see and be seen by no man, they also knew that God with His manifold duties might not always remember to replenish the suffering hermit's diet of worms and locusts.

From first light to last he bent over the sheaves of his thickening manuscript, unaware of the incessantly chewing sand flies and the swarms of insects that rose to feed on his frail body at dusk, so absorbed he no longer blinked when an ant crossed his eyeball, his act of creation witnessed only by an occasional ibex or gazelle or mole, a wildcat or jackal or leopard, the timid and ferocious beasts who came to stare at the unfathomable patience of this fellow animal, while in the invisible sky beyond the mouth of the cave eagles swooped through the thousand-year lives granted them in the desert and thin flights of quail and grouse and partridge passed briefly in their seasons.

Until one morning Wallenstein found himself raving about legions of locusts as large as horses, wearing lurid crowns and iron breastplates, atrocious beasts with the hair of women and the teeth of lions and the tails of scorpions, relentlessly charging the cities on the plain to trample and poison and dismember transgressors in the valley of his Book of Revelations, blood running in rivers in the name of God.

And reverently one evening he lifted his eyes from the riot of plague and slaughter to behold a great high mountain with a great city upon it, the holy Jerusalem descending from heaven amidst incandescent jewels.

And the building of the wall it was of jasper, he wrote in his stately fourth-century Greek, *and the city was pure gold.*

A few days later he made his final warning, saying that if any man ever took words away from this book of prophecy God would take him out of the book of life and out of the Holy City.

And then he wrote, *The grace of our Lord Jesus Christ be with you all, Amen,* and suddenly he found his enormous apocalyptic forgery at an end.

Wallenstein stared at the rags in his lap. He had turned the last sheet of parchment and his lap was empty. All at once he was frightened. He reached out and touched the walls of the tiny cave.

No more pages in the book of life? What place was this?

He gazed at the reed in his hand. How straight and beautiful it was and how grotesque the bits of skin and bone that clasped it. Crooked repulsive fingers. Why were they so ugly now when the slender reed was unchanged?

Wallenstein shuddered. The reed fell from his hand. He crawled out of the cave and squinted up at the mountain. The sun had just set. A mole was watching him with wide eyes. Humbly Wallenstein knelt and the mole asked him a question.

What have you done today for God?

Wallenstein bowed his head. He drew his rags around him in the dying light and his head slipped lower until his brow rested in the dust, where the answer was given.

Today in His name I have rewritten the universe.

And there he remained all night, not stirring, accepting the last hours he would know on Mt Sinai, the last lucid moments of his life as well.

What he had done he had done only for God, yet all the same he knew what would happen to him now.

At dawn he gathered up his materials. Once more the cave was as he had found it, small and bare and crumbling.

Wallenstein limped down the mountain toward the

gate of St Catherine's. The monks came running to appraise the wild hermit unseen in seven years, but when the gate was opened all but the older fell back.

What face was this? What body? No man could possess them. Had the soul already been taken up by God?

The older monks knew better. Meekly they bowed their heads and prayed as the abbot ordered the bells of the monastery to be rung in celebration. The bells pealed, the abbot stepped forward to address the twisted figure with the terrible face.

The task is done? You have found what you sought?

Wallenstein groped to find a voice men could understand. His contorted mouth opened and closed in agony. He made a harsh uneven sound.

Done.

The abbot crossed himself.

Then will you rest with us, o brother of the mountain? You have succeeded after all, you have accomplished what you set out to do. Nourish yourself now and let your wounds heal, and let us help you. It will be an honor to serve you, brother.

Wallenstein staggered. A jagged scar had appeared on the horizon of the desert, some indelible hallucination. He tried to wipe away the scar but his hand couldn't reach it.

God's creatures had done it, the ants in the cave crossing his eyes for seven years, tracing a path with their footprints. Each day the scar would grow more jagged until soon there would be no landscape at all and the scar would be all there was to see. How much time did he have? Weeks? Days?

You will rest with us? repeated the abbot.

One night, whispered Wallenstein. A cell for one night if you will.

The abbot crossed himself again. The hermit in front of him was clearly near death. He began to protest but the anguish in Wallenstein's face stopped him.

As you wish, he murmured sadly. Will you be traveling then tomorrow?

Yes.

Where must you go?

Jerusalem.

The abbot nodded. Now he thought he understood. The hermit was taking his soul to the Holy City to relinquish it. Who knew? Perhaps his task wasn't yet completed. Perhaps there was this last covenant he had made with God during his suffering on the mountain.

Jerusalem, he said softly. Yes I see.

That night while the monks slept Wallenstein's forgery of the Sinai Bible found its way to the back of a dusty shelf in one of the storerooms of St Catherine's. Most of the other books there were of little value, but not so insignificant that some future scholar would fail to examine them.

As for the original manuscript with its terrifying ambiguities, he was going to take that with him to Jerusalem, having no intention of destroying it. For although written by an anonymous blind man and an anonymous imbecile who had lost their way in the desert, hadn't the great St Anthony also gone into the desert in search of the Word?

Yes, Wallenstein told himself, St Anthony had also done that. And if other poor souls had made the same attempt and been confused by ghosts and mirages and succumbed to untenable visions, still their work couldn't be destroyed for they too had tried, only the Word as they heard it had been wrong. So it had never entered Wallenstein's mind to destroy the original manuscript, a work of God's like any other. Rather it would be laid to rest in a dry dark grave just as his own once blank parchment had been before it.

And given his humility it also never occurred to Wallenstein that in the course of his long sojourn in a desert cave, following the example of St Anthony, he might have performed a monastic feat equal in magnitude to St Anthony's and thereby become a new St Anthony.

Or simply the real St Anthony, a hermit who knew no era in his love for God.

Or what could have been stranger still, that in the course of his trial of fatigue and hunger, tormented by the glaring sun and lonely stars and yet surviving in his cave, he had in fact relived the lives of those two unknown wanderers whose recitations in dusty waysides had finally led them to the foot of the mountain three thousand years ago.

That Wallenstein had thus found nothing and forged nothing.

That instead, in bewilderment and wonder, no less than a blind man and an imbecile, he had construed his own sacred chant to the mystical accompaniment of an imaginary lyre and flute and ram's horn.

Intricate possibilities and revolving speculations, in any case far beyond Wallenstein's ravaged mind. With the last of his strength he dragged himself out of the desert and up to the gates of Jerusalem, which immediately overwhelmed him with its multitude of sights and sounds and smells, so shocking after seven years of solitude in a Sinai cave.

In fact Wallenstein was totally lost in the maze of alleys. He wandered in circles and might have kept wandering until he collapsed in Jerusalem, an insignificant clump of rags on the cobblestones clutching a precious bundle in death, if he hadn't chanced to stumble upon the antiquities shop where he had once bought the parchment for his forgery.

The elderly owner of the shop, Haj Harun, didn't

recognize his former acquaintance at first, but when he did he quickly offered food and water and a bed, all of which Wallenstein refused, knowing his time was almost at an end. Instead he begged Haj Harun to lead him to the Armenian Quarter, to the basement hole where he had acquired the skills for his task so long ago.

You're not going down into that again? said Haj Harun, disturbed as always by the filth and darkness of the hole.

I must, whispered Wallenstein, for my bundle's sake. Good-bye and God bless you, brother.

With that Wallenstein turned and painfully crawled down into the hole. He searched the dirt floor. Where should he dig?

A crack appeared in the dirt, the scar on his eyes.

He bent over the crack and pawed furiously at the earth, ripping his nails and tearing his fingers, desperately working to dig the well of memory while there was still time. Whenever another scar appeared in the earth he attacked it savagely, in dismay, boring ever deeper into the spreading cracks in his mind.

The bones in his hands broke against stone. He had dug down into a paved hole, old and dry and airtight, what might once have been a cistern before it had been swallowed up by the endless razings and rebuildings of Jerusalem. An ancient well in an underground horizon? Exactly what he needed.

He laid his bundle in the cistern and replaced the stones and repacked the well, trampled down the basement floor until it was hard and flat. No one would ever suspect. The heretical book was safely hidden forever.

Wallenstein screamed. The smooth earth at his feet had suddenly shattered and broken into a thousand scars. His terrible presumption on Mt Sinai had led to an end in the desert footprints of God's ants and now he had to flee, an outcast to the wastes, his Holy City lost to him forever because he had created it.

Moaning softly he dragged himself up the stairs and away from the basement hole, blinded by the scars on his eyes and thus oblivious to the thin figure who had been watching him from the shadows, the man who had led him back to his former home in the Armenian Quarter and then lingered on out of curiosity, a gentle dealer in fourth-century parchment and other antiquities, Haj Harun.

Deaf now to the raucous cries of Jerusalem and blind to its walls, Wallenstein stumbled out of the city and crawled north, reaching a first ridge and then a second. Each time he looked back he saw less and less of the great high mountain and the great city upon it. The jasper was gone and the gold, the domes were splintering, the towers and minarets were toppling.

The landscape cracked a final time and the city was lost in haze and dust. As promised, the raw network of scars had engulfed his brain.

Wallenstein sank to his knees and collapsed on the ground. A white film covered his eyes, fevers shook him, open sores spotted his skin, his hands were immovable claws, one ear hung by cartilage and his nose was eaten away, to all appearances a leper in the final stages of decay, utterly broken by his nineteen years in the Holy Land.

And untouched by the world. So of course he never knew that a German scholar, searching the shelves of St Catherine's a short time later, came across the issue of his unparalleled devotion and proudly announced the discovery of the most ancient of Bibles, a beautifully written manuscript that both refined and authenticated all subsequent versions, irrefutable proof of the distant origins of traditional Holy Scripture.

Scholars were entranced, the young German was world-famous. And after some decent haggling the exquisite manuscript was acquired by Czar Alexander II, at that time as powerful as any defender of any faith and appropriately enough, like the now insane lost hermit, a namesake of one of the military heroes the original storyteller and scribe had seen fit to have die at the early age of thirty-three along with one of their spiritual heroes.

Alexander the Great and Christ, a blind man and an imbecile, the czar and Wallenstein all steadfastly sharing their profane and sacred concerns over the centuries.

5
The Haj

In the end nothing could be said of his work except that it was preposterous and true and totally unacceptable.

❖

After Strongbow disappeared from Cairo his botanical monographs appeared less and less frequently. A year might go by with only one page published in Prague. Yet his exercises were so masterful and obscure it was generally believed he had begun some extraordinary project of which these meager presentations were but random footnotes. Given his brilliance in botany, no other explanation could be found for his apparent indifference to it.

After the middle of the century this opinion was strengthened when nothing whatsoever was heard from Strongbow for a dozen years. By then botanists everywhere were convinced the eccentric scholar had taken refuge in some remote corner of the desert to assimilate his findings, which he would soon present to the world as a monumental new theory on the origin of plants, much as his contemporary Darwin had recently done with the origin of species.

And indeed Strongbow was assimilating findings and formulating a theory but it had nothing to do with plants, a phenomenal change brought on by his brief encounter with the gentle Persian girl. And there was no way his subject could elude him in his endless disguises as a poor camel driver or a rich Damascus merchant, a harmless haggler over pimpernel or a desert collector of sorrel and similar spring herbage, an obsessed dervish given to trances and an inscrutable hakīm or healer, dispensing quinine and calomel and cinnamon water, a few grains of rhubarb and one of laudanum.

It was true no European had the opportunity to speak with him during those decades of wandering, yet there were suggestions of what was to come.

In one of his flower monographs, published in 1841, he hinted that Englishwomen in the Levant were known to sweat and that their sweat had a strong odor. If anyone at the time had considered the unholy implications of this statement it might have been realized that Strongbow was already moving inexorably toward some vast and unspeakable indecency.

But no one did notice. Scholars concentrated on his daring descriptions of new flowers, and thus while his peers rummaged through the English countryside awaiting a botanical study, Strongbow continued his epic journey across a quite different landscape.

Then too, all the accounts of Strongbow brought back to Europe over the years were more than misleading. Without exception they were totally false, the ludicrous fancies of other Europeans.

With genuine Levantines his behavior was prodigious and volatile. With them he devoured whole lambs and braces of pigeons, washing down these mountainous meals with gallons of banana beer and quarts of a frighteningly powerful alcohol he made by tapping certain palm trees and letting the juice ferment, which it did rapidly, doubling its potency every hour.

When the eating bout had been a serious one he often slept for a week, his immobile and immensely long frame stretched out like a python digesting a kill. And if the alcohol consumption had been greater than usual he might lie in his tent for as much as two weeks letting his head and organs repair themselves.

Nor did he disdain tea. On the contrary, Strongbow probably consumed more tea than any Englishman who had ever lived. Regularly each month a tea chest ordered from Ceylon arrived for him in Aqaba. In the course of a single month he drank it to the bottom, then packed the tight dry chest with the notes and journals he had accumulated during the same period.

Tea out. A great stream of piss. Notes and journals in.

As for conversation of any kind, he could find no end to it. For three or four weeks he would sit with a man, any man, feverishly discussing cryptology or music or the course of an invisible planet, the manufacture of transparent beehives, the possibility of a trip to the moon or the principles of a nonexistent world language. Wherever he found himself he would instantly seize on any stray topic that chanced to arise in the flames of a campfire or the dimness of a smoky tent, in a bazaar back room or under the stars in a watered garden.

In Tripoli, having long noted the affinity between sleeping and mysticism, wakefulness and madness, he learned the techniques of hypnotism while curing some prostitutes of their price-reducing habit of snoring.

In Arabia he observed that the temperature in the summer at five thousand feet was one hundred and seven degrees in the shade at midday, while in the winter all land above three thousand feet was covered with snow.

Miracles of rain occurred in the desert but not in every man's lifetime. The Wadi er-Rummah, forty-five camel marches or one thousand miles in length, had once become a mighty river with lakes three miles wide where Strongbow had lived for a time on a raft, ferrying stranded bedouin from side to side.

On one day alone, a twenty-third of June, he recorded sixty-eight varieties of a minor sexual act practiced by a remote hill people in northern Mesopotamia. And in a single small notebook he catalogued no less than one thousand five hundred and twenty-nine types of sexual activity practiced by an even more remote tribe unvisited by an outsider since the age of Harun al-Rashid, a people who had spent their entire history circling an oasis on the tip of the Arabian peninsula.

Darwin was said to have performed a feat similar to the first of these with a species in Brazil, and a feat similar to the second with specimens in Uruguay.

But Darwin's species had been a minute beetle and his specimens had ranged from fish to fungi, which he then shipped home in wine for later classification, whereas Strongbow's Levantine subjects were life-sized, could only be plied with wine on the spot and even then tended to alter their characteristics incessantly before his eyes.

Deep in the Sinai, Strongbow sat with the elders of the Jebeliyeh tribe and asked them what unusual information there might be in those parts. They replied that not too long ago a hermit had spent ninety moons in a cave on the mountain above the monastery of St Catherine's.

The monks had thought the hermit was praying but the Jebeliyeh knew better. Actually the hermit had been scribbling on old paper, composing a thick volume which also appeared to be very old. They hadn't seen it closely but they knew it was written in ancient languages.

How do you know? asked Strongbow.

One night, they said, an old blind man familiar with many tongues happened to come to our camp and we led him up the mountain to hear what he could hear. The old man said the hermit was muttering a mixture of archaic Hebrew and archaic Greek and some tongue he'd never heard before.

Did the old man just listen?

No, being blind he was also clever with sounds. He listened long enough to know the hermit thought he was talking to a mole, then he cast his voice as if speaking for the mole, making the squeaks but using words as well. Since the hermit was mad he wasn't surprised at the mole's questions and he answered them. But of course the answers didn't make any sense.

The mole asked what was being written?

He did, and the hermit replied that he was rewriting a sacred book he had unearthed nearby, perhaps in the monastery.

Why was he rewriting it?

Because it was chaos, a void containing all things.

And what was he going to do with his rewritten copy?

Leave it where the world would discover it.

And the original?

Bury it again so the world wouldn't discover it.

Strongbow leaned back by the fire and considered this dialogue between a mole and a hermit. As he knew, the Bible manuscript known as the Codex Sinaiticus had only recently been found in St Catherine's. But what if it was a forgery? What if the real document presented a totally different view of God and history?

After a time he took a Maria Theresa crown from his cloak and placed it on the ground in front of the Jebeliyeh elders.

This marvelous tale well pleases me. Is there more to it?

Only that the old man who was the mole forecast the hour of his death upon his return from the mountain and went to bed to await it. He never woke up. Subsequently the hermit left the cave and never came back. We can take you up there if you like.

Strongbow agreed and they climbed the mountain in darkness. Outside the cave he lit a candle. The opening was too small for him to crawl inside but he pushed one arm in and took measurements. Then he thanked the elders for their information and left toward midnight for Aqaba, normally a distance of eight marches. But Strongbow was intrigued by what he had heard and the next thing he knew a dog was yapping around his heels, a sure sign he was near an Arab village. For the first time he laid aside his speculations and raised his eyes from the ground. A shepherd boy was watching him.

What place is this?

Aqaba, answered the boy.

And the day?

He was told. He looked back at the desert and smiled. He had walked through two sunsets and three sunrises without noticing them. The shepherd was saying something. He turned to the intent little face.

What's that, son?

I asked, master, whether you're a good genie or a bad genie?

Strongbow laughed.

And why might I be a genie?

Because you're twelve feet tall and because you've just walked out of the Sinai without a waterskin or a pouch of food or anything else.

Nothing?

Only your empty hands.

Yes only those, said Strongbow slowly. But a genie isn't always tall, is he? He may be small and live in a tiny cave and never go anywhere in ninety moons.

And in all that time he may speak only once and then only to a mole.

The boy grinned.

So that's what you were doing out there, master, and now you've just changed your shape and size again the way your kind is always doing, from a mole to a giant as it pleases you, in an instant or after ninety moons. Well the water is that way if you want to wash your face, I know you don't need to drink it. But before you go, genie, won't you tell me the one thing you said to the mole?

How's this? Confide the whole truth to a shameless scamp, a mere slip of a rogue?

I'm not a rogue, master.

Promise?

Yes, please tell me.

And you won't repeat a word of the secret to anyone?

No, master.

Briefly then Strongbow recounted an obscure tale from the *Thousand and One Nights* and walked on, leaving the little boy gazing dreamily down on the gulf where a dhow was approaching with spices from India and a bulky wooden chest bearing a familiar inscription in Singhalese stating that therein was to be found the finest selected tea from Kandy, site of the temple that housed a tooth of the Buddha.

After the middle of the century there was a period of a dozen years when nothing was heard from Strongbow, the time he spent producing his study, not in a remote corner of the desert as was generally assumed but rather in the very heart of Jerusalem, where he both lived and worked in the back room of an antiquities dealer's shop.

For Strongbow those were peaceful years. The

sturdy tea chests filled with his notebooks lined the walls. He used several tea chests as his desk and a giant Egyptian stone scarab, cushioned with pillows, was his seat. An antique Turkish safe was his filing cabinet and a rusting Crusader's helmet served as an object of contemplation, much as a skull might have rested in front of a medieval alchemist.

With its heavy masonry the vault was snug in the winter, cool in the summer and nearly soundproof. When he was at his desk small cups of thick coffee were sent in every twenty minutes from a shop down the alley along with a fresh handful of strong cigarettes. During that period of concentration he seldom spoke with anyone but the antiquities dealer who was his landlord, and, less frequently, with a fat oily Arab in the bazaar from whom he bought his writing paper on the first Saturday of every month.

A cognac with your coffee? asked the stationer as Strongbow settled himself on the cushion indicated, at the front of the shop.

Excellent.

The usual order of fifteen reams?

If you please.

The man shouted instructions to his clerks and then arranged his robes on the cushion opposite Strongbow, where he had a clear view of the narrow street outside. He patted his glistening hair and puffed lazily on his hookah while they waited for the order to be counted out.

The composition goes well?

It seems to be on schedule.

And it still concerns the same subject? Only sex?

Yes.

The sleek Arab listlessly applied a fresh coat of olive oil to his face and gazed at the passing crowds. Occasionally he exchanged a nod or a smile with someone in the alley.

In all truth, he said, it seems extraordinary to me

that seven thousand sheets of paper a month could be required to write about such an ordinary matter. How can that be?

Indeed, said Strongbow, sometimes I don't understand it myself. Do you have a wife?

Four, Allah be praised.

Of all ages?

From a matronly housekeeper down to a mere feather of a girl who giggles life away in brainless inactivity, praise Him again.

Yet you are often not home in the evenings?

Work demands it.

And in the evening who are those young women I see parading near Damascus Gate?

The barefaced ones who gesture obscenely and sell themselves? It's true, Jerusalem's appalling.

And the young men there in equal numbers?

Painted no less? Winking as they curtsy? Shameless.

And the little girls in the shadows so young they only reach a man's waist?

Yet who make all manner of suggestive signs? Yes it's shocking for a holy city.

And the swarms of little boys no taller, also in the shadows?

Yet who are so lascivious they will hardly let a man pass? Disgraceful.

Who was that old crone who passed the shop just now wagging her toothless smile in this direction?

An elderly slattern who runs a private establishment near here.

She comes to visit you on occasion?

In the slack periods of the afternoon.

To barter?

Allah be praised.

Offering to arrange spectacles and diversions?

Quite so, praise Him again.

But also in her toothless state to act in confidence on a specific matter?

Quite specific.

Continuing vigorously, this crone, until business revives?

Very vigorously.

And the leering old man in front of her who also threw a secret smile in this direction?

Her brother or cousin, who can remember.

He also comes to barter on occasion?

Work must go on, Allah be praised.

This man has ingenious episodes to recount?

Very ingenious, praise Him again.

Tales offering unheard-of excursions?

Quite unheard of.

Yet he always visits at different times from his sister or cousin?

If acts and tales were to coincide we would be dizzy.

And in addition to all else, both this man and this woman have innumerable orphans of every description at their disposal?

Innumerable. Every. In addition.

A clerk bowed and announced that Strongbow's order was ready. He rose to leave. The sleek stationer smiled through half-closed eyes.

Won't you have just a puff or two of opium before you go? The quality is excellent this month.

Thank you but I think not. It tends to cloud my work.

Are you sure? It's only ten o'clock and you have the whole day ahead of you, a whole night too. Ah well, perhaps next month.

Strongbow nodded pleasantly and stepped down onto the cobblestones, leaving the fat man languidly massaging olive oil into his face as a clerk refilled his hookah.

The owner of the antiquities shop whose back room he rented was quite a different sort of man. Meek,

thin and otherworldly, he seemed to live more in the
past than in nineteenth-century Jerusalem. With objects that dated back to 1000 B.C. he had a phenomenal
familiarity, but when a piece was older than that he
was always confused and had to ask Strongbow's
opinion.

When Strongbow returned, the dealer, Haj Harun,
was examining some of his better jewelry, transferring
the stones and rings from one tray to another. Strongbow bent his long frame over the counter to admire
the splendid gems sprinkling light to all sides, dazzling
him with their colors.

Would you mind? asked Haj Harun timidly, holding
up a ring. I just acquired it from an Egyptian and I'm
not sure at all. What do you think? More or less the
middle of the New Kingdom?

Strongbow pretended to study the ring with his
magnifying glass.

Did you make a haj twenty-one years ago?

Haj Harun looked startled.

Yes.

But not in a caravan? Not following the regular
routes? Keeping by yourself to remote tracks that
weren't tracks at all?

Yes.

Strongbow smiled. He remembered the dealer although of course the man couldn't remember him
since he had been disguised as a dervish at the time.
The man had stumbled across him one afternoon near
the great divide of the wadis of northern Arabia and
remarked that the sky seemed strangely dark for that
hour, which indeed it was, because a comet happened
to be passing overhead.

In fact Strongbow had been in that particular spot
precisely for that reason, to take measurements with
a sextant and chronometer and prove to himself that
the unknown comet actually existed, Strongbow before then only having deduced its cycle of six hundred

and sixteen years from certain celestial evidence to be found in the lives of Moses and Nebuchadnezzar and Christ and Mohammed, in the Zohar and the *Thousand and One Nights*. That afternoon he had explained this to the frightened Arab, who had then nodded vaguely and gone dreamily on his way.

Strongbow's Comet. He hadn't thought about it in years. For a moment he considered the possibility of writing it up in an astronomical monograph, but no, it would be an idle indulgence. His method for dating the comet was difficult, he already had enough to do and couldn't afford to be deterred by heavenly matters.

Strongbow licked the ring. Older, he announced.

Really?

Yes.

The Arab sighed.

I can't see it. The very oldest I might venture would be early New Kingdom.

No. Older still. End of the XVII Dynasty to be exact.

Ah the Hyksos, an obscure people. How did you know?

Taste.

What?

Metal content.

Haj Harun thanked him profusely. Strongbow smiled and disappeared into his vault. To him it seemed appropriate and comfortable here. Out front the Arab dealer was trading baubles from the past while in back he was cataloguing the evidence for the present on a mountaintop called Jerusalem.

And more than once as he sat down at his desk he recalled a conversation between a mole and a hermit in the moonlight on another mountain. Who had he been, that recluse? What had driven him to undertake such an incredible task?

Of course he would never know. There was no way to know.

Saturday morning. Another fifteen reams of paper for the month ahead. He drew a file from the antique safe and drank a cup of thick coffee and lit a strong cigarette. Briefly he gazed at his rusting Crusader's helmet, then patted the nose of his giant stone scarab and went back to work.

Only once did Strongbow falter in the course of those dozen years of work in Jerusalem, but the consequences were so significant it caused his study to be almost three times longer than he had planned originally.

The episode occurred one hot summer Sunday afternoon in his vaulted room at the back of the antiquities dealer's shop. Toward midnight the night before he had finished a chapter as usual, and the next morning at six o'clock, also as usual, he had arranged himself on the giant stone scarab and gazed at the rusting Crusader's helmet before picking up his pen.

Sometime later he found himself still gazing at the Crusader's helmet. The pen was in his hand but the two hundred and thirty sheets of paper scheduled to be covered with handwriting that day still stood untouched in a neat pile. With his sundial strapped to his hip Strongbow marched outside to see what time it was. He brought the bronze piece up to the level and gasped.

Three o'clock in the afternoon? He couldn't believe it. Frowning deeply, he wandered back inside.

Haj Harun was stretched out in a corner of the front room perusing old manuscripts, as he often did on Sunday afternoons. Although he was always respectful of his tenant's privacy, the man's face looked so troubled at that moment he decided to venture a few words.

Is something the matter? he asked in a voice so low

the question could have been ignored. But Strongbow abruptly interrupted his stride and stopped, causing the sundial to swing into the wall and noisily knock loose a shower of plaster.

Yes. Time is. It seems I've done nothing for the last nine hours and I don't know what to make of it. It's unheard of for me to do nothing.

And you were doing nothing at all?

Evidently. It seems I was just sitting at my desk staring at my Crusader's helmet. Nine hours? It's incomprehensible.

Haj Harun's face brightened with hope.

But that's not nothing. That's daydreaming.

He waved his arms enthusiastically at the shelves which were crowded with artifacts.

Look at all these memories from the past around us. I spend most of my time daydreaming about them. Who owned that and why? What was he doing then? What became of it after that and what became of it later? It's enchanting. You meet people from every era and have long conversations with them.

But I don't daydream, said Strongbow emphatically.

Not even today?

Well it seems I did but I can't imagine it, nor can I imagine why, it's simply not my way. If I'm walking to Timbuktu I walk there. If I'm floating down the Tigris to Baghdad I don't get out of the water before Baghdad. And if I'm writing a study I write it.

Well perhaps you're leaving something out of your study that should be included. Perhaps that's why you were daydreaming.

Strongbow looked puzzled.

But how could I be leaving something out? That's not my way either. I don't do that.

The old Arab smiled and disappeared into the back room. A moment later he stuck his head out and Strongbow burst into laughter at the ludicrous sight.

Haj Harun had put on the Crusader's helmet, which was so big on him it floated around on his head.

Here, he said happily, a regular thinking cap, this will help us. When I want to daydream I gaze at one of my antiquities and pretty soon I'm slipping back in time and seeing Romans and Babylonians in the streets of Jerusalem. Now let's see what you see. What's your study about?

Sex.

Then it must be a woman you've left out. Who was she? Look deeply.

Strongbow stared at the old man in the helmet and it worked, suddenly he saw her again as clearly as if she were standing in Haj Harun's place. He clasped his hands and lowered his eyes.

A Persian girl, he whispered.

And you were young?

Only nineteen.

A gentle Persian girl, mused Haj Harun softly.

Yes, said Strongbow, so very gentle. There was a stream in the hills far from any city, where I chanced to pause in a glen one day to rest, and singing to herself she came upon me there. She wasn't frightened, not at all, it was as if she had expected the meeting. We talked for hours and laughed and splashed in the water, played in the water like two little children, and when darkness fell we were lying in the shadows promising each other we'd never leave that beautiful place we had found together. The days and nights that followed were boundless in their minutes of love, they seemed to stretch on forever, but then one day she returned briefly to her village and soon after she came back she collapsed on the grass, cholera, and I could only whisper to her and hold her helplessly in my arms as the life ran out of her and all at once she was gone, simply that. I buried her in the glen. A few weeks we had, no more, yet I remember every blade of grass there, every spot of sun and every sound made by the water on the rocks. A memory by a stream, the most rapturous and wretched moments I have ever known in life.

Strongbow sighed. Haj Ḥarun came over and rested a frail hand on his shoulder.

Yes, he said, a gentle Persian girl. Yes, you certainly must include her.

Strongbow got to his feet and shook himself out of the mood.

No it's not that kind of book. And anyway, that was all too long ago.

Too long ago? said Haj Harun dreamily. Nothing is ever too long ago. Once I had a Persian wife myself. She was Attar's daughter.

Who do you mean? The Sufi poet?

Yes.

But he lived in the twelfth century.

Of course, said Haj Harun.

Strongbow studied him for a moment. There was something startling and transforming about the old Arab shyly smiling out from under the large Crusader's helmet. Haj Harun was rubbing his hands and nodding encouragement.

Won't you do it? Please? At least a few pages? Just to prove to yourself that nothing is ever too long ago?

Strongbow laughed.

All right, why not, I will include her. But I think you should keep that helmet. You'll obviously be able to put it to better use than I can.

Strongbow turned and went into the back room humming to himself, eager to begin on this whole new aspect of his work. Behind him he saw Haj Harun already beginning to nod over the faded manuscript in his lap, the helmet slipping slowly down over his eyes as he drifted away on some reverie in tʰ stillness of that hot summer Sunday afternoon.

A curious man, thought Strongbow. He actually seems to believe what he says. Perhaps someday there'll be time to get to know him.

Strongbow's forty-year haj ended with the publication of his gigantic thirty-three volume study, the volumes containing some sixty thousand pages of straight exposition and another twenty thousand pages in fine type listing footnotes and allied contortions, all together a production of well over three hundred million words, which easily surpassed the population of the Western world.

Most of the footnotes could only be read with a magnifying glass equal in power to Strongbow's own, but a glance at any one of the volumes was sufficient to convince the most skeptical reader that Strongbow had immersed himself in the details of his subject with unerring scientific skill, making full use of the rational premises of the nineteenth century.

And this at a time when the authoritative English medical manual on sex stated that the majority of women had no sexual feelings of any kind, that masturbation caused tuberculosis, that gonorrhea originated in women, that marital excess led to a full spectrum of fatal disorders, and that other than total darkness during a sexual act caused temporary hallucinations and permanent brain damage.

Strongbow's dismissal of these and other absurdities was nothing compared to the demented esoterica that followed, such as the Somali practice of slicing off the labia of young girls and sewing their vulvas together with horsehair to assure virginity upon marriage.

Nor was the massive presentation in any way hampered by the engraving on the frontispiece which showed a scarred determined face swathed in Arab headgear, permanently darkened by the desert sun yet still undeniably that of an English aristocrat whose family had been honored in England for six and a half centuries, despite a certain inherent lethargy.

Nor was the impact lessened by the author's note in the preface that for the last forty years he had been an absolute master of every dialect and custom in the Middle East, and that he had spent those forty years variously disguised in order to penetrate freely every corner of the region.

Strongbow's study was the most exhaustive sexual exploration ever made. Without hesitations or allusions, with nothing in fact to calm the reader, he thoughtfully examined every sexual act that had ever taken place from Timbuktu to the Hindu Kush, from the slums of Damascus to the palaces of Baghdad, and in all the shifting bedouin encampments along the way.

All claims were substantiated at once. The evidence throughout was balanced in the Victorian manner. Yet the facts were still implacable, the sense and nonsense inescapable, the conclusions terminal.

Given his subject matter, it was only to be expected that the great majority of people would find the work revolting. For even if such practices did occur in the infamous hot lands of the Eastern Mediterranean, there was still no reason to put them into words.

And especially such explicit words, *wogs* for example, which had always been used to designate everyone east of Gibraltar but had never before appeared in print, even in the most scurrilous publications. But here was Strongbow making it the contents of his entire first chapter, tirelessly repeating it line after line and page after page together with its customary prefix *bloody, bloody wogs bloody wogs bloody wogs bloody wogs bloody wogs bloody wogs bloody* as if to signal the utter contempt for all known standards of decorum that was to follow.

Yet other revolutionary thinkers in the nineteenth century were also confronting topics subversive to society, and what was surprising at first was that unlike them, Strongbow solicited no initial support whatsoever. Instead his thesis outraged both the contemporary defenders of Darwin and Marx and the future defenders of Freud.

And always for the same reason. In both cases Strongbow contradicted the new masters by denying all precepts and mechanisms whether subtle or bold. He had the effrontery to suggest that far from there being any laws in history or man or society, there weren't even any tendencies toward such laws. The race was capricious, he said, thrusting or withdrawing as its loins moved it at the moment.

Nothing else was discernible. In the framework of Strongbowism events were random and haphazard and life was unruly and unruled, given to whimsy in the beginning and shaken by chaos at the end, a kind of unbroken sensual wheel made up of many sexes and ages revolving through time on the point of an orgasm. Thus those who courageously held liberal views, and who might have been expected to be Strongbow's natural champions, found themselves forced to denounce him bitterly with personal cause.

For there was an unmistakable hint in Volume Sixteen, and again twenty million words later in Volume Eighteen, that all unorthodox thinkers were being indicted for secret crimes. Under the tenets of Strongbowism, these seemingly brave believers in modern times stood accused of an abominable retreat into respectability because they embraced grand schemes of order.

This they did, said Strongbow, solely to conceal from themselves the rank disorder of their true natures, the inner recesses where sexual fantasies somersaulted down slippery slopes with the gamboling abandon of lambs drunk on spring grass.

So much for his possible defenders, Darwinians and Marxists alike. Having been apprehended as undercover sex maniacs, they had no choice but to become vehement enemies of Strongbowism.

As for the great bulk of his countrymen, who were traditionally in favor of dispatching large armies overseas, they were appalled by Strongbow's assertion that any military expedition was merely a disguised sexual sickness, more specifically a profound fear of impotence.

In Volume Twelve, repeated ninety million words later in Volume Twenty-two, he pointed out that *fuck you* and *fuck them* and *fuck off* were the common terms of hostility preferred by imperialists and patriots. Thus armies were raised, he said, because it was likely their raisers could raise nothing else.

As for the very foundations of imperialism, the profits accruing from military expeditions overseas, he likened them in a vulgar manner to excrement. The revolting passage appeared in Volume Eight.

There is nothing a young child values as highly as his own feces, for the simple reason that it is the only product he can produce at such an early age.

Therefore builders of empires and others with a concern for money are the perennial children of every era, at play with their feces, and in yet another guise we find men contriving to clothe their formidable sexual chaos in respectability.

For it is axiomatic in the West that it is improper to spend one's life playing with shit, whereas a thoughtful accumulation of lucre is seen commendable and even noble.

Nor did Strongbow limit his anal assaults to those caught with money in their hands. He also included all club members and anyone who propounded ceremonies or band music. The offensive material could be found in a few short sentences in Volume Twenty-six.

What are these enthusiasts actually up to? Could it be they fear the slippery and slithering and wholly unmarchable rhythms of true sexuality? Is that why they organize themselves into a counter-orgy of numbing rituals and dreary Sunday after-noon concerts? Because they are reduced to expressing pride in the only sensual act of which they are capable?

Taking a shit?

Strongbow's text was equally offensive to many who cherished romantic notions of the East, such as those who wanted to believe a rumor long current in the more exclusive London men's clubs that there was a unique male brothel in Damascus, with a special dungeon, where a man could pay to have Moroccan mercenaries cane him for the rest of his natural life.

Not true, said Strongbow, who then listed all the brothels in the Middle East along with their equipment and activities.

In addition many of Strongbow's more homely observations on life among the bedouin were simply misconstrued, such as a minor aside on camel cows. When they gave birth, he said, two of the four teats were bound with twine by the bedouin so the family could share the food by halves with the new calf.

This was seen to imply incest complicated by bestiality, the whole further debauched by mutilation and bondage and aberrant lactation methods, the striking multiple perversions at work so complex as to be unthinkable.

So too some of his simpler travel notes. A passing remark that shrimps eight inches long were generally available in the markets of Tunis, only one entry

among tens of thousands on food and eating habits in
the region, was singled out as a confession that proved
for all time the patient treachery and general depravity
long associated with the Eastern mind, trapped as it
was in an erotic coma caused by excessive sun and
blue skies, deprived of the fogs and mists and rain
that maintained human composure in Europe.

But above all there was that major aspect of Strongbow's work that had been suggested by his landlord
of twelve years in Jerusalem, the shy antiquities dealer
Haj Harun. As a result of their brief discussion on
daydreaming one hot summer Sunday afternoon, when
the old Arab had put on the rusting Crusader's helmet
and smilingly insisted that no event was ever too far
in the past to be forgotten, Strongbow had devoted
two-thirds of his entire text to his memories of the
gentle Persian girl he had loved so long ago.

These tender passages described his few weeks with
her in exquisite detail, the stream in the hills where
he had found her and the new flowers of spring and
the soft grass where they had lain under the sun and
under the stars, the words they had whispered and
the joy they had shared in those endless minutes of
springtime when he was only nineteen and she a few
years younger, love from long ago recalled now in a
tale that spanned two hundred million words and was
thus the most complete love story ever told.

Yet that part of Strongbow's work was completely
ignored. The beautiful passages devoted to the gentle
Persian girl were passed over in their entirety as if
they didn't exist, of no interest at all to his Victorian
audience when compared to such possibilities as a
Damascus dungeon where Moroccan mercenaries
could be hired to administer secret canings for life.

Clearly Strongbow had already abused most occupations and all political positions. But he refused to let

matters rest there. Indomitably he pushed deeper into
a licentious morass of insults until in Volume Twenty-
eight, provoked by his own obscene ardor and raving
out of control, he went on to pose the possibility that
everyone alive, regardless of status or opinion, was
sexually suspect.

Men have a tendency to project their own
personal cause as the general cause at large. Thus
a cobbler sees the world as a shoe, the state of its
sole dependent upon him.

A naturalist with the wit to realize he has
evolved upward since infancy by selecting this
and not that, or that and not this, views all the
species of the world as having done the same
thing. And lastly a political philosopher with
heavy unmovable bowels finds the past turgid
and ponderous, the future necessarily destined to
experience explosive upheavals from the lower
regions or classes.

Of course each of these hypothetical men is
right as far as he goes, which is to say all men are
right when describing themselves.

As seen by a cobbler, the world is a shoe. Men
do evolve out of their infancies and pent-up
bowels may well and probably will explode. But
all these innumerable individual acts must not be
allowed to obscure what they only take part in, a
chaotic universe boundlessly mad.

Strongbowism, it was apparent, ranged wide. It
could and did attack every sort of person. And it was
especially damaging to those who wanted to believe
there was some kind of scheme operating in the
universe, preferably an imposing or dramatic scheme
that could provide an overall explanation for events
either through religion or nature, society or the psyche.

Or at least a partial explanation. And if not daily

events then events that occurred once in a lifetime. Or once in a century. Or even once in an epoch.

Or at the very least one reassuring explanation for some event somewhere since the beginning of time, some tiny structure no matter how pathetic. For otherwise what did it all mean?

And here Strongbow appeared to be smiling. Exactly the point, he seemed to be saying.

For nowhere in his thirty-three volumes was there to be found even a nascent conspiracy. Not even that. On the contrary, as seen by Strongbow all yearnings for the existence of a conspiracy in life were hopeless illusions from childhood that surfaced later in idle moments, the illusions having been caused by a child's false perceptions of order above him, the subsequent yearnings arising from an adult's inability to accept the sexual chaos beneath him.

To the whore's interim statement, I'm sitting on a fortune, Strongbow now added a vastly enlarged final statement, I'm sitting on everything which is also nothing.

This argument appeared in its most cogent form in a barely legible footnote in Volume Thirty-two, printed in such fine type an acuity of eyesight worthy of a bedouin was needed to decipher it.

All of these various Levantine acts, heretofore described in detail and accounting for life as it is, I have found to be repeated incessantly among the nine sexes, in low stations and high, but never with a view toward organization or design.

The effect everywhere and at all times has been incoherent, and as much as I would like to think someone has known what he or she was doing at these most crucial moments in life, or even paused to consider the matter, I can't honestly say I do.

Rather the obverse obtains. Forty years of research have taught me that men and women fuck

with great avidity. When they finish they fuck
again and if they are not fucking when next you
see them, or gathering the strength to do so, it is
only out of some bizarre lack of opportunity.

In point of fact there is a great deal of fucking
in the world but no one is in charge of it, no
organization controls it, no recommendations
affect it.

Instead men and women fuck right along as
they always have and always will, paying no
particular attention to kingdoms or dynasties,
ignoring the universal theorems that are regularly
announced over the ages as applicable to all when
they aren't, in rapture and headlong chance,
spinning round and round the sensual wheel.

It would be comforting news indeed if we
could find a scheme or a plan or even a hint of a
conspiracy in life, some stationary point where
we could sit and be still at last. But having long
studied the spin of our wheel, I have to admit
there is none. Alas we are only right there. Each
of us.

Blasting away in another orgasm.

Nor did Strongbow defend his depraved attacks on
everyone by claiming his aim was to diagnose the
rampant sexual pathologies of his age in order for
them to be cured. In fact cures were inconceivable to
him, for it was obvious he believed man was insane
by definition.

This he made plain in Volume Thirty-three.

Within the animal kingdom we are an incorrigible and lawless member, deathly ill, a species
suffering from an incurable disease. Wise men of
all ages have known this, ignorant men of all ages
have suspected it. It amounts to congenital in-
sanity and because of it man has always wanted

to return to the orderly and ordered conditions of the animal state where he once found contentment.

All memories of lost paradises verify this, as do all visionary dreams of future utopias.

Whenever a prophet or a philosopher speaks of a new man in a new age his creation is invariably the same, the old man in the old age, the animal in his animal kingdom, the beast in the grazing herd that browses for forage digesting and rutting and evacuating in a seemingly timeless eternity, untroubled because unaware of the troubles on every side, undying because unaware of death, unliving because unaware of life.

For an animal this is most certainly a happy existence. But for you and me it can never be again.

Yet in the closing lines of Volume Thirty-three, Strongbow revealed that in spite of everything he was still willing to live with his findings and even do so with a certain gusto.

It's true that life is crumpled and mindless and covered with hairs. But for the few years we have its good memories we also have to admit it remains as pleasantly soft to the touch as an old well-used wineskin.

Or for that matter, as an old man's well-used balls.

Thus Strongbow's thesis was nothing less than a vicious onslaught on the entire rational world of the nineteenth century, where sensible solutions were considered available to all problems. In his systemless universe no one was safe and there were no solutions, just life itself.

In proof of this he had offered three hundered

million words in thirty-three volumes with no deviations from the facts.

So perhaps it was understandable that Strongbowism never acquired a single adherent in the West. In the end nothing could be said of his work except that it was preposterous and true and totally unacceptable.

When the manuscript was ready Strongbow sent it by caravan from Jerusalem to Jaffa, where a large chartered steamship was waiting to carry both camels and manuscript to Venice. There the caravan would be re-formed by its wild bedouin drivers and traverse a stately swaying course across the Alps to Basle, which he had chosen for publication because of traditional Swiss neutrality. Strongbow himself, feeling the need for a vacation after twelve years of uninterrupted work in the back room of the antiquities dealer's shop, left Jerusalem for the shores of the Dead Sea where the sun was both warm and perpetual.

At the lowest spot on earth Strongbow lolled comfortably in sulphur baths while his volumes duly appeared in a private edition of twelve hundred and fifty copies, the same number used by Darwin for the first run of the *Origin of Species*. But the only other comparison with Darwin's study was that *Levantine Sex* also sold out on its day of publication.

There was therefore no need for the British consul in Basle to attempt to have the remaining editions confiscated as he had been ordered to do by Her Majesty's government. Instead the consul went with his staff to the leading local British banker, who added his staff for the joint visit to the leading local Swiss banker, who closed for the day and collected his considerably larger staff for the march across town to Strongbow's printer.

Thus it was a large and mixed group that gathered at sunset behind the locked doors of a foundry on the outskirts of Basle. The furnaces were fired to maximum temperature and Strongbow's manuscript was dumped in and consumed. Then they began wheeling in the towering stacks of plates used to print the study and shoveled them into the furnaces, where they were reduced to huge identical ingots of solid dead metal.

The furnace doors clanged, shadows danced on the walls, sudden flashes of sparks shook the air and the printing history of *Levantine Sex* lasted less than twenty-four hours, over before the next sun rose. Having learned patience in the desert, that much Strongbow might have accepted. But not the act that had occurred during the night.

For it seemed that Parliament had secretly met on the night of publication to review his study, and to booming cries of *Shame Shame* had found it despicably un-English without debate, thereupon unanimously enacting emergency legislation stating that his title as the Duke of Dorset was from that moment forever null and void, that all rights not specifically granted him as a private citizen were to be ignored and denied him, and that he was to be deplored in perpetuity throughout the Empire.

So a contest had been joined. But there was never any doubt who would be the victor.

6

YHWH

Undoubtedly God passed His time in some other way, but how?

❉

Around the middle of the century a ghostly figure became familiar in certain villages in central Albania. Barefoot and hairless and mostly naked, a skeleton with gaping holes in its head, this diseased apparition lurked near water holes muttering insanely in an unknown tongue.

Normally the peasants of the place would have wasted little time beating such a grotesque derelict with their staves, but the appearance of this apparent leper was so unworldly they offered him vegetables instead. Dumbly the ghost accepted their onions and carrots and floated away on an arcane route that always brought him back in a few days.

The language the peasants heard by the water holes was Aramaic and the ghost was none other than the last of the Skanderbeg Wallensteins, who in the course of six or seven lost years had somehow found his way home from the Holy Land. The villages where he now begged had once belonged to him and the mysterious circle he traced lay around the Wallenstein castle, although his eyes were too weak to make out the cliffs above, where it had once stood.

A change came when he chanced to be near a church where Bach's Mass in B Minor was being

played. The music stirred dim memories of a tower
conservatory and the Albanian dialects of his youth,
allowing him to ask questions that led him to the
castle, where he collapsed in delirium. By then only
two people were living there, a mother and her young
daughter, the mother having once been a cleaning
woman attached to the stables. All the other servants
had long since died or moved away after Wallenstein
had consumed the family fortune in Jerusalem.

The castle itself was in a terrible state of ruin. The
roofs were gone and the upper storeys had fallen in.
Bushes grew where generations of Skanderbeg Wallensteins had once sneaked down corridors, peering
suspiciously down at the surrounding countryside.
One room alone remained intact in the foundations,
a small kitchen in which the mother and daughter
lived.

They too would have left had the mother not been
crippled by kidney stones which made it impossible
for her to walk. But as it was they had nowhere to go
and couldn't have hired a cart to take them there anyway. So the daughter tended a meager vegetable
garden in an upper storey and collected firewood from
the debris of former window frames and furniture.

It was the daughter who found Wallenstein unconscious in the empty moat. Although a small girl she
easily shouldered the light sack of bones and carried
him down through the rubble to the kitchen, where
she and her mother ripped their skirts into bandages
and applied herbal plasters. That night they lay on
the bare stones while Wallenstein slept on their pile
of straw.

After being nursed for several months Wallenstein
began to recover. His skin ulcers healed, his fingers
uncurled and his eyes cleared, he could hear through
one ear and control his bowels and spittle. He still
lacked the other ear and nothing could be done about
the nose eaten away by ants, but the daughter

cleverly carved a wooden ear for him and a lifelike wooden nose, which were held in place by a thin leather thong tied at the back of his head.

The herbal remedies had a remarkable effect on Wallenstein's maladies save for one, a high fever of unknown cause. Wallenstein was running a steady temperature of one hundred and three degrees and would do so as long as he lived, yet for some reason he was capable of sustaining this feverish new condition. What worried mother and daughter alike was the way he talked upon emerging from his coma.

For it seemed that after completing the greatest forgery in history, Wallenstein had inexplicably been converted to the very heresies he had meant to correct. Twice before he had committed himself to extreme religious positions, once to the silence of the Trappists and later to the even more severe silence and solitude of a desert hermitage.

Now came this third upheaval, an absolute belief in the stupefying contradictions of the Sinai Bible he had nearly died rewriting. And since he felt he was living at the end of time, he was convinced he had to recite the entire text of the buried original lest its striking confusions be lost forever.

Thus did Wallenstein plunge from utter silence into utter volubility, talking and talking as if he could never stop.

When he awoke on the straw in the morning some of what he said was still comprehensible. As he sat up in bed he had the habit of shouting *I am that I am* over one shoulder, the shoulder below the wooden ear.

And then as if to reinforce this notion, or perhaps simply because he couldn't hear through that ear, he would turn his wooden nose to the other side and shout with equal conviction over the other shoulder *He is that He is*, these primal announcements often repeated a dozen times before he was satisfied with their authenticity, whereupon he would leap from bed ignoring the breakfast laid out for him and go striding off naked through the barren ruins of his ancestral castle in search of the innumerable shifting characters once imagined by a blind man and an imbecile, inevitably finding a crowd of their faces in a collapsed wall and stopping there to harangue the blocks of stone tirelessly for the rest of the day.

Or he would lecture a tree for weeks, the crumbling castle and its wild grounds having become a mythical land of Canaan whose dusty waysides were thronged with shepherds and priests and cobblers and traders of every description, not to mention the forty thousand prophets rumored to have sprung from the desert since the beginning of time.

Darkness and snow, autumn and winds, spring and rain and the heavy heat of summer, nothing could keep Wallenstein from preaching his inspired message to the rocks and trees and bushes he mistook for the multitudes swirling through his brain, Isaiah and Fatima and Christ listening to him and munching olives, Joshua and Judas and Jeremiah listening and sharing a wineskin, Ishmael and Mary holding hands and listening, Ruth and Abraham sitting on the grass and listening while Mohammed's flying horse hovered overhead and Elijah and Harun al-Rashid eagerly pushed forward, everyone surging around him intent on not missing a word that fell from the lips of Melchizedek, legendary King of Jerusalem.

For Wallenstein now realized who he was. This secret of antiquity had been well kept, but he knew, so down the open galleries of the castle he marched casting blessings and warnings, raising a hand in hope or instruction, arms spread wide as he assayed meaningless proverbs and retold in an impressively loud voice, to no one, the thousand and one dreams tumbling through his mind.

As his body healed these verbal seizures increased in eloquence and speed, the words coming so fast there was no time to form them anymore. Powerful tirades were delivered as mere noise. Whole sermons were encapsuled in half a breath, where they disappeared before being uttered, the unspoken syllables solidly entangled and indistinguishable.

Until the slightest sound from the outside world, even his own footstep, might cause him to forget where he was. When that happened he thrust his wooden ear forward timidly and for a few seconds it seemed he might be lost, driven back once more to the profound silence of that tiny cave he had known near the summit of Mt. Sinai.

But then just as suddenly he was all smiles. A hundred faces appeared in a rock, a thousand faces lined the trunk of a tree, a new sea of admirers surged around him.

Wallenstein straightened his wooden nose and adjusted his wooden ear. He was ready. Forcefully he launched himself into an even more incoherent monologue.

Sophia, the daughter, was eight years old when Wallenstein returned to the castle. Having always lived as a recluse in its ruins and never really known anyone but her mother, she had no reason to consider Wallenstein insane. Her mother had a bloated body and never spoke, Wallenstein had wooden features and never stopped speaking. Such was the world for Sophia, who was humble and retiring by nature. Gradually she came to love him as a father and he was able to feel her tenderness despite the swarms of hallucinatory events clamoring for his attention.

When she was old enough she tried to teach herself the intricacies of business in hopes of repairing the castle to make his life more comfortable. Money could still be borrowed in his name but the money-lenders were shrewd and she was often humiliated.

Sophia the Unspoken she came to be called in the villages, because she never said more than a few words at a time. People thought this was due to shyness but actually it came from a simple and gentle fear that too many words on her part might somehow reveal the joyful secret of her new love, and in so doing, in some unexplained way, cause it to go away.

At night she cried alone in the castle, the next day she went back to face the moneylenders, in time learning to manage the investments. Painstakingly she paid off the debts on the castle and bought back its farms and villages, so that eventually the Wallenstein holdings were as extensive as ever.

While Sophia was still young her mother's kidney stones finally burst through the organs and she died, leaving the adopted father and daughter alone in the castle. Almost at once they became lovers and remained so for twenty years. During that time, moved by a physical contact he had never known before, Wallenstein had moments of lucidity when he was able to recall the original Bible he had found and describe its wonders to Sophia, recalling as well the forgery he had made.

I had to do it, he whispered, I had no choice. But someday I'll go back and find the original again.

His voice cracked when he said those words and he began to cry helplessly in her arms, knowing he would never go back because the moments of lucidity were too rare, too brief, for him ever to do anything important again.

The Armenian Quarter? he said with hope. It's there where I left it. I can find it again can't I?

Of course you can, answered Sophia, holding him tightly and wiping away his tears, her simple love no match for the memory of nineteen years in the Holy Land and the terror of a mountain cave, the scars in the dirt floor of a basement hole in Jerusalem.

You can, she said, *you can you can,* she repeated

desperately as she felt his body loosen and he drifted away in her arms, the sorrowful cast of his face already lapsing into an imbecilic grin.

After twenty years Sophia became pregnant. She didn't want to have the baby but Wallenstein pleaded with her and finally she agreed. She also agreed to name the child Catherine in honor of the monastery where he had discovered his new religion.

The child was a boy and Sophia duly named him Catherine, but his birth was the great tragedy of her life. From that day on Wallenstein never again spoke to her, never touched her, never saw her when she was standing in front of him. Unknown to her, behind his grin, he had been pondering for some time the possibility that he might not be merely Melchizedek, no matter how august that primary priest of antiquity.

Secretly, for some time, he had been considering the possibility he might be God.

Now with the birth of a son his own daring overwhelmed him and the already incredible profusion of his brain was pushed into an ultimate or original chaos. In his mind Catherine was Christ and he at once descended into the limitless prophecies of the Bible he had buried in Jerusalem, a vision from which there was no return.

And now that he was God the legions of his creation were so vast, the dimensions of his universe so grand, he could never stop talking, not even for an instant. Yet he also sensed it was beneath him to continue addressing rocks and trees and bushes. Those were the duties of Melchizedek, bringer of the divine message.

Undoubtedly God passed His time in some other way, but how?

Wallenstein raised his wooden ear hoping to catch a familiar sound. When he had become God, not surprisingly, he learned that God was also never silent. Not surprisingly, God talked just as incessantly as he had when he had been Wallenstein. But what was so important that only God could say it?

A name? The very name he had been invoking for years in his rapid deliveries? A name spoken so reverently, so quickly, there had never been time to include any vowels in it? A name, therefore, that could only be pronounced by Him? A name that was nothing but noise to anyone else?

Wallenstein tried it. He said it quite loudly.

YHWH.

It sounded right and he repeated it, astounded that he could sum up the entire universe and describe everything in it simply by identifying himself, exactly what he had been looking for during all those years of tirade, one unpronounceable word at the end of time, his own name.

YHWH.

Yes he had the timbre of it and it was a surpassing method for affirming the truth.

Suddenly he grinned. All at once he had advanced from the blind man's secret three thousand years ago in the dusty waysides of Canaan to the secret of the imbecile scribe. Now never again would he bother to lecture a stone or a tree or a bush. Never again would he eat or sleep or put on more or less clothing or march down corridors and gardens varying his accounts to verify the truth. Now there would be no more winters and summers for him or days and nights at the foot of the mountain.

He had finished his autobiographical footnote, *saith end ending of endings end,* and now he could stand absolutely still through all eternity repeating his own name.

Sadly Sophia watched him shouting his senseless noise and knew there was only one way to save him, only one way that he could live, so she took him by

the hand and led him down through the deepest
recesses of the castle to a soundless black dungeon
many hundreds of feet below the ground, sat him
down on the cot and locked the iron door, thereafter
faithfully visiting him three times a day with food and
water and lovingly stroking him for an hour or more
as he shouted out his incomprehensible name to the
entire assembly of worlds he had made, tenderly
adjusting his wooden nose and his wooden ear before
kissing him good-bye and locking the door once more
so moments might come in the black stillness when
he could forget his manifold duties as creator of all
things and grow silent, finding at last each day the
food and sleep necessary for life, which the former
hermit and forger did for another three decades,
surviving beneath the castle until 1906, through
Sophia's love living to the advanced age of one
hundred and four deeply buried in the boundless
darkness or light God had found for Himself in the
universe of His cave.

7

The Tiberias
Telegrams

*The desire of the stranger is to
his people. Speed the stranger
home.*

❧

News of the triumphant book-burning episode in Basle
and Parliament's emergency legislation against him
reached Strongbow by way of a Roman newspaper
months out of date.

While tarrying in the cabalist center of Safad he
had gone down to Galilee one morning to fish. The air
was fresh, the land still, the water unruffled. In due
time he caught a fish and searched his robes for something to wrap it in, but all he had with him was a
worn copy of the Zohar.

A clamor from the hillside above attracted his attention, a noisy band of Italian pilgrims climbing up to
have a breakfast picnic on the site where Christ had
preached the Sermon on the Mount. As they trudged
along one of the men impatiently broke out a large
salami and ripped off a mouthful of meat, discarding
the wrapping paper, which floated down the hill in
Strongbow's direction.

Strongbow was about to wrap up his fish in the
newspaper page when he saw his own name looming

up in a greasy headline that led into the fish's mouth.
The dispatch was slimy but included all the essential
facts.

At once Strongbow strapped his heavy bronze sundial to his hip and marched down the shore to Tiberias,
where a small Turkish garrison was quartered. Without a word he pushed aside the guards and slammed
his way into the private apartment of the Turkish
commandant, a young man who was sipping his
morning coffee, not yet dressed.

The commandant grabbed his pistol from the night
table and wildly fired off all nine rounds at what he
took to be an immensely tall old Arab holding a fish
and wearing a sundial and carrying a book of Jewish
mysticism. When the bullets stopped crashing into
the walls the Arab calmly laid the fish on the night
table and placed a Maria Theresa crown beside it.

I've just caught a herbivorous fish that thrives on
algae and I want to send news of the catch to England.

What?

A St Peter's fish, rather bony but tasty. Are you in
contact with Constantinople by telegraph?

Yes, whispered the terrified Turk, staring first at the
fish and the book, then at the gold coin, then at the
cryptic Arabic aphorisms engraved on the sundial.

Good. Send two telegrams for me to Constantinople,
to someone you can bribe or trust, with instructions
that they are to be taken to a commercial telegraph
office and forwarded to an address in London I will
give you.

But I don't even know who you are.

Strongbow placed a second gold coin on the table
beside the fish. The Turk's eyes narrowed.

How can I be sure your catch is authentic and your
fishing expedition isn't meant to harm the Ottoman
Empire?

Strongbow placed another coin on the table and the
Turk's eyes widened as he stared at the six glistening

gold breasts of the former Austrian empress, largely bare and bulging impressively after having nursed sixteen children.

Or perhaps even meant to destroy the Empire?

Strongbow placed a fourth and last coin on the table, surrounding the fish with gold. He raised his sundial and studied it.

At this moment in your life the Prophet has presented you with a choice.

He has? What is it?

Pocket this money, send my telegrams, order the fish cooked for your lunch and shoot any of your men who are insubordinate. Or conversely, refuse the money and I will shoot you and all your men, send the telegrams myself and cook the fish for my own lunch.

The tall Arab checked his sundial again. In fact this apparition from the desert was so unnaturally tall and self-assured the Turk wondered if he might not be the Prophet himself, in which case it made no difference what he decided. And although he was still afraid to send the telegrams on his military circuit, the eight large breasts of Maria Theresa made a handsome sum of money.

Time, said the apparition, startling the Turk out of his thoughts. Instantly he reached into his night table for pen and paper.

Allah must have willed it, he sighed.

Indeed it seems likely, murmured Strongbow, who had begun printing rapidly in four-letter groups.

Naturally Strongbow's codes were unbreakable and could only be read by his London solicitor, who had certain sealed envelopes locked in his safe to be used for deciphering when so directed.

The first telegram instructed the solicitor to sell the Strongbow estate in Dorset and the numerous holdings that went with it. He was also to liquidate all the other Strongbow assets scattered throughout the industrial north and Ireland and Scotland and Wales, using hundreds of intermediaries so the enormity of these financial transactions would remain unsuspected.

The huge sums of money accruing from the sales were then to be forwarded in a devious manner to banks in Prague for eventual deposit in a Turkish consortium. Only when every shilling of the Strongbow fortune was safely out of England was the solicitor to decipher the second telegram that had been sent from Tiberias.

Whereas the first telegram had been long and detailed, the second was brief. And although Strongbow refused to address it properly, this second telegram was directed to Queen Victoria.

In it, citing his own family as an example, Strongbow noted that the quality of sexual life in England had deteriorated disastrously over the last seven hundred years. He admitted the queen was probably incompetent to do anything about it, but at the same time he said his self-respect would no longer allow him to participate in such a dreary decline.

Therefore he was renouncing his citizenship. Never again would he set foot west of the Red Sea. He then concluded with an array of scabrous allegations that surpassed even the obscenities found in *Levantine Sex*.

MADAME, YOU ARE A SMALL AND SMUG MOTHER RULING A SMALL AND SMUG COUNTRY. CERTAINLY GOD MADE YOU BOTH SMALL, BUT WHOM ARE WE TO BLAME FOR THE SMUGNESS?

IT WOULDN'T SURPRISE ME IF YOUR NAME IN THE FUTURE BECAME SYNONYMOUS WITH UGLY CLUTTER AND DARK PONDEROUS FURNITURE AND HIDDEN EVIL THOUGHTS, WITH ARROGANT POMPOSITY AND CHILD PROSTITUTION AND A WHOLE HOST OF OTHER GROSS PERVERSIONS.

IN SHORT, MADAME, YOUR NAME WILL BE USED
TO DESIGNATE THE WORST SORT OF SECRET SEXUAL
DISEASE, A PRIM HYPOCRISY INCOMPARABLY RANK
BENEATH ITS HEAVY LAVENDER SCENT.

The address on the telegram was *Hanover, England.*
It was signed *Plantagenet, Arabia.*

Thus the former deaf boy, lance in hand, who had
once cleared his family manor of six hundred and fifty
years of frivolous history, now felt he had found his
vocation at last. The huge magnifying glass and
bronze sundial were to be left behind. At the age of
sixty he had decided to become a hakīm or healer
curing the poor in the desert.

Of course he had no way of knowing that the influx
of his immense fortune into Constantinople, nominal
ruler of the desert in his day but already corrupt
beyond hope, would ineluctably cause repercussions
far beyond that city, until by the end of the nineteenth
century not only the desert but the entire Middle East
would in fact be the property of one man, a lean
barefoot giant who spoke humbly as an Arab and was
occasionally humiliated as a Jew, who was by then
both an Arab and a Jew, an indistinguishable Semite
living in a ragged opensided tent tending his sheep.

From Galilee he walked to Constantinople and began to set up the banks and concessions and sub-
sidiaries that would allow his fortune to run without
him. One day he was a Persian potentate, the next an
Egyptian emir, the third a Baghdad banker.

He obtained a controlling interest in the posts and
telegraph system, bought up all government bonds
and issued new ones, became the secret paymaster of
the Turkish army and navy, bribed the descendants
of the Janissaries, consulted with pashas and ministers
and laid aside trust funds for their grandsons, ac-

quired rights to the wells in Mecca and all wells on all routes leading to Mecca, bought two hundred of the existing two hundred and forty-four industrial enterprises in the Turkish realm, dismissed and reappointed the Armenian and Greek and Latin Greek and Syrian Greek patriarchs in Jerusalem and the Coptic patriarch in Alexandria, leased four thousand kilometers of railway lines, established dowries for the daughters of the principal landowners between the Persian Gulf and the Anatolian highlands, refurbished the gold mosaics and polychrome marbles of Santa Sophia, so that by the time he was ready to leave the city anyone who could ever be in a position of power in that part of the world was under his control.

Although no one knew it, he had bought the Ottoman Empire.

Nor did anyone know he had already assured the destruction of the British Empire by sending it into a slow decline from which it could never recover. Some might date the decline from the day when his barbaric caravan had disembarked at Venice with its monstrous load of Eastern lore. Or a dozen years earlier when he had first sat down on the giant stone scarab in Jerusalem to expound that ruinous lore. Or even many years before that when he had hinted in a monograph on flowers that Englishwomen were known to sweat in the Levant.

But all these dates were too recent. One hundred years was a more likely span for the disintegration of a great empire, so probably the irrevocable course had been set on that warm Cairo night in 1840 when a laughing naked young Strongbow had turned his back on the reception celebrating Queen Victoria's twenty-first birthday and leapt over a garden wall to begin his haj.

And now forty years later it was a rainy October

afternoon when a tall gaunt man solemnly concluded his business in Constantinople and walked to a deserted stretch of the Bosporus, saw the clouds part and stood in a dripping olive grove watching the sun sink over Europe, then ceremoniously removed the rings and jeweled sandals and filigreed headgear of his last disguise, threw them into the passing waters and climbed back through the gnarled grove to disappear forever, barefoot now and wearing only a torn cloak, without even a bundle to carry, making his way south toward the Holy Land and perhaps beyond.

No one suspected the loss but Strongbow had taken far more than a great fortune away from Europe. He had also taken an irreplaceable vision that saw new worlds and sought them, a spirit that fed itself on the raw salads of mirages.

Never again would the West send out another Strongbow. After him there would be delegations and commissions, engineers and army garrisons, circulating judicial bodies and stray wanderers on camelback. These events were still to come but the greatest of all conquests was over, the expedition that could only be launched by one man from the vast legions he found in his heart.

As a destitute hakīm he no longer carried calomel or quinine or rhubarb grains. Now he cured solely through hypnotism.

His usual practice was to seat himself behind his patients so he couldn't see their lips and read the words they thought they were saying, thus freeing himself to use his knowledge of the desert to listen to their true feelings. After a time he told the man or woman to turn and face him.

By then the patient was thoroughly accustomed to an empty vista and the sudden confrontation with the hakīm's huge immobile presence, especially his gaze, was overwhelming. Powerful, musing, contemplative, the great eyes bore down upon the patient, who was immediately under their control.

The hakīm said nothing in words. With his eyes he reshaped and repeopled the barren desert from the rich landscape of his patient's mind, detecting distant drifts of sand and adjusting veils, adjusting costumes and revisiting forgotten corners, sampling the sound of the wind and sipping water from tiny wells.

As a botanist might, he planted seeds and nursed the seedlings into flowers. Gently he blew the flowers to and fro until their contours shimmered in the sun. Steadily he gauged the sweep of the horizons.

The eyes spoke a final time and the patient awoke from the trance. The hakīm told him to come again in a day or a week, and if the asthma or astigmatism hadn't improved by then he would suggest they sit together once more staring at the desert.

At the same time the hakīm took the opportunity to explore a more personal question. Ever since he had left Jerusalem he had pondered deeply that obscure conversation in archaic languages between a mole and a hermit outside a cave on Mt Sinai. And having considered it carefully, he had come to believe that an astounding transformation had indeed occurred in that tiny cave, and that the Bible accepted as the oldest in the world was nothing more than a forgery of stupendous proportions.

Of course he had no way of knowing what was in the real Sinai Bible, he could only guess at its contents. Yet for some reason he was convinced it held the secret to his own life. A strange idea came to him then and he began asking his patients the questions he had been asking himself for so long.

Have you heard of a mysterious lost book in which all things are written? A book that is circular and unchronicled and calmly contradictory, suggesting infinity?

His patients stirred in the depths of their hypnotic trances. Sometimes they were slow to answer but the answers seemed always the same. They thought they had heard of the book. Parts of it might have been read to them when they were children.

The hakīm went on with his cures until the end of the day, when he sat alone and wondered at the sameness of these replies. Since so many people knew of the lost book, could it be they were all secret contributors to it? That the lost original could thus be retrieved only by probing the hypnotic trances of everyone on earth?

The hakīm reeled under the weight of this revelation. The truth was staggering, the task without hope. For the first time in his life he felt helpless.

Bleakly he recalled his decades of ceaseless wandering through tides of sand in the wake of the moon in search of a holy place once mentioned by Father Yakouba. The memory of that serene and gentle dwarf now filled him with a terrible sadness, for his haj was over and he knew he hadn't found his holy place. Why had he failed? Where were the footprints in the sky?

Enormous and solitary in the twilight, the greatest explorer of his age sank to his knees and gazed slowly around at the shadows, lost and knowing he was lost, remaining there until a young man approached him at dawn.

O revered hakīm?

Yes, my child.

I am sick and weary.

Yes, my child.

Can you help me, as they say you can?

Yes. Sit now and turn your back and fix your eyes on that distant eagle as he swoops and soars in the first light of day living a thousand years. Are we able to follow such paths? Could it be his flight traces the journey of the Prophet, the actual footsteps a man takes from the day of his birth to the day of his death?

The swirls of the Koran shape and unshape themselves as do the waves in the desert and yes the oasis may be small. But yes, we will find it.

One afternoon a shepherd watched the hakīm healing on a hillside in the Yemen and came to him when he was finished. He was a small plump man given to continual smiles who waddled more than walked. The waddle carried him along the hillside where he stood dancing from one leg to the other.

Salaam aleikoum, respected hakīm. And who might you be?

Aleikoum es-salaam, brother. A man astray.

Ah but we're all astray, yet isn't it also written that each man has an appointed place?

It is, and also that man knows not in what country he must die. Now what is it that ails you, brother?

So businesslike, hakīm, but you see it's not me. I only have the usual aches to be cured when that day arrives. It's you I've come to talk about.

Me, brother?

Yes. You're ailing and no one likes to see a kindly man ail.

As you said, when that day arrives.

No no, hakīm, I didn't mean that at all. But won't you come to my tent for coffee? The day's over and it's time to leave the dust. Won't you come along now? Come.

The little man tugged the hakīm's sleeve and when the hakīm rose the little man laughed loudly.

What is it?

Why the two of us, don't you see? When you were sitting I was as tall as you but now suddenly I'm only half as tall. What's to be done? Must a hakīm always sit while a poor shepherd always stands? A marvel, that's what it is.

What?

His variety, His gifts. But come, brother, as you call me, the day's over and there's good coffee to drink. Yes come at once. Ya'qub is my name, come.

He laughed again and they started off, the tall gaunt hakīm dignified despite his rags, the short plump shepherd humming happily as he skipped along trying to match the solemn strides of the man he had come to lead home.

The hakīm arranged his rags, Ya'qub made coffee. And now the little man's face was serious and his voice urgent.

I've watched you curing the sick with your eyes, hakīm, and it's good work you do. But don't you know your own eyes can be read as well? They can and today I read them. Would it be wrong to say you've traveled so much you've seen everything?

It may be so.

And that these things you've seen and done no longer interest you?

That's true.

Yes of course, because you're growing old like me. But we're not really that old, hakīm, only sixty and a little more, not much of anything. And isn't it also true you're very rich? Not at all the poor man you appear to be?

How's that, brother?

Here I mean, in your heart, because you've seen so much. Isn't it true you're one of the richest men in the world? Perhaps the richest of all?

It may be.

No no, sadly for you it isn't true. You certainly should be but you're not at all. And when you said before you'd seen everything, that wasn't true either. You're a good man and kind but a sickness has come to you in the second half of your life.

I grow old, that's all.

No no it's not age, it's something else. With all your travels and your wisdom don't you know it? Don't you see it with those powerful eyes of yours, you who see so much in everyone else? Well if you don't I'll have to tell you. It's loneliness, hakīm, that's your sickness. You're all alone. Haven't you ever loved a woman and had a child?

The first but not the second.

You mean you have loved a woman?

Yes.

But it was long ago in some faraway place?

Yes.

But how long ago, simply years and years? A very long time?

If forty years is a long time, yes.

And this faraway place, would it be strange to a poor shepherd from the Yemen?

It might be strange, yes.

You mean it has palaces and fountains and elephants? These and other wonders without count? All that and more? What could such a place be called?

Persia.

The little man clapped his hands and now all the gravity was gone from his face. He laughed and hugged himself.

Oh I've heard of it, hakīm, I've certainly heard of Persia with its elephants and fountains and palaces but I've never known anyone who's been there. So won't you tell me all about it? About the woman too? It's good for men of our years to recall love, nothing is better save to have that love still. So please tell me everything, hakīm. This is rich news you bring to my hillside.

Yes yes, he whispered, jumping to his feet and scurrying around the tent searching in vain for more coffee to boil, bumping into a lamp in his haste and knocking it over, laughing at the lamp and bumping into the tent poles and laughing at them, finding coffee at last and seating himself with great pleasure, rocking and smiling and wrapping his stubby arms around his body as if to feel the joy that would be his with a story of love and Persia.

The tale Ya'qub heard wasn't at all what he had expected. The hakīm began slowly, for once unsure what he was going to say, not even sure why he was telling this stranger about the gentle Persian girl he had once known for a few weeks, no more, before she died in an epidemic and he too had fallen ill and been partially blind for a time, memorizing the Koran in his sadness and becoming a Master Sufi before moving on to encompass the rituals of a thousand tribes.

As Ya'qub listened to this tall gaunt man he realized he wasn't merely a hakīm no matter how good and powerful, but a wanderer who had been many men in many places, a figure disguised in many robes, truly a vast and changeable spirit.

A genie?

Yes a genie, but that was before. Now he was a man with a sickness.

Ya'qub listened to his guest and watched his eyes. He nodded when the hakīm ended.

You're deaf?

Yes.

No matter. Anyone can be deaf or something else and all men are.

Only one other person has ever guessed that.

And he heard it too, just as I did, and of course his name was also Ya'qub, wasn't it?

Yes, but why?

But why and why? repeated Ya'qub happily. How could it be otherwise? When things are a certain way that's the way they have to be. But you're smiling now, hakīm, and why is that? How can a man who's done nothing and been nowhere make you smile? And there was more to your wandering than just wandering, wasn't there? All that time when you were pretending to be on a haj you were really looking for a lost book, isn't it so? The story of the gentle Persian girl was in it but also other things and that's why you picked up so many jokes and riddles and scraps of rhymes in so many holy places. Admit it, because you thought they were also part of the book.

Rhymes? asked the hakīm. Jokes and riddles?

Ah I've caught you haven't I? Now listen to me retell your tale exactly as I heard it.

The little shepherd swelled himself up and began to hum. He rocked back and forth and whistled, spread his short arms and clasped himself, floated naked down the Tigris at night and swam the Red Sea and penetrated Mecca and Medina and tarried in Safad, walked twenty-five hundred miles to Timbuktu to meet the other Ya'qub and soaked his feet in Lake Chad coming and going, marched out of the Sinai oblivious to two sunsets and three sunrises and plotted the passage of a secret comet in north Arabia, conversed with an oily stationer and an ethereal dealer in antiquities while composing three hundred million words in a Jerusalem vault, acquired one empire and destroyed another and finally rode an elephant to a palace, finally sat down beside a fountain in the palace to rest, finally leaned back with a small cup of coffee to read the old new lines in the palm of his hand.

Do you see? said Ya'qub. Isn't that how it was? Scraps from a magical book that's always being written? Or was written once? Or will be written someday? Well I know all about that book, hakīm. What? Of course I do, I couldn't have been more than three or four years old when I first heard people talking about it. But the point is, hakīm, why go on looking for it when we can write it ourselves? Or better yet, just talk it out in our old age? Why seek what can be lived? Could it be this very tent is the palace referred to in the tale? Don't the two of us know enough by now? An old man who's been nowhere, an old man who's been everywhere? Between us all the gifts and marvels, every one? Now admit it, hakīm, you like this hillside don't you? Of course you do and that's why you're going to stay here. There must be an Arab saying for that. What could it be?

The desire of the stranger is to his people, said the hakīm. Speed the stranger home.

Yes yes, good, speed the stranger home, that's it certainly. Yet it took you more than sixty years you say, and that's why you smile now when you look around your new home. Well that's just one of His little riddles, where would the world be without a few riddles and scraps of rhymes? All solemn ceremony, nothing but grave purpose. Anyway, how good you must feel to be with your people at last, to be home at last. Surely that's the greatest gift but one. No two.

And what are they, Ya'qub?

The first is the woman you love, the second is the child she gives you. But we don't have to think about that because soon you will have both.

I will?

Of course, it's in your eyes, nothing was ever clearer. Now just let me tell my daughter we have a guest for dinner, all this talk about faraway places has made me hungry. To find something at the end of the day that's been lost, how sweet it is. But there you go again and not just smiling but laughing as well. Why laugh at a man just because he's never been anywhere or done anything? There'll be laughter enough when people see us out walking, your head in the sky and mine on the ground. We'll look ridiculous together and they'll laugh but no matter, it can't be helped since that's the way it's going to be.

What is, Ya'qub?

What I glimpsed in your eyes just now, why were you trying to hide it? Your marriage to my daughter of course. One year from now or less, a son. But why are you laughing a third time, o former hakīm? Hadn't you even read that in your lost book when I found you this afternoon? Didn't you know it was written long ago that this hillside in the Yemen would one day be your home? That what you have been seeking so long is the peacefulness of this very tent?

PART TWO

8

O'Sullivan Beare

We ourselves.

❖

Some thirty years before the once great Generalissimo
Wallenstein had become a fugitive in the mists of
northern Bohemia, an Irish chieftain named O'Sullivan
Beare was having his castle burned and his people
slaughtered by the English in County Cork. He had
no choice but to abandon his land and go on the run,
which he did, from the south to the north of Ireland
with one thousand of his people.

The month was January and the weather was severe
as usual. Armies were in pursuit and the country was
starving as usual. O'Sullivan Beare marched two
hundred miles in fifteen terrible days and arrived in
the north with only thirty-five survivors. After that
heroic march the clan became famous in southwestern
Ireland, where they were alternately known as the
O'Sullivan Foxes when sober and cunning and the
O'Sullivan Beares when drunk and blustering.

The bear and fox who would smuggle the first arms
to the Haganah for Strongbow's son was born on one
of the tiny Aran Islands that lay to the west of the
country, a barren windswept outpost in the Atlantic
so poor it had never been gifted with soil. The island
had never supported a population of more than a few
hundred souls, yet over the centuries fully one hundred
saints had been born there. No area in Christendom
had ever produced so many saints and it was generally

believed this was because the place was so desolate its people had no choice but to be canonized or emigrate or stay drunk.

Or have large families, which they also did in abundance. Seven or eight children was normal and fifteen or twenty was not unknown, but Joe's family was unusual because he was one of thirty-three brothers, the youngest, this enormous brood fathered by one poor fisherman who was himself the seventh son of a seventh son, which meant he had an infallible gift of prophecy when moved to use it. Given the traditional shyness of the islanders it wasn't surprising he was so moved only when thoroughly drunk, which happened exactly three times a year, after mass on Christmas and Easter and June 14, the feast day of the island's patron saint.

On those days a barrel of stout was set in the corner of the room and all the men in the neighborhood dropped in to dance and sing and tell tales, since Joe's father was the undisputed king of the island, not only because he had the gift but also because he had thirty-three sons.

For young Joe there was magic in those special nights, the doings of the pookas and banshees and especially the *little people*, the trooping sly fairies who were seldom seen but often experienced, knee-high and dressed in bright green jackets and flat red hats and buckled shoes, mischievously passing the ages feasting and singing and holding their hurling matches brazenly on the strand. And then the doings of his brothers around the world with his father's prophecies interspersed, supernatural events to a young boy growing up on a bleak and rainy slip of land in the Atlantic where the rest of the year was spent at sea in a canoe made of cowhide, fighting the cold waves to lay miles of nets before daybreak.

Wondrous and special evenings for young Joe until

the most fateful of all prophecies arrived on that June night in 1914.

That evening his father had neither sung nor danced, in fact he hadn't even spoken. Instead he sat by the hearth drinking and brooding until well after midnight.

Some of his friends made an effort at singing and dancing but nothing much came of it. The whole room was waiting for the king's customary accounts of miracles past and future, and without them they didn't know what to do. Yet still the king sat staring at the turf fire, downing his pints of stout and not saying a word.

It was ominous. This wasn't the king's way on a party night. Finally signs were made around the room in desperation and the oldest man among them broke the silence with a question.

Joe, would something be bothering you then?

For a long moment there was silence and then at last the king stirred. He muttered a word no one could hear.

What's that, Joe?

Trouble. I see trouble ahead.

What kind of trouble, Joe?

War.

But wars are always leaving or coming, Joe. What's that to us poor folk?

The king's face darkened. He prodded the fire.

Leaving or coming they are like the sea, but not like this one for me. In two weeks' time, you see, a duke is going to be shot in a place called Bosnia and they're going to use that as an excuse to make a great war. How great? Ten million dead and twenty million maimed, but that's not for me. What's for me is that seventeen of my sons are going to fight and die in that war, one in every bloody army that makes up that bloody war.

The silence deepened. The king took a long drink of stout and everyone took the opportunity to do the same. The king gazed into his mug and all the men in the room followed his example.

Terrible, whispered a voice.

Terrible? said the king. No they're men now and they can do what they want. What eats at this old heart is that not one of those seventeen sons of mine will die fighting for Ireland. Fight they will and bravely, die they will too for seventeen countries and not one of them my own. I sent them out and that's fair, it's their life to lead. But that's also our people for you, everyone's cause but our own. Fill the mugs now. We need a drink because I have something to say about this.

The men in the room quickly did so. Somberly they filed up to the barrel and filled their mugs and went back to their seats. The king's mug was refilled and returned to his gnarled hand.

He sat by the turf fire staring at the floor. When he sipped they sipped, when he cleared his throat they cleared their throats. Prophecy was a gift and couldn't be hurried. A man who was about to lose seventeen sons fighting in seventeen foreign armies had a right to weigh his thoughts. Still the question escaped once again from someone.

What's to be done, Joe?

A sip. Sips across the room. The king cleared his throat, they did the same. Now was the moment.

What's to be done? I'll tell you what's to be done. In two years time there'll be an Easter rebellion, a rising of the nation, and I'll have a son in that rebellion, one son fighting for Ireland, a mere lad it's true but he'll be there. So that's the full truth on this June 14th in 1914. I've had thirty-three sons in my time and I saved my name for the last of them, and what will happen will be and that lad will do as he has to and I know what it is, and after that he's going to go on and become the King of Jerusalem for some reason.

The last words startled everyone in the room. Even the king's head jerked back in surprise.

Don't blaspheme, cautioned a voice.

And none intended. I have no idea why I said that. And now what's your name? he shouted suddenly to hide his embarrassment, staring between the shoulders of his friends who crowded the room.

Everyone turned. They hadn't noticed the small dark boy huddled in a corner at the back, struck dumb as always by his father's oracular sessions. With all eyes upon him he was afraid to speak, but with his father's eyes upon him he was even more afraid not to speak.

Joseph, he whispered.

Joseph what?

Joseph Enda Columbkille Kieran Kevin Brendan O'Sullivan Beare.

Saints of this island, answered his father, and that's my name too, saved for you so you can fight for Ireland as I once did, two years hence in the rising. Now there's no need to swear by those saints, lad, but we're going to raise a mug to you for what's to come, that much we can do. And the evil eye be off you and the *little people* be with you, and as your mother has taught you to say, If you haven't a shilling a ha'penny will do, and if you haven't a ha-penny God bless you.

Solemnly the men in the room raised their mugs and emptied them. In the corner young Joe, fourteen years old, stood perfectly straight and terrified.

On Easter Monday in 1916 the rising came as predicted and the Irish revolutionaries managed to hold the Dublin post office for several days. One of the few to escape from the post office was young Joe, who then walked two hundred miles south to the mountains of County Cork, thereby reversing the route of his famous ancestor.

What's to be done? he wondered as he walked. A man fighting alone needed distance from the enemy, so he decided to teach himself to use his rifle at long range.

The rifle itself was a curious antique, a modified 1851 U.S. cavalry musketoon that had last seen service with czarist dragoons in the Crimean War. But Joe soon discovered that with its short thick barrel, its heavy stock and enormous bullets, the musketoon could be used with extraordinary accuracy when fired in the manner of a howitzer, aimed in the air rather than at the target so the bullets traversed a high arc and struck from above.

For the next three years Joe practiced with his musketoon in the mountains mastering the trajectories of a howitzer, careful to let himself be seen only from far away. He moved at night and never slept in the same place twice, a phantom figure in a bright green jacket and buckled shoes and a flat red hat whom the farmers of Cork, with their sure knowledge of pookas and banshees and trooping sly fairies, quite naturally came to refer to among themselves as *the biggest of the little people*.

Then too he had to scavenge for food at night and that added to the legend. In the morning a farmer would find a chair in an outbuilding out of place and four or five potatoes missing.

He was here last night, the farmer would whisper to his neighbors, and of course no one had to be reminded who *he* was. The neighbors would nod gravely, perhaps recalling a soft crack of thunder they had heard in the distance at dawn.

In 1919 guerrilla warfare broke out and the English later sent in the Black and Tans, who roamed the countryside looting and beating and spreading terror. Until *he* manifested himself and the terror in southern Ireland was suddenly on the other side.

The pattern was always the same. A band of Black and Tans galloping down a road, a lone farmer running across his fields trying to dodge their bullets. From far away a soft crack of thunder. Another and another. Two or three Black and Tans tumbling to the ground, each with a bullet wound in the top of his head.

One day in western Cork, the next in eastern Cork. The third day near a fishing village. The fourth day far inland.

And the bullets always striking from directly above as if fired from heaven. All at once the Black and Tans found themselves facing divine intervention or at least a division of elusive sharpshooters armed with some secret new weapon. They refused to leave their barracks and *he* seemed to have won.

But the private war waged by *the biggest of the little people* couldn't last forever. When ballistic tests proved the enemy was only one agile man armed with an old modified U.S. cavalry musketoon, the Black and Tans began ravaging the countryside with renewed vengeance. And the informers informed and young Joe's hiding places in the mountains disappeared.

Gone now were the bright green jacket and the flat red hat and the buckled shoes, gone the reassuring soft cracks of thunder in the distance, gone the mysterious presence in southern Ireland, gone even the old cavalry musketoon, buried now in the ruins of an abandoned churchyard along with the tiny hope that someday he might return to reclaim it.

It was Easter Monday again, four years to the day since the rising, and young Joe sat in a vacant lot in a slum of the city of Cork passing his last afternoon in Ireland. His trousers were worn with holes, his bare feet were blistered and what served as his shirt was a lacework of rags tied together with string. Sea gulls screeched overhead. He blinked at the sky and sadly gazed back at the turf fire on the little island in the Atlantic where his father sat surrounded by the crowd of poor fishermen.

Jaysus, he whispered, I just hate to disappoint but I have to give it up now. I can't run and I can't hide and people are clubbed because of me and I can't help them, I only make it worse. You know what they're saying now? They're saying *he's* gone and it's true, I'm lost to them.

The roomful of men solemnly raised their mugs to him.

I know, he whispered, Jaysus I do know and I'd do anything rather than disappoint, I'd stay and stay if it could do any good but it can't. I tried and it worked for a while but the while's up and what I told you just now, Jaysus it's the truth and I'm done, they've done me in, *he's* gone.

He raised his hand in farewell and limped away from the vacant lot across a bridge and crawled down a coalbin into a cellar. There an elderly carter told him the plan for his escape was ready, adding that the Black and Tans had tortured someone on the west coast and discovered their old enemy of the musketoon was in Cork. By noon the next day they would arrive in force, seal the city and begin the search.

The Black and Tans arrived well before noon but still too late. Early that morning a small freighter had sailed from the harbor with a cargo of whiskey and potatoes for the English garrison in Palestine. In addition the freighter carried a dozen nuns bound on a pilgrimage to the Holy Land.

The journey the nuns were about to make was exceptional, for they were Poor Clares who ordinarily would never have been allowed out of their convent, let alone out of the country. The cause of their going was a request for a pilgrimage made by a reverend mother from a less strict order who had been in charge of the convent at the end of the eighteenth century, before the Poor Clares had acquired it. But the Napoleonic wars had intervened and after that the convent changed hands.

Just what had happened to the request during the nineteenth century was uncertain. In any case it reappeared when the Vatican's files were reorganized at the end of the First World War, and thus one hundred and twenty-five years later a decree suddenly arrived at the convent directing the reverend mother to take eleven of her nuns on the pilgrimage.

The reverend mother was stunned. She wrote to her bishop, who was equally stunned, but he could only reply that an order from the Holy See was an order to be obeyed. Although it was incomprehensible, the Holy Father must have had his reasons for sending Poor Clares on this fearful voyage.

The nuns were chosen on the basis of age and ranged from seventy to ninety years old. All were unusually tall save for one who was small and dark with a shadow of what might have been newly shaved hair above the lip.

The Poor Clares weren't allowed to speak and the formalities on the wharf were handled by the bishop, the nuns rustling their beads and fluttering in circles so that it was even difficult to count them. But their excitement over visiting the Holy Land after waiting a century and a quarter seemed reasonable enough to the English officials, so their documents were processed quickly and they disappeared on board the freighter in a flurry of swirling black habits.

The nuns were not seen again until the freighter

docked in Jaffa. The dusty journey up through the hills was made. The carriages approached New Gate and were soon surrounded by the usual crowds of thieves and mastic-sellers and pilgrims spitting and cursing and praying as they squeezed into the narrow alleys of commerce and paradise. Just outside the gate a small dark man in a shabby Arab cloak and Arab headgear was seen to cringe on one of the running boards, hand outstretched to beg.

But the policeman on duty at the gate was quick to give the beggar a solid blow on the head with his baton, thereby reducing the Poor Clares to an even dozen and sending *the biggest of the little people* sprawling across the cobblestones of Jerusalem.

Joe squatted outside the entrance to the Franciscan enclave in the Old City still dressed as an Arab beggar, whispering furtively in Gaelic when a priest came by, assuming a priest from any country other than Ireland would mistake his words for some garbled Arab dialect.

He spent a day at the main entrance and successive days outside the wine cellar and the olive-oil press. Famished by nightfall, he dragged himself to the entrance of the bakery.

No one appeared at the door in the morning. Soon the sun was overhead. With the heat overcoming him he slipped lower, into the gutter. Sometime during the afternoon he had a dream the door was opening.

We ourselves, he whispered in Gaelic into the dirt, repeating the name of the Irish revolutionary party. In his dream a shadow fell across him.

What's that? said a soft voice, also in Gaelic.

Love, the forgiving hand to victory, whispered Joe, repeating the legend of the O'Sullivan Beare clan.

Is that so? Is that who you are, lad? But what ails

you lying in a Jerusalem gutter dressed like that? Inside with you before a policeman comes by.

The old priest pulled him out of the alley into the cool depths of the bakery. He locked the door and poured water over Joe, then stuffed his mouth with bread and watched him eat. When Joe was able to talk he told his story, the old priest nodding his head vehemently at each new turn in the account.

Was your father in the Fenian movement? he said at the end.

That he was, Father.

Well so was I but the Church made me leave it. Of the seven men in my cell six were O'Sullivan Beares named Joseph. Your father might have been one of them. Anything special for me to go on?

Prophecy.

Ah that one, I knew him all right. He used to say he was going to have twenty or thirty sons and I admonished him to be happy with what God gave him. Happy I will be, he said, it's just that I already know. Well that's fine for seventy years ago but what are we going to do now? Here you are a former terror of the Black and Tans wanted for patriotism and other heinous crimes, in English territory without papers. Drop our lovely mother tongue and repeat after me. *Yes I am English actually but I was born with faulty vocal cords and multiple speech impediments.*

Joe did so.

Atrocious, said the priest. That wouldn't even begin to fool an Arab.

We ourselves? whispered Joe hopefully.

Not this time, it's just not enough. We'll need some help if you're not to be caught. Now sit there while I stoke up the oven. I've been the baker here for sixty years and I do my best thinking at the oven, so you sit and I'll bake.

The old priest began kneading dough and baking loaves of bread that came out in various irregular shapes. One was clearly a cross and another had roughly the shape of Ireland. The third might have been meant to represent the shape of the walls of the Old City, but the fourth was an unrecognizable oval slightly angular at the top and more so at the ends. Before long the corners of the bakery were heaped with bread.

What's that loaf? asked Joe.

Which one?

That corner there.

The Crimea of course.

The priest turned back to the oven but all at once his cassock twirled and his sandals slapped the stones. He had broken into a dance.

But that's the answer, lad, why didn't I think of it? You're the reason why I wasted that time in the army, old Joe's son on the run's the reason.

The priest, dripping with sweat, renewed his little dance in front of the open oven door. Right there, thought Joe, and at it sixty years no less. Been doing it so long the brains have melted. Out of the gutter but as finished as ever.

Which army was that, Father?

Her Majesty's own, what else. Before you jigs a former officer of light cavalry with several medals from the allies not to mention the Victoria Cross from herself.

He was bouncing back and forth now dropping a loaf in the oven, now plucking one out. Hopeless, thought Joe, totally melted. Sixty years of that could turn anyone's brains to bread.

The Victoria Cross you say?

The very same, lad. Before I found my vocation I was so stupid I joined the army and off we went to the Crimea, where some deluded ward of God ordered a suicidal charge. My mount fell and broke its leg and

I couldn't keep up on foot, so it turned out I was one
of the few survivors. That's right my boy, 1854 was
the year in question and the English public was
furious. The army had to find some heroes who were
still alive, that was me and in came the medals.

Joe shifted on his buttocks. His bottom hurt. Maybe
that charge had been a disaster but sitting here was
a disaster too. The old priest danced across the room
and dropped a ribbon over his head. Joe stared dumbly
at the cross. Once he had seen one on an English
officer before the Easter Rebellion.

That's it and there you are, young Joe, an official
hero of Her Majesty's forces and one of the few to
survive the charge of the Light Brigade. Two years
after that piece of madness in the Crimea, you see,
Her Reigning Presence decided to honor God and
herself by creating a new and highest honor for
Britannic valor on the battlefield, named for herself,
this Victoria Cross we now see around your neck. Her
advisors naturally agreed with that and suggested the
first VC ever to be go to the most decorated man
presently in the forces. Who's that? asked Victoria R.
Right here on the rolls, said the advisors, checking, it
appears to be none other than the illustrious hero who
was loaded with Sardinian and Turkish and French
medals only two years ago, our very own MacMael
n mBo of Crimean fame. MacMael *what?* asked the
queen, suddenly weary with the tasks of empire.

The old priest smiled.

No matter. Presently she recovered and they were
able to find the last sober Irishman in the islands to
teach her how to pronounce the name and the ceremony was held and there I stood, first recipient of the
famous Victoria Cross. Well then a few years after
that some worthy people established a retirement
charity in Jerusalem for veterans, the Home for
Crimean War Heroes it's called, and since there
aren't many of those veterans around by now as you'd

imagine, heroic or not, the quarters are more than
spacious. In fact you'll have it practically to yourself.
Commands a decent view of part of the Old City and
the bread's excellent, I bake it myself. So, lad, I'll give
you my old documents and that's that.

That's what? thought Joe. Were the old priest's
brains melted or not? He was twenty and the
Franciscan must have been at least eighty-five.

Won't apparent age be a problem then?

Not here, not in Jerusalem, answered the old priest
merrily. Here young or old is about the same. Our
Holy City, everyone's Holy City, is an odd place as
you'll come to see, not an everyday commonplace
matter.

We ourselves, said Joe.

Exactly, and just the three of us in on the trick, you
and me and God. And some trick it was, choosing
those Poor Clares.

How's that, Father?

The trip. This dreadful journey the Poor Clares had
to make over here seeing and being seen by all
manner of creatures and smelling all smells known to
the species. That's not their usual business is it? Not
what they signed up for is it? No, direct intervention,
that's what it was.

What?

Oh you wore a bright green jacket and buckled
shoes and you set your flat red hat at a properly
jaunty angle, and you kept on the move as best you
could but He knew trouble was coming and He said
to Himself, The lad's going to have to get out of
Ireland and how's he going to do it?

Well naturally He took a look in the files of the
Vatican, which is where He goes when dealing with
historical matters, and what does He find but an old
request for some nuns to make a pilgrimage to the
Holy Land. Right you are, He says to Himself, that's
the job. Who's ever going to suspect the terror of the

Black and Tans sneaking out of the country disguised as a Poor Clare when everybody knows Poor Clares aren't even allowed out of their convents? Who would even conceive of such a thing? So after He has His little laugh He arranges for the document to be found and processed, and after one hundred and twenty-five years the frightened Poor Clares do their duty and you're saved.

Father, I didn't realize any of it.

It's true you didn't but there you have it, said the old priest, who went dancing off into the corners of the bakery collecting a loaf in each of the four shapes and proceeded to pile them in the fugitive's lap.

9

Haj Harun

They simply didn't have time to believe a man who had been born a thousand years before Christ. Whose mind, moreover, teemed with facts no one else had ever heard.

❊

One afternoon after he had gone to live in the Home for Crimean War Heroes, O'Sullivan Beare was wandering in the Moslem Quarter when he found himself facing a blank wall at the end of an alley. Near him a wizened old Arab stood forlornly in a doorway. The Arab wore a faded yellow cloak and a rusting helmet tied in place with green ribbons. Unaware that anyone was there, the old man raised his cloak and pissed weakly into the alley.

O'Sullivan Beare jumped out of the way. The man's legs seemed too spindly to support him. The heavy helmet rolled when he moved and crashed down on his nose. After dropping his cloak he sighed, readjusted the helmet and once more stared sadly ahead at nothing.

Just as the baking priest said, thought Joe. He was right as right about Jerusalem and here's another one off in a different bog. He stepped back and saluted.

Beg pardon sir, could you tell me what campaign the helmet's from?

The old man was puzzled. He stirred and the decomposing metal released a shower of rust in his eyes. He wiped away his tears and the helmet went awry again.

What's that?

The helmet. Which campaign might it be?

The First Crusade.

Jaysus and that must have been a hard one...

The old Arab lowered his head as if expecting a blow. He wept quietly.

Ridicule and defeat, abuse and humiliation, I've never expected anything else.

Oh no sir, no insult intended.

The eyes drifted in the direction of O'Sullivan Beare, the voice less far away now.

What? You don't mean you believe me when I say I fought in the Crusades?

No reason not to.

There isn't? But no one has believed anything I've said for a very long time.

Sorry to hear that sir.

Not for over two thousand years.

Dreadfully sorry sir.

And I wasn't on the Crusaders' side, I have to tell you that. I was defending my city against the invader.

I know how that is.

So naturally I was on the losing side. When you're defending Jerusalem you're always on the losing side.

I know how that is too. Terrible position to be in sir.

The old Arab tried to focus his eyes more closely.

See here, why do you keep calling me *sir*? No one's shown me any respect for centuries.

Because you're nobility and it's only proper.

The Arab made an effort to stand more erect, which he did for a few moments despite the arthritis crippling his back. His face showed surprise and confusion and a tiny hint of pride.

That was at least as far back as the reign of Ashurnasirpal. How did you guess?

Your eyes sir.

It's still there?

As clear as the last muezzin.

The Arab looked even more surprised and also embarrassed.

Don't call me sir, my name's Haj Harun. Now please tell me why you believe what I say instead of beating me when I say it?

What else would I be doing? Do you recognize this uniform?

No, I've never been too good with uniforms.

Well it's genuine Her Majesty's Forces, 1854, and I'm only twenty years old but I'm a hero of that war, here you behold the medals. And this special one was given to me by Victoria R herself although I was only a year old when she died. So there we are and that's Jerusalem for you in 1920, me back from the Crimea and you back from the Crusades, and as one veteran of the wars to another I thought I'd look you up.

The Arab studied the Victoria Cross. He smiled.

You're Prester John, aren't you. I was sure you'd get to Jerusalem sooner or later and I've been waiting for you. Please come right in so we can talk.

He disappeared through the doorway. For a moment Joe lingered in the alley undecided, but the sun was hot and his uniform heavy, so he followed. The first thing he saw was what appeared to be a bronze sundial set into the wall, a large ornately-cast piece. Attached to it near the ceiling was a set of chimes.

From Baghdad, said Haj Harun, noticing him eyeing the sundial. The fifth Abbasid caliphate. I used to deal in antiquities before I dedicated myself to defending the Holy City and lost everything I owned.

I see.

It was a portable sundial once.

I see.

Monstrously heavy but somehow it didn't seem to bother him. He wore it on his hip.

Did he now. And who might that have been?

I can't remember his name. He rented my back room one afternoon to do some writing and gave me that in appreciation.

Rented it for just one afternoon?

I think that's all it was but he got a good deal done anyway. Then he packed up all his papers and sent them by camel caravan down to Jaffa where there was a ship waiting to transport the caravan to Venice.

And why not, I say. In good weather Venice would be a natural destination for a camel caravan.

Suddenly the chimes began to strike. They pealed twenty-four times, paused, pealed twenty-four times again and once more. Joe fingered his Victoria Cross uneasily.

Jaysus they shouldn't be doing that now.

Doing what?

Striking off three days just like that.

Why not?

They just shouldn't that's all, time's time.

Time is, said Haj Harun airily. But the sun doesn't fall on the dial every day, sometimes it's cloudy and then the dial has to make up.

Haj Harun went over and sat in a decrepit barber's chair. Near the door was a small press for squeezing fruit with a rotting pomegranate beside it. Next to the barber's chair was a stand holding a bottle of murky water, a pan for spitting in, an old toothbrush with flattened bristles and an empty tube of Czech toothpaste. He picked at the moldy chair as he gloomily surveyed the room.

I went into the toothbrushing business at exactly the wrong time. Very few people find their way to the end of this alley and anyway, brushing teeth hasn't been the same since the war. Before the war you might have done well in it, the Turkish soldiers had awful teeth. But since they left and the English soldiers came it's been hopeless. Their teeth are certainly just as bad but they won't let an Arab brush them.

Bloody imperialists.

They also won't have them brushed in public. The Turks never minded but the English aren't the same.

Bloody hypocrites.

A wail rose down the alley. Haj Harun pulled his helmet down and braced himself. A moment later a crowd of shrieking men and women burst into the shop and raced back and forth clawing at the air. The Arab stared fixedly over their heads trying to maintain his dignity, and in a few seconds the looters had snatched up every movable object in the room and swept out the door. Gone were the pomegranate and press and barber's chair with its equipment, even the empty tube of Czech toothpaste. Haj Harun moaned softly and shrank back against the wall, yellow and emaciated and half dead from hunger.

Jaysus, who was that mob?

The Arab shuddered. He managed to wave his hand in resignation.

Mercantile elements of the citizenry, it's better to take no notice of them. They come to raid me sometimes. They want things to sell.

Bloody outrage.

There are worse. Look here.

He opened his mouth. Most of his teeth were gone and those that were left were broken off near the gums.

Rocks. They throw them at me.

Bloody shameful.

And these scars from their fingernails. They have very sharp fingernails.

Bloody terrible.

All true, but I suppose we have to accept certain

troubles when going from Ceca to Mecca. All the
women I ever married were dreadful.

Do you tell me that. Why did you marry them then?

That's so, but of course they didn't have an easy
time of it either. You know that don't you?

O'Sullivan Beare nodded and walked into the back
room of the shop. After the assault by the mob of
Jerusalem mercantilists only two objects were left
there, both far too heavy to move. He gazed at them
thoughtfully.

An antique Turkish safe about four feet high,
narrow, shaped like a filing cabinet or an impregnable
sentry box.

A giant stone scarab about four feet long, a sly
smile carved into its flat face.

You know that don't you?

So much rust had fallen into Haj Harun's eyes his
cheeks were running with tears.

I mean of course they didn't have an easy time of
it. Take my wife who was a Bulgarian Greek. The
Greeks up there were educated and they also had to
serve as moneylenders because there were no banks.
The Bulgars could only sign their names with Xs, so
every now and then they came around and massacred
the Greeks to cancel their debts and cheer themselves
up. My wife's family escaped during the massacre of
1910 and when they finally arrived in Jerusalem they
were destitute, so you can't blame her for taking all
my plates and cups and pots when she left me.

Joe studied the iron safe more closely. Why was it
so tall and thin?

Then another of my wives was born in the deserted
city of Golconda which used to be famous for its
diamond trade, but it's been deserted since the
seventeenth century and that's not a pleasant memory
to have either, to come from a totally deserted city I

mean. So look here, no wonder she wanted to have the security of some furniture and carpets and took all of mine when she left. You can see that can't you?

Joe rapped the antique safe. The muffled echoes were out of all proportion to the size of the safe. Haj Harun was roaming around and around the bare walls.

Still another wife was the daughter of a twelfth-century Persian poet whose song told of a pilgrimage made by a flock of birds in search of their king. Since the pilgrimage was over water most of the birds died, and when the survivors finally reached the palace behind the seven seas what did they discover but that each of them was actually the king. So see here, given a father who saw things that way it's not surprising she took all my vases and lamps. Naturally she wanted to surround herself with flowers and light.

Joe got down on his knees and rapped the safe more loudly. The reverberations were uncanny. Deep hollow echoes boomed up into the room. Something was going on here that he didn't understand.

Why do you wear a yellow cloak?

It was bright yellow when it was new but that was seven hundred years ago and since then it's faded.

Do you tell me so. But why yellow?

There must have been a reason but I can't recall it at the moment. Can you?

Joe shook his head. He still needed time to think.

What's that cord in the corner?

I had an electric light once but a dog was always sneaking in behind my back and biting the wire. He liked the shocks. Finally it was so full of holes I had to go back to using a candle. Did you know I discovered a comet no one else has ever heard of?

Did I? No I didn't. Tell me about it.

Well I knew it had to exist because of certain events in the lives of Moses and Nebuchadnezzar and Christ and Mohammed. I knew there had to be an explanation for all those odd things happening in the sky so I went to my copy of the *Thousand and One Nights* and was able to date it from some of the episodes.

Good, very sound. What's the cycle of your comet then?

Six hundred and sixteen years. It's been over five times since I've been in Jerusalem although the first four times I didn't know it, and I still don't know what happened in 1228 that was so important. Do you?

No, but I haven't studied the records for that year closely.

Nor have I as far as I know. Anyway the last time I saw it was in the desert on my annual haj. I met a dervish in a place where no man should have been and the strange light thrown by the comet's tail made him look seven and a half feet tall. It plays tricks, that comet.

Comet tricks, muttered Joe, as he continued noisily sounding the safe. Now he was sure of it. The echoes rose from deep in the ground.

He left the safe and went over to examine the giant stone scarab in another corner of the back room. Why was it smiling in such a cunning way? He thumped its broad nose. He rapped his way down its back.

Yes he was sure of that too. The massive stone beetle was hollow. He sat down with the flat nose between his legs and began beating the nose with his fists, rapping out a rhythm. Haj Harun had stopped in front of a bare wall to adjust his helmet in a non-existent mirror. The noise startled him and he peered toward the alley.

What's that out there?

Not out there, in here. I'm riding the scarab. It's hollow isn't it?

Oh just the scarab. Yes it is.

There's a secret latch hidden somewhere?

In the nostrils. A combination of latches, very clever. Built for smuggling.

What?

Mummies and bones. The Romans had strict sanitation codes and wouldn't allow dead bodies to be transported from one province to another. But the Egyptian traders here would pay well to have their mummies smuggled home when they died and the Jewish traders in Alexandria would also pay well to have their bones brought back here. An Armenian made quite a bit of money out of that trade. I must have bought it from him when he retired.

Ever use it yourself?

Not for smuggling but for something else. What was it?

Haj Harun backed away from the empty wall and gazed at the crumbling plaster.

I seem to remember taking naps in it. Is that possible? Why would I have done that? Age. My memory's going, all the years slide together. Now when were those naps, under the Mamelukes? I had the falling sickness then, at least I think it was then, and that might have been a reason for crawling inside the scarab and curling up there. But no, it must have been earlier. I also seem to recall bumping my head so that I was paralyzed from the neck up for a while. When? Under the Crusaders?

His voice was doubtful, then suddenly he smiled.

Yes that's it exactly. Those knights were always clanking around in their armor so I used the scarab for my siestas. It was the only quiet place I could find.

Still as still as stone, said Joe, who climbed off the scarab and went over to examine the mysterious safe once more.

Noisy days, said Haj Harun, his memory suddenly jarred into place by the prospect of a pageant of

Crusaders banging their swords on the cobblestones.

Noisy but not the worst. When the Assyrians took the city they put rings through the lips of the survivors and led them away as slaves, everyone except our leaders, who were blinded and left behind in the deserted ruins to starve.

The Romans thought the people in the city were swallowing jewels, so they cut open stomachs and slit intestines but all they found was worn leather. The famine was so bad during the siege we had been eating our sandals.

The Crusaders killed about a hundred thousand and the Romans almost five hundred thousand. The Babylonians murdered less than the Assyrians but blinded more. The Ptolemies and the Seleucids also murdered on a smaller scale, as did the Byzantines and Mamelukes and Turks, generally speaking just the religious leaders and anyone who was educated. Naturally the people were made to change the churches into mosques and destroy the synagogues, or change the mosques into churches and destroy the synagogues, depending on the new conqueror. What came after that? Where was I? Oh yes, my last wife came after that.

Joe drummed loudly on the safe. The swelling echoes shook the walls of the empty shop.

She was the one who took what I had left, my books. She was a failure in life you see, and being an Arab the only explanation was that someone had betrayed her. There had to be a traitor in the house and who else was in the house but me?

Haj Harun sighed and straightened his helmet, which fell forward with a new rain of rust. The tears began running again.

But you have to remember I still wore socks in those days and the socks were always wet because my feet were always wet, and wet feet aren't pleasant in bed. She put up with it for a time and I don't deny it.

Where does it lead? asked Joe quietly.

Always having wet feet?

No, the shaft below the safe. It is a bottomless safe, isn't it?

Well not really. Deep but not bottomless.

How deep?

Right here about fifty feet.

And there's a ladder?

Yes.

To where?

A tunnel that leads to the caverns.

How deep are the caverns?

Hundreds of feet? Thousands of feet?

Joe whistled softly. He sat down beside the safe and pressed his ear to the iron door. Far away a wind hummed. Haj Harun was retying the green ribbons under his chin.

What's down there?

Jerusalem. The Old City I mean.

Joe looked out at the alley. A lean cat was sneaking in front of the shop with some kind of wire clamped between its teeth.

Isn't that Jerusalem out there? The Old City I mean?

One of them.

And down below?

The other Old Cities.

O'Sullivan Beare whistled very softly.

How's that now?

Well Jerusalem has been continually destroyed, hasn't it. I mean it's been more or less destroyed several hundred times and utterly destroyed at least a few dozen times, say a dozen times that we know of since Nebuchadnezzar and before that another dozen times that we don't know of. And being on top of a mountain no one ever bothered to dig away the ruins when it was rebuilt, so the mountain has grown. Do you see?

So I do. And down there where your ladder goes?

What's always been there. A dozen Old Cities. Two dozen Old Cities.

With some of their treasures and monuments still?

Some. Things that are buried tend to be overlooked, and then in time they're forgotten altogether. Look here, in my lifetime I've seen a great many things forgotten, the dents in my helmet for example. Does anyone remember how I got those dents?

The wizened Arab paced aimlessly around the room.

Jaysus, thought Joe. Haj Harun's ladder. We are descending.

Being a native of the city, which had always been thronged with conquerors or pilgrims, Haj Harun had quite naturally spent most of his life in the service trades. During the Hebrew era he had begun his career by raising calves and later lambs. Under the Assyrians he was a stonecarver specializing in winged lions. He was a landscape gardener under the Babylonians and a tentmaker under the Persians.

When the Greeks were in power he ran an all-night grocery store and when the Maccabees were in power he poured candles. During the Roman occupation he was a waiter.

For the Byzantines he painted ikons, for the Arabs he sewed cushions, for the Egyptians he cut stones again but this time with emphasis on square blocks. He was a masseur for rheumatic ailments during the Crusader occupations, shoed horses for the Mamelukes and distributed hashish and goats for the Ottoman Turks. In the beginning he had also spent intervals as a sorcerer and prophet and in the less demanding field of general medicine.

To succeed in sorcery he had shaved his head and had his credentials engraved on his skull with a stylus, so that in moments of crisis he could ask that his head be shaved and thereby prove his authenticity.

As a prophet he didn't wear a collar and have himself led around on a rope from customer to customer as was the common practice, preferring instead to sit in the bazaar shouting unsolicited warnings to passersby.

In medicine he dealt entirely with the pasty residue of a plant with star-shaped flowers known as Jerusalem cherry, a form of nightshade. These mixtures he prepared by mashing them on the filthy cobblestones around Damascus Gate, where he was frequently seen down on his hands and knees, doing a kind of dance to escape the feet of the crowds.

He also used a more potent juice from the wilted leaves of deadly nightshade, an effective narcotic which also caused severe vomiting. This left Haj Harun weak most of the time, since by necessity he had to take his own cures several times a day. To give some substance to his vomit he consumed large bowls of mush made from Jerusalem artichokes.

During that period he still had the ability to address all men in their own tongues even when he himself didn't understand the language, a great advantage in Jerusalem. In this manner he soon acquired a reputation for being able to transform a loquat or a jackass or even the unintelligible cries of hawkers into astonishing portents of grandiose events.

In the course of time he had been known by many names he couldn't now remember, but after his first haj in the eighth century he had permanently taken the name Aaron, or Harun as the Arabs pronounced it, in honor of Harun al-Rashid who figured so prominently in the tales he loved above all others, the *Thousand and One Nights*. It was also after his first haj that he had dedicated himself to defending Jerusalem and its past and future inhabitants against all enemies. Yet despite his good intentions he had to admit his accomplishments remained vague.

Perhaps, as he said, because such a task is both immense and perpetual. Am I making myself clear?

Not quite, replied Joe dizzily. Could you be just a little more specific?

Haj Harun looked embarrassed.

I doubt it but I'll try. What about?

Oh I don't know. How about that time when you were practicing medicine. That's a good profession, why did you give it up?

Had to. The market for deadly nightshade disappeared overnight.

Why?

Someone started a rumor that wiped out the business. You see most of it was bought by women to enlarge the pupils of their eyes, to make them more beautiful. Well a young man whose wife was a customer of mine came to confide in me. They'd only been married a short time and it seems she wouldn't take him in the mouth. She thought it was unnatural or unsanitary or both. So I advised him.

What advice for such a problem?

I told him to tell her it was perfectly natural and sanitary and furthermore there was no better substance in the world for instantly enlarging the pupils of the eyes. For best results, I said, the dosage should be repeated every few hours. It was only a little lie to help their marriage you see, or maybe it wasn't a lie at all. Maybe it works, who knows. Do you know?

It is true that I do not. What subsequent developments in the matter?

Well he told her all that and she asked me, as her physician, if it was true and I said it was, and after that her husband went around looking so happily exhausted his friends began to wonder what was going on and asked him.

And?

And he told them, and they told their friends, and

overnight all the men in Jerusalem were looking happily exhausted and I couldn't sell any more deadly nightshade because the women were getting too much of the other substance.

So the rumor that drove you out of business was started by yourself?

Haj Harun moved his feet uneasily.

It seems so.

Not exactly the way to maintain yourself in a profession is it, would you say?

No I guess not but look at it the other way. Didn't I help to make a lot of marriages happier?

Agreed, that help you must have been. Well what else?

What else what?

What else can you be specific about?

Let's see. Did you know that when the bedouin are starving they cut open the vein of a horse, drink a little and close the vein? I learned that on a haj.

I did not know it. And if they're horseless?

They make the camel vomit and drink that.

I see. I won't ask about camel-less days.

And that bedouin girls wear clusters of cloves in their noses? That they paint the whites of their eyes blue? That the hills around Kheybar are of volcanic origin? I learned all that on different hajes.

I see. Where's that?

A haj? Where does it lead you mean?

No, the place with the surrounding hills and so forth.

Oh that's near the great divide of the wadis of northern Arabia.

Good. What else?

Well once I supplied an Armenian antiquities dealer with some parchment that was fifteen hundred years old.

Had some left over did you?

I did. In the caverns. In a grave down there. I don't know why, do you?

Could you have been thinking of writing your memoirs fifteen hundred years ago and laid in a burial stash just in case?

It's possible, anything is. Anyway he was very desperate to get his hands on it. But you know, he wasn't really an antiquities dealer at all.

No, not at all. He spent all his time practicing penmanship, learning to write with both hands, I used to go and talk with him sometimes. And you know he wasn't really Armenian either. We spoke Aramaic together.

What's that?

The language that was used in Jerusalem two thousand years ago. And now that I think of it, that's probably the only time I've used it since then.

And very sensible too, taking advantage of the opportunity I mean. Probably non-Armenians who write with both hands and speak Aramaic don't turn up that often, not even in Jerusalem.

Haj Harun stirred. He frowned.

That's true. You know I didn't see him for seven years after that, not until he wandered into my shop one morning looking like a ghost. You've never seen a man so dusty. And his nose gone and one ear falling off and a bundle under his arm.

Hard times in the desert, you think?

It would seem so. He said something about having been in the Sinai and talking to a blind mole down there but it wasn't clear at all, I couldn't make any sense out of it. He was lost, poor man, he couldn't even find his way around Jerusalem. He begged me to lead him to the Armenian Quarter, to the basement hole where he used to live there, so I did.

Excellent. What event occurring thereby?

None really. He began digging in the basement and

dug down a few feet until he came to an old unused cistern. Then he put the bundle he'd been carrying in the cistern and filled up the hole. Why did he do that? Do you know?

Not at the moment but fresh ideas are always coming to me.

You see he didn't realize I was there, he seemed to have lost hold by then. He was muttering all the time and passing his hand over his eyes as if he were trying to wipe something away.

Muttering, losing hold, do you tell me so. Well that's a good one too. Is there anything else now?

Only those two discoveries I made as a child.

Only two you say?

The first had to do with balls.

Playing kind?

Well, my own.

Oh I see.

Yes. When I was a little fellow I always thought they were for storing piss. Looking at them it seemed reasonable enough, but then when I was a little older it turned out to be not that way at all.

That's true, it didn't. What second and final discovery?

That women and even emperors took shits just like I did. Once a day more or less with the same explosions and gases.

A curious proposition.

Yes. Very. It took me at least a year to get used to the idea and you know how long a year can be when you're a child. Doesn't it often seem like forever?

Forever, true. Often.

You know how I made those two discoveries?

Not precisely I believe.

Well it was from a blind storyteller who was chanting beside the road while an imbecile wrote down what he said. They were adult stories and I shouldn't have been listening but I was. I was very young then.

I see.

Yes, added Haj Harun wanly. But isn't it true we were all young and innocent once?

By far the most striking influence on Haj Harun's early years was his birthmark, an impressive phenomenon that had long been dormant and now appeared only on rare occasions.

This birthmark was an irregular shade of faded purple that began above his left eye, gathered momentum around his nose, cascaded down his neck and swirled intermittently over his entire body in a restless proclamation of stops and starts, tentative here and emphatic there, now lashing out boldly and now retreating, lapsing and flowing by turns as it swung across his loins and drifted down one leg or the other to vanish near an ankle in the manner of a map of some fabulous land of antiquity, Atlantis perhaps or the unknown empire of the Chaldeans, or the known but constantly shifting empire of the Medes.

When the purple pattern had still been largely visible there were those who professed to see in it a general layout of the streets of Ur before that city had been silted over by the primordial flood. To others it offered indistinct clues to the essential military strongpoints throughout the Tigris and Euphrates valleys, while still others claimed it was an accurate diagram of the oases in the Sinai.

In any case the birthmark drew attention to Haj Harun early in his career. By the time of the first Isaiah he was a well-known figure in Jerusalem, variously respected or held in awe by men of many races and creeds.

But during the Persian occupation a change set in.

He was no longer considered totally reliable by either natives or foreigners, and when Alexander stopped off on his way to India, Haj Harun was already viewed as an obscure oddity, despite the fact that he had lived in the city much longer than anyone else. Certain disreputable soothsayers still sought his advice in private, but even they had to be mindful of public opinion and ignore him in the street.

Once begun the erosion was rapid. Haj Harun's confidence in himself steadily declined. He lost his forthright habits of speech and with them his fearless presentations. Well before the Roman era no one in Jerusalem took him seriously. By then he had already seen too many peoples come and go and witnessed too many eras erupting and ending. He had a muddled way of lumping all events together as if they had occurred yesterday, and when strangers happened to make the mistake of listening to him they were sent reeling in all directions, reality changing before their eyes as swiftly as the borders of the purple landscape that curled around his frail body.

Therefore from about the time of Christ there was a total eclipse in Haj Harun's credibility. The inhabitants of Jerusalem were forever piling new walls and gates and temples and churches and mosques on the ruins of the past, forever covering the old rubble with new bazaars and gardens and courtyards, forever massing and rearing new structures.

They were busy and they simply didn't have time to believe a man who had been born a thousand years before Christ. Whose mind, moreover, teemed with facts no one else had ever heard.

10

The Scarab

*An Egyptian stone beetle and
great secret scarab stuffed with
the first arms for the future
Jewish underground army.*

❖

Nearly three thousand years later in 1920, young
O'Sullivan Beare was far from being ready to retire.
As soon as he entered the Home for Crimean War
Heroes he began to scheme, looking for ways to make
money, hinting in various Arab coffee shops that he
had extensive experience in illegal affairs. Before long
a man of indeterminate nationality approached him.

Smuggling arms? He nodded. He described his four
years on the run in southern Ireland and the man
seemed impressed. From where to where? Constantinople to here. For whom? The Haganah. What's that?
The future Jewish underground army. Who's it going
to fight, the English? If necessary. Good, bloody
English.

You'll have the honor of bringing them their first
weapons, added the man. If the money is right,
thought Joe.

Money. He remembered Haj Harun's lost treasure
map, which he was sure existed. The old Arab had
referred to it only in passing as *the story of my life*,
but Joe had been too intrigued to let the matter rest
there.

You wrote it down? he'd asked Haj Harun.

The old Arab had waved his arms in circles. He couldn't remember whether he had or not but to Joe the implication was that he had and later lost or misplaced it, this real or secret history of the riches he'd discovered in the caverns beneath Jerusalem, in the Old Cities he'd explored down there and then mixed up in his mind with tales from the *Thousand and One Nights* and the other fancies that obsessed him, a detailed guide to the incalculable wealth brought to Jerusalem over the millennia by conquerors and pious fanatics.

He'd pressed Haj Harun about it.

Are you sure you don't have any idea what you could have done with it?

With what?

The story of your life.

Haj Harun had shrugged helplessly and wrung his hands, certainly wanting to please his new friend by recalling this or anything else yet simply unable to, his memory slipping as he said and the years all sliding together, pumping his arms in circles and sadly admitting he just couldn't be sure, just couldn't say, the past was too confusing.

Was he forgiven? Were he and Prester John still friends?

That they were, Joe had answered, nothing changed that. But the treasure map had never left his mind and now he wondered whether to mention it to his new employer, who seemed to know a good deal about Jerusalem. Why not chance it? Carefully, without enthusiasm, he asked the man if he had ever heard of a document that supposedly included three thousand years of Jerusalem's history, written by a madman and worthless, thought to have disappeared not too long ago.

The man studied him curiously. Was he referring to the myth of an original Sinai Bible? An original version totally unlike the forgery later bought by the czar?

The czar. Even the czar had been after it. So eager to get his hands on the map he'd been going around snapping up forgeries.

That's it. What do they say happened to it?

Supposedly it was buried. But no one has ever seen it and of course it's all nonsense, the fabrication of a demented mind.

Demented certainly, nonsense of course, buried assuredly. Haj Harun unlocking his antique safe one evening and putting a foot on the ladder, a short time later padding steathily away down a tunnel fifty feet below the ground for a long private night in the caverns.

What do they say was in it exactly?

The man smiled. That's the point. Supposedly everything is in it.

Everything. Persian palaces and Babylonian tiaras and Crusader caches, Mameluke plunder and Seleucid gold. A map so valuable the czar had been willing to trade his empire for it.

When do they say it was buried?

In the last century.

Yes that would be right, Haj Harun would still have had his wits about him then. He'd have written it and hidden it and then forgotten where he'd hidden it when he was seized by the idea of his holy mission. He saw the old man stumbling around the walls of his empty shop staring into corners. Mission to where? The moon. Residence? Lunacy. Occupation? Lunatic.

Jaysus that was his Haj Harun all right. Explorer of secret caverns and discoverer of two dozen Old Cities, mapmaker of the centuries, the former King of Jerusalem now reduced to peering at blank walls and absentmindedly adjusting his helmet, which released a shower of rust to fill his eyes with tears and blur the figure he'd hoped to see in his nonexistent mirror.

The man on the other side of the table was talking about routes from Constantinople. Trails, roads, paths, English border posts and sentries, defiles to be crossed at night. Joe held up his hand.

Here now, aren't we talking about the first arms ever to be smuggled to the Haganah? What's an everyday wagon with a false bottom doing on such an occasion? Figs for cover? I have a better idea. There's a giant stone scarab I happen to know about, hollow inside so that it could hold a lot. A scarab, I said. A giant Egyptian stone scarab.

The man gazed at him. Joe lowered his voice.

Picture it now. From the heart of the enemy's camp a huge beetle inches across an ancient parched homeland one day to be fertile again. A relentless scarab creeping forward, an Egyptian scarab as patient and hard as stone because it is stone as still stone. A scarab as old as the pyramids, as determined as the people who will now escape those pyramids, a giant stone scarab scaling the slopes of the mountain to reach Jerusalem at last in the first light of a new day, an Egyptian stone beetle and great secret scarab stuffed with the first arms for the future Jewish underground army.

O'Sullivan Beare leaned back and smiled, suspecting this man Stern might pay him well.

He had the baking priest's papers and Stern's instructions, now all he had to do was get Haj Harun to agree to the trip, since there was no hope of parting him from the scarab. This morning, he said, I overheard someone mention a man named Sinbad. Who is he anyway? A local trader?

Ha Harun abruptly stopped pacing along the walls.

A local trader? Do you mean you've never heard of Sinbad's mighty adventures?

No. What were they then?

Haj Harun took a deep breath and launched into a headlong account. Twenty minutes passed before the sundial chimes struck, causing him to pause.

Midnight though the sun's out, said Joe. When was the last time you went to sea?

Haj Harun's hands hung in midair.

What?

To sea.

Who?

You yourself.

Me?

Yes.

Haj Harun lowered his head in embarrassment.

But I've never been to sea. I've never left Jerusalem except to make my annual haj.

The hell you say. Sinbad did all that and you've never been to sea even once?

Haj Harun covered his face, overwhelmed by the pathetic failure of his life. His hands shook, his voice quivered.

It's true. How can I ever make up for it?

Why we'll make a trip of course. We'll follow resolutely in the wake of Sinbad.

I can't. I can't leave my treasures unprotected.

No need to. No one can make off with the safe, it's too heavy or too deeply rooted or both. Your helmet you can wear, Sinbad probably wore one himself. And the scarab we'll take with us.

We will? Would a ship captain allow it?

We'll tell him it's cargo. We'll say we're in the antiquities business and we're lugging it to Constantinople to sell for some lighter pieces. He'll understand. Who wants to own something that heavy? Then when we come back we'll say we couldn't get a proper price for it, all neat and tidy and no one suspecting a thing. What do you say?

Haj Harun smiled dreamily.

Resolutely in the wake of Sinbad? After all these years?

The same afternoon the sea voyage was proposed Haj Harun noticed something that bewildered him. All at once his new friend had begun to refer to his past as a Bible. More specifically he called it the Sinai Bible.

What did it mean? Why was his past a Bible to his friend and what did it have to do with the Sinai? Was he being accepted as Moses' spiritual companion and brother in the wilderness because his name was Aaron?

He pondered the problem as best he could and kept returning to Moses. After forty years of wandering Moses had arrived somewhere, and although he had been wandering about seventy-five times that long he hadn't gotten anywhere at all yet. But in the near future? Did his friend have faith in the eventual success of his mission? Was that what he was saying?

Haj Harun peeked shyly at the crumbling plaster in his nonexistent mirror. He straightened his helmet.

Was it blasphemous? Should he accept this new information as he had accepted so many apparently incomprehensible truths over the centuries?

Humbly he agreed it was his duty. His friend was insistent and he couldn't turn away from facts just because they seemed unlikely. Facts had to be believed. Although he had never suspected it until this moment, he, Haj Harun, was the secret author of the Sinai Bible.

And once having accepted it as fact he easily fitted it into his background. That very evening he was referring to the Sinai Bible as his diary, an account of adventures recorded in the course of a Jerusalem winter during some earlier epoch of his life.

By epoch you mean the last century? asked O'Sullivan Beare.

Haj Harun smiled, he nodded. He couldn't quite recall why he had written down what he had, but probably it had been to pass the time and forget the icy drafts in the caverns where it was likely he had been living then.

Why this likelihood? asked O'Sullivan Beare.

Haj Harun looked doubtful, then laughed.

Because the caverns have been my winter residence as far back as I can remember.

They have? Then you admit the Sinai Bible deals solely with what you found in the caverns?

Oh yes indeed, answered the old man grandly. Didn't you know that's been my routine for some time now? Wandering around the Judean hills in the summer enjoying the sunshine, back to my shop and the streets of the Old City for the brisk clear air of autumn, the caverns of the past in winter and a haj in the spring? I've kept to that schedule for millennia and why not? What could be more exhilarating?

The morning they were due to leave O'Sullivan Beare was locking up the safe when he noticed a small piece of paper caught in a crevice at the back. He pulled it out and passed it to Haj Harun.

A reminder you wrote yourself before the Crusaders arrived?

Not mine. It's a letter in French.

Can you read it?

Of course.

Well who's it to then?

Someone named Strongbow.

Bloody myth, muttered O'Sullivan Beare, who had heard stories about the nineteenth-century explorer in the Home for Crimean War Heroes. Never existed. Couldn't. No Englishman was ever that daft. What's it say?

It thanks this man Strongbow for a present he sent across the Sahara in honor of a special occasion.

What's the present?

A pipe of Calvados.

All that way and only a pint?

No, pipe, a kind of measurement I believe. About one hundred and fifty gallons. Say about seven hundred bottles.

And why not, might as well say that as anything else. What's the special occasion?

The birth of his nine hundredth child.

Do you say so. Whose nine hundredth child?

The man who wrote the letter.

How's he sign himself?

Father Yakouba.

Oh I see, a priest. Where's he writing from?

Timbuktu.

What?

That's all there is except the number on the letter. They must have had a large correspondence.

Why this opinion?

The number is four thousand and something. The script is faded there.

Well Jaysus it should be. A priest fathering nine hundred children? Seven hundred bottles of Calvados marching to Timbuktu? Four thousand letters each way? What's the date on it?

Midsummer night, 1840.

What were you doing then?

Haj Harun looked puzzled.

Never mind. At least you weren't tramping around the Sahara boiling your brains in the sun. Come on, here comes the cart for the scarab.

Sinbad's hour arrived. In Jaffa they boarded a Greek caïque and a course was set for southern Turkey.

Haj Harun was sick from the beginning, unable to go below decks because of the engine fumes and unable to keep his balance topside because he was so weak from vomiting. He was afraid the waves would wash him overboard and eventually O'Sullivan Beare had to lash him to the gunwale beside the scarab to keep him from tumbling around and hurting himself.

The Irishman crouched astride the scarab holding its ropes like reins, riding it backward to Constantinople. The boat pitched violently. As each new wave broke over the bow Haj Harun clenched his jaw and closed his eyes. The waves smashed down, his body writhed, a stream of water shot out of his mouth.

How many? shouted O'Sullivan Beare.

How many what? groaned Haj Harun.

Like I said, how many others know about the Sinai Bible?

The bow of the boat sank out of sight, a wall of water loomed in the sky. Haj Harun pressed himself against the gunwale in terror. The sea swept over them with a roar and the boat began to climb.

What did you say?

Two or three.

That's all?

At any given moment, but after all we're talking about three thousand years of moments.

Jaysus.

Haj Harun screamed. A new wave rose majestically. Haj Harun turned his head.

How many does that add up to all together then?

Twelve?

Only twelve?

More or less.

But that's nothing at all.

I know it's nothing. Could the number have something to do with the moon or the tribes of Israel?

Are you sure only twelve more or less?

Haj Harun wanted to be brave. If he had been standing on solid ground in Jerusalem he would have straightened his shoulders at least a little and pushed back his helmet and fixed his gaze on the domes and towers and minarets of his beloved city. But here he was helpless.

Yes, he whispered, trembling and ashamed. Then once again he tried to be hopeful as he had by invoking and aligning himself with the twelve tribes and the moon.

There's an old saying that there are only forty people in the world and we get to know only a dozen of them in our lifetime. Might that explain it?

O'Sullivan Beare nodded solemnly as if weighing this information. It might explain the moon and lunacy but not much else.

I've heard that saying, he shouted, but does it apply to a life as long as yours? I mean if you've lived three thousand years how can so few people have known you?

Not quite three thousand, whispered Haj Harun. I'm sixteen years short of that.

All right, not quite three thousand. Now who are these dozen people? Emirs and patriarchs? Chief rabbis? Princes of the church? People like that?

Oh no, whispered Haj Harun.

Well who?

Do you remember that man who walks back and forth on the top of the steps that lead down to the crypt in the church?

The Church of the Holy Sepulchre? The one who never stops? The one who's always muttering to himself? The man you said has been doing that for the last two thousand years?

Yes that's him. Well he believes me. Or at least he didn't beat me when I told him about it.

Did he stop walking back and forth?

No.

Stop muttering to himself?

No.

Did he even look at you?

Haj Harun sighed. No.

All right, who else then?

There was a cobbler once. I went into his cubbyhole and told him about it and he didn't beat me either.

Where was that?

Somewhere in the Old City.

Where?

I can't quite recall.

When?

I don't remember.

Who else?

I can't think of anyone else but it may come to me.

Beautiful, thought the Irishman, just no competition at all. The map's there for the taking.

By Jaysus is that the truth? he shouted.

Oh God the truth, moaned Haj Harun as the boat shot down and down, as a monstrous wave leapt into the sky and he turned his head to receive the vicious blow on his other cheek.

The day they docked in Constantinople the stomach of the stone scarab was tightly packed with dismantled Czech rifles. The return voyage was just as rough and by the time they arrived Haj Harun had gone without food for three weeks. In Jaffa the heavy scarab was lowered off the boat into a cart. There was little traffic on the pier and the English customs official seemed to want to pass the time.

Couldn't make a sale up there?

Not offered enough this trip but next time we'll make it.

The official was staring at Haj Harun, at the rusting

helmet that kept crashing down on his nose. The old man was walking in circles, anxious to finish the last stage of the journey.

Who is he? whispered the official. I mean who does he think he is?

He doesn't think, he knows. He's the last King of Jerusalem.

The what?

That's right.

And the scarab's his?

Yes.

Where'd he get it?

From the former king.

And when was that?

The twelfth century I think. He's not too good on dates, uniforms either.

The official smiled and picked up his pen.

Name?

MacMael n mBo, baking priest.

Permanent place of residence, Mr. Priest?

The Home for Crimean War Heroes, Jerusalem.

Nationality?

Crimean.

Status of traveler?

Retired war hero.

Present occupation?

Keeper of the royal scarab, second class.

The customs official smiled but O'Sullivan Beare's face was serious. He was having difficulty holding Haj Harun, who seemed ready to walk off the side of the pier at any moment.

Expect you'll be seeing a promotion soon?

Within the decade probably.

Fine. Now just point the old man in this direction so I can ask him a question or two.

I wouldn't, not if you want to keep your sanity.

The official laughed.

Name? Residence? Profession?

Haj Harun muttered his name, then repeated *Jerusalem* three or four times.

How's that? Profession?

Jerusalem, said Haj Harun.

That's a profession?

For him it is.

Now listen, just have him tell me something he's done in his life. Anything at all, I don't care, I just want to fill out this form.

Go ahead and tell him then, said Joe.

Indeed I will, answered Haj Harun. Once I wrote the Sinai Bible.

The what?

The Bible. I'm sure you've heard of it.

Well that's just lovely. And what, my friend, is the Sinai Bible?

The original Bible, whispered Joe. I mean it's the oldest one that's ever been found only now it's lost again. He misplaced it.

The customs official swore.

Who misplaced it?

This Arab here called Aaron. The man who wrote it.

Get your arses off my pier, shouted the official.

O'Sullivan Beare nodded pleasantly. He bent and heaved, Haj Harun broke into a wheezing cough. Pushing and pulling they wheeled the heavy cart with its secret load of weapons down the quay, gathered momentum midway and had to run to keep up as the giant stone beetle went hurtling into the Holy Land.

The next day they were trudging up the heights toward Jerusalem in a cloudbank. They climbed in silence beside the cart, Joe prodding the donkey and Haj Harun struggling along behind. Toward the end of the afternoon Haj Harun spoke for the first time.

It's my last trip.

Why this sentiment?

No food in three weeks. I'm sick.

And Sinbad and all the voyages he made? You can't forget that can you and just give up?

No I guess I can't. It's true there's much to bear and we have to keep trying.

His chin fell to his chest, slamming the helmet into his nose. There was little light from the overcast sky and his eyes were watering as usual so he was having trouble finding the path. For several hours he had been straying off into the wastes stumbling over rocks and bushes. His hands were scratched and cut, he limped from a bruised knee on one leg and a sprained ankle on the other. Blood oozed out of a jagged gash in his cheek.

The cold wind ripped at them. Joe plodded along with his head down. All at once there was a loud crash. The donkey stopped, Joe went back down the path to see what had happened.

Haj Harun lay stretched on the ground on his face next to a tall narrow boulder. He had walked over it blindly, one foot on each side, or rather he would have walked over it if the boulder hadn't been waist-high. The rock had smashed into his groin tearing muscles and cracking bones. He had lost his balance and fallen on his head twisting a leg as he went down. Only his helmet, newly dented down the middle, had saved him from crushing his skull.

Joe rolled him over. One leg looked broken and the entire pelvic region was soaked in blood. He groaned and lay still.

That's it, I can't take any more, you might as well go on without me.

The leg?

Numb, it won't move, I can't move, my insides are all torn apart. For centuries I've been trying to do it, trying to go on, but this time it's over, I'm finished and I know it. I'm too old and tired, just a miserable sack of pains, nothing but aches and more aches, no

I can never move again. Oh I know you thought you could help and you did but I'm beyond helping now, I've reached the very end. There's a limit after all, sadly there is. So take the kingdom, Prester John, it's yours, and take the scarab and the safe and the sundial, they're yours too. You know, I used to think I'd have no regrets when the end came but now I know I'm no match for Sinbad and all those other people I dreamed about, no match for anyone at all. Once I thought I could do something but it never worked out. That cobbler and that man on the top of the steps who doesn't even know I'm there, they're the only ones who will listen to me, you're right about that. Other people just beat me, they always have. They beat me because I'm foolish. They call me a fool and I know I am. Just an old fool who has never done anything, never accomplished one thing, nothing at all.

Stop this now, said Joe. Stop it right here. The city depends on you, it's survived because of you. Where would it be without you to defend it? Who would rebuild it? How would it keep growing higher? What would happen to the caverns?

Haj Harun sobbed quietly.

No, I wanted to think all those things but they're not true. You know my wives were probably right after all, I should have been content to live like other people. I was comfortable, there was more than enough to eat and I was never cold, and since then I've done nothing but starve and shiver and never sleep, never get any rest at all because my gums hurt so much when I lie down. And they warned me, I don't deny it. Don't be a fool, they said. Why give up everything for this hopeless mission? Do you want to be cold all the time? Do you want to starve? You must be mad.

Haj Harun's crumpled figure was all but lifeless. He lay on the stony ground gasping painfully for breath, his face smeared with blood. Blood and rust filled his eyes. The circle of blood below his waist was spreading. The broken leg was bent awkwardly to one side.

Joe knelt holding the old man's hands, which were so cold it frightened him. His pulse was uneven and growing weaker.

It couldn't be. Was the old warrior really dying?

A sudden warmth fell on his shoulders. He looked up. The sky had opened and a fierce wind was peeling the clouds back over the hills. Directly above them, lit by the sun, was Jerusalem.

Look, he shouted.

Haj Harun's lips moved. There was a gurgle deep in his throat.

It's no use, I can't see. I tried and failed and it's over.

No, look.

He gathered Haj Harun up in his arms and wiped the blood and rust out of his eyes. The old man's head rolled back. He gasped.

Jerusalem.

Yes.

Right there.

Yes.

Haj Harun struggled out of his arms. He crawled to his knees and planted one foot. He grasped the boulder and pulled himself up never taking his eyes off the mirage above him. Wildly he lurched away from the boulder, slipped and nearly fell but somehow kept going, staggering and coughing and spitting, cackling and stumbling, half naked on his spindly crooked legs tottering up the hillside, laughing and trailing blood and no longer caring whether he was on the path or not, waving his arms frantically as he yelled.

I'm coming, wait I'm coming.

II

Maud

*Once more a dream and a place
to dream.*

✵

The bleak first memories better to be forgotten as they
had been for forty years.

A farm in Pennsylvania where she was born toward
the end of the century, her poker-playing father gone
before she knew him, abandoning his wife and child
to go west. Her mother managing a few years before
she swallowed a dose of Paris green in despair and
when that didn't work went out to the barn and
hanged herself.

Maud hungry and thinking it was time for supper,
calling her mother and going to look, stepping through
the open barn doorway with a little skip.

A taut stiff rope. A straight stiff body hanging in the
shadows.

Screaming and running, too young to understand
everything could be taken away by a footstep through
a doorway. Running and screaming, *Why have they
left me?*

The desolate mining town where her silent grandmother lived alone, an old Cheyenne woman whose
husband had been a murderer, sent away. The old
Indian woman not saying a word for days at a time,
her face flat and dead behind the counter of the small
saloon she ran, a dark filthy place where little Maud

171

poured beer at ten o'clock in the morning and stared at the tense blackened faces of the miners as they whispered about another broken lift cable and mangled bodies three hundred feet below the ground, learning arithmetic by adding up what the exhausted miners drank.

An ugly world and she was frightened. People left you, why? What had you done? Everyone always went away and there was no one to trust, so she dreamed. At home alone she took off her clothes and danced in front of a mirror, dreaming because dreams alone were safe and beautiful.

All else was grime and coal dust and dangling ropes, old women who never spoke and murderers who never came back and haggard worn-out faces, hopeless whispers and the terror of doors and footsteps.

She worked hard to escape, to become the best skater in the world, it was her whole life as a child. The clean white ice sparkled as she flew across it on the glittering hard surface of her dream, a still silent surface so white and yet so thin above the swirling currents of life that could spin ever deeper into blackness and a blind world of twisting creatures unknown in a young girl's dreams.

She won competitions and more competitions and when she was only sixteen she was chosen to join the future American Olympic team that was going on an exhibition tour in Europe. The year was 1906 and the first exhibition was in the resort town of Bled, which was where she met a man with the curious name of Catherine and where it all began.

A strange name for a strange man, a rich Albanian who was the head of one of the leading Albanian clans, whose native tongues were Tosk and Gheg, who lived in a seventeenth-century castle.

Tosk and Gheg, a castle in a mysterious land. Within a week she left for Albania with Catherine Wallenstein to become his wife.

Almost at once she discovered she was pregnant and at the same time Catherine ceased to take any notice of her. Increasingly he was away on what were called his hunting trips. Toward the end of her pregnancy Maud learned the horrible truth about these forays from an elderly woman named Sophia who had a peculiar hold over the castle, a woman referred to by everyone for some reason as Sophia the Unspoken.

Her mysterious position in the castle was beyond explanation. Sometimes Maud had the impression she might once have had some intimate connection with Catherine's dead father, yet she also hinted her mother had been no more than a lowly servant in the place, a cleaning woman attached to the stables. In any case she had been born in the castle and passed her whole life there, and now she seemed to be its real master while Catherine was little more than a stranger who came and went. The old woman completely ignored him and he did the same to her, even to the point where they never addressed one another. To both of them it was as if the other didn't exist.

Yet she was kind to Maud and often talked to her, especially about Catherine's father, who had died insane. The old woman was obsessed by his memory and whenever she mentioned him she became a little mad herself. Her voice was hushed and childlike with a peasant's awe for superstition and she told preposterous tales about the last of the Skanderbeg Wallensteins almost as if he were still alive, although from what the other servants said he must have died at least three decades ago, long before any of them had come to the castle. Of Catherine's mother, who apparently had died in childbirth, Sophia the Unspoken never said a word.

And then having mentioned Catherine's birth, the old woman suddenly went into a rage. She clenched her fists and muttered wildly, spewing out the monstrous visions of a demented mind.

A vicious child, she hissed. At first he killed only wild animals. He trapped the females in the mountains and ripped them open to roast the embryo. But later he began going into the mountains disguised as a holy man, just as he does today, hunting for stray boys. When he finds one he carries him off and ties him up and uses him, uses him and cuts him until the boy's nearly dead, then hacks off the head and eats the mouth. Do you understand? The peasants suspect it's him but they can't do anything about it because he's a Wallenstein. All they can do is never let their little boys out of their sight for an instant, but that makes no difference to him because there are always gypsies wandering through the mountains to provide new victims for his ecstasies, more sacrifices for his rites.

Thus Sophia raved in her boundless hatred for Catherine until finally Maud had to lock her door and refuse to see her.

A few weeks before Maud was to give birth, Sophia broke into her room one night. Maud had never seen the old woman so crazed. She screamed at her to leave but Sophia seized her by the arm and pulled her to the door with an unnatural strength.

Tonight you must see it all, she hissed, dragging her down the hall to Catherine's room where she worked a concealed lever in a desk. Inside the secret compartment was a thick book in a pale covering.

His life, she said, bound in human skin. Touch it.

Maud pulled away in terror but Sophia still held her tightly. She dragged her down a corridor to the back of the castle and lifted a tiny shutter in the darkness. They were looking down on a small windowless courtyard Maud had never seen before and there in the moonlight crouched Catherine, naked and thrusting, the hindquarters of a ram between his legs, his strong hands wrapped around the animal's neck.

To break it at exactly the moment, hissed Sophia. Now do you believe me?

Sophia had a carriage waiting and Maud left at once. By noon the following day she had gone into labor. Catherine, in pursuit with forty horsemen, found the farmhouse where she lay and slaughtered all the inhabitants before ordering some of his party to carry his newborn son back to the castle. His left eyelid was drooping in the familiar Wallenstein manner of past generations and to Maud he said nothing. His only interest now was to return to the castle and murder Sophia before she escaped.

But as it happened Sophia hadn't tried to escape. She was waiting for him, standing rigidly in a window of the old tower room where her lover had first learned to play Bach's Mass in B Minor nearly a hundred years ago. As Catherine neared the castle he caught sight of her. She glared at him, slowly making the sign of the cross and at that moment his furious gallop came to an end. His horse reared, a convulsion seized him and he was thrown to the ground.

His men propped him against a tree. His arms twitched violently, his mouth frothed, his knees jerked against his chest in successive spasms. Blood trickled over his lips and the veins in his face began to rupture.

In a few seconds it was over and the once powerful body of Catherine Wallenstein lay dead, not struck down by some primitive paroxysm of rage as it appeared, rather felled by the terminal onslaught of a massive and incurable disorder that had been ravaging him for years with a fever resembling paratyphoid, noncommunicable among humans, a condition visited upon him during the onset of puberty when he had first contracted a rare and largely extinct mountain strain of Albanian hoof and mouth disease.

Maud meanwhile, dazed and sickly and understanding none of it, crept on toward Greece with her two gifts from Sophia the Unspoken, a purse of Wallenstein gold and the secret of the Sinai Bible.

In Athens she eventually found work as a governess and came to know a Cretan visitor to the house, a fiery nationalist and soldier whose father had been one of the leaders of the Greek war for independence. Although raised in the wealthy Greek community in Smyrna, Yanni had run away when he was sixteen to join the Cretan insurrection against the Turks in 1896.

He had the tall powerful frame and deep blue eyes common to the remote mountain area in southwestern Crete where he and his father had been born, an isolated enclave of shepherds who were said to be direct descendants of the Dorians, their harsh region notorious for both the savage bloodshed of its vendettas and the fierce independence of its people, so unyielding the Turks had never fully subdued them in their two-hundred-year occupation.

Yanni was proud of this heritage and always wore the costume of his native mountains, high black boots and black jodhpurs and a black scarf tied around his head, in his waistband a long pistol with a white grip and a knife with a white handle split at the end in the Minoan symbol of a bull's horns, a wild and dashing sight on the quiet streets of Athens where he looked like a ferocious corsair from another era, eyes alert and quick in his step, mouth set in such a way men often crossed the street to avoid him.

Yet there was another, softer side to him when he was with Maud. Then the powerful man who bristled with weapons and honor and courage fell into moods so awkward his direct and tender feelings were almost childlike in their simplicity. Suddenly he would look bewildered and fumble for words, lose them and end up staring at the floor helplessly gripping his huge hands.

It was flattering but she didn't prolong it. My eagle, she called him as she asked him to tell her about his mountains in Crete, and then all at once his awkwardness was gone and he was off soaring on the heroic words that had brought his people sweeping out of their mountain retreat again and again to fire yet another revolution in Crete down through the long nineteenth century, every ten years freedom or death, just as soon as a new generation of young men was old enough to fight and be slaughtered.

After a courtship that lasted a year his friend came to her with Yanni's formal proposal of marriage in which he stated that since she was an American, where the custom didn't prevail, he didn't expect a dowry, Maud smiling when the man gravely emphasized the depths of Yanni's love by pointing out that for a man of his name and reputation even a dowry of two hundred healthy olive trees would have been modest in Crete.

After they were married he took her to Smyrna to meet his half-brother, a man then almost sixty, nearly thirty years older than himself.

Not at all like me, he said with a smile, but family's important in Greece so that doesn't matter. And he's a kind man who means no harm, I think you'll like him.

Maud did like him immediately, fascinated by the strangeness of it all as they sat having tea in the garden of his beautiful villa overlooking the Aegean, Yanni nodding respectfully in his fierce costume and trying not to crush the delicate teacup in his hands, his worldly half-brother Sivi immaculate in one of the elegant dressing gowns he always seemed to wear until sundown, languidly passing pastries and discoursing on the opera he was to see that evening or relating the latest gossip of Smyrna's sophisticated international society.

When they returned to Athens, Yanni left her almost at once to enlist in the Greek army that was preparing defenses in the north. He came back a few times during her pregnancy but was away in 1912 fighting the Turks in Macedonia when their daughter was born, and away again a year later fighting the Bulgarians when the baby died. Maud tried not to be bitter but the resentment was there deep within her.

After the Balkan wars came the fighting on the Salonika front and in 1916 she received a telegram saying Yanni had died in a malaria epidemic. Maud cried but it also seemed she had been alone almost from the beginning, a young woman in a foreign land whose childhood dreams had briefly come to life only to slip away again after her first few months with Yanni, still not admitting to herself that once more she felt someone she loved had left her.

Sivi came to see her and helped her with money. He offered to pay her fare back to America if she wanted to go but she said she wasn't ready yet, she wanted to be alone and study, languages she thought so she could earn a living doing translations. Over the next few years they wrote to each other and she saw him several times in Athens and Smyrna, always enjoying the visits yet always puzzled how the brothers could have been so unalike.

He was away so much, she said, sometimes I have the feeling I never really knew him.

Oh you knew him all right, said Sivi. What you saw was what he was, mountain men like that take their freedom or death in an uncomplicated manner.

And as for us being so different, he added mischievously, one of us was obviously an anachronism, either Yanni in his guise as an eighteenth-century brigand or me with my tastes that run farther back in history, several thousand years shall we say.

She met several men who weren't important to her, summers she went to the islands. When the war had been over two years she turned thirty and then she decided the time had come, she was ready to go but where? It couldn't be far, she had saved only a little money.

She looked at a map of the Eastern Mediterranean and put her finger on it. She laughed. Of course. Where else but that unparalleled theater of bazaars and races and faiths above the deserts and wastes, for so long the hope of wandering and lost and searching peoples, once more a dream and a place to dream.

So Maud made her way to Jerusalem.

12

Aqaba

Whispering do it again right now.

❖

One afternoon when she was treading slowly up the steep steps from the crypt beneath the Church of the Holy Sepulchre, a figure suddenly emerged from the shadows and began whispering to her. He was a small dark man with a thin beard and burning eyes but she hardly noticed that. It was his voice that held her.

Beneath the city, that's where I've just been and that's where I've just come from, down there exploring places lost for millennia, Solomon's quarries I've seen and Roman circuses and Crusader chapels and the cognac is eight hundred years old and the lances are two thousand years old and the carved stones are three thousand years old will you believe me.

On down through the past rushed the hushed Irish voice tracing caverns and corridors, spiraling through pageants and spectacles and the innumerable triumphs and devastations of Jerusalem over time, finally after three days and two nights to emerge by chance on this very spot, so astonished by what he had seen he had to describe it all to the first person he met.

And you're the first person, whispered the soft Irish voice, and what would your name be then?

But Maud said nothing, not wanting to break the magic between two strangers suddenly brought together in the holy crypt. Instead she smiled and silently slipped to her knees and took him in her mouth, leaving him afterward leaning dizzily against the stones in the shadows.

She lingered in the magic a day or two before going back and of course he was there waiting. And on top of the steps that led down to the crypt, as before, was the same muttering man pacing back and forth in the darkness, privately pursuing the secret duties of his unfathomable vocation. As before they took no notice of him, and he of course took no notice of anyone.

Maud led him from the church to the immense and quiet esplanade beside the Dome of the Rock, and there sitting in the shade of a cedar she touched the collar of his patched and ragged uniform and spoke to him for the first time.

What in the world is it?

Officer of light cavalry, Her Majesty's expeditionary force in the Crimea, 1854. Ragged because old, patched because of a fall suffered in a renowned suicidal charge.

And how did you survive that charge?

Two are the reasons. With God's blessings and also because my father said I had other things to do in the future. Do you see these medals and especially this cross? They indicate I'm an established hero from the middle of the nineteenth century, when I foolishly aided the cause of the British Empire in a substantial and dangerous manner.

Maud held the cross and laughed.

How old does that make you now?

Twenty, just. Although sometimes I feel older, even as aged as my father. He was a fisherman and a poor man like myself.

And all those things you told me the other day were true?

Jaysus and yes they were true, each and every one
of them more than the last and as much as the next.
True to the end as only the end can be. I know. My
father had the gift.

What gift?

Seeing the future as the past, seeing it as it is. The
seventh son of a seventh son he was and in my land
that means you have the gift.

Maud laughed again.

And what did your father see about your future
that allowed you to survive the suicidal charge?

Fighting for Ireland he saw, not rowing over to
Florida as good St Brendan had the sense to do some
thirteen hundred years ago. That's one of my names
too you see. I come from an island of saints and I
would have been glad to row to Florida for the sake
of the Church from all I hear of the climate there but
that wasn't for me, fighting in the mountains of Cork
was for me lugging around a monstrous old weapon,
a modified musketoon it was, U.S. cavalry issue 1851
and sixty-nine caliber, me firing it like a howitzer to
keep my distance, but after a while they caught onto
my faraway game and I had to escape so God allowed
me to join an order of nuns known as the Poor Clares,
temporarily of course, because some of these Poor
Clares were going on a pilgrimage to the Holy Land
that had been requested at the end of the eighteenth
century, God waiting to grant permission until the
moment was opportune, and that's how I happened
to come to Jerusalem as a nun but now I'm not a nun
anymore, now I'm a retired veteran living in the
Home for Crimean War Heroes because the baking
priest decided to award me this Victoria Cross for
general valor because the bread was getting to his
brains, only natural after sixty years at the oven
baking the same four loaves of bread, and if I seem
to be rambling and this is confusing it's just because
I've been keeping company with a peculiar Arab, a

quite elderly sorcerer, an unusual old man who is so unusually old he has that effect on you. Sorry, we'll start again. Ask me something.

Maud took his hand and smiled.

What would your father see if he were here now?

Surely the desert. We must be away from this babble of Jerusalem with its roving fanatics of every kind. Did you see that item pacing the top of the stairs to the crypt?

Yes.

Well he's been doing that for two thousand years, just pacing and muttering and never stopping. How could we even begin to think clearly in a place where such things go on?

Who told you that?

About the man on the top of the stairs? My sorcerer friend. And he knows because he's been watching him all that time. Around the beginning of every century he drops in to compare notes and see if there's been any change in the general situation but there never is. But what do you think, will we be going to the desert then? I've never been but the old Arab says it's a wonderful place for filling your soul. He's been making a haj for the last ten hundred years or so and he says nothing compares to it in the springtime, wild flowers and all that. Shouldn't we be going?

Yes my love, it must be a wonderful place and I think we should be going.

From Aqaba they rode south along the shore of the Sinai until they found a small oasis where they camped. Through the foothills in the moonlight they circled the colors of the desert, swam at noon in the brilliant gulf and lay on the hot sand of the beach, asleep in each other's arms in early evening and awake again at dawn to slip down to the shore and embrace in the shallows, laughing over their figs and pomegranates and toasting the new sun with arak, whispering *Do it again right now* and spinning, sinking through the quarters of a moon.

On their last evening they sat on a rock by the water watching the sunset gather silently, passing the arak back and forth as the Sinai burst into flames behind them and the last of the light settled on the barren hills where darkness was coming to Arabia. The rustle of the waves and the fingertips of the wind, the desert cast to fire and the rush of arak in their blood, the air lapsing into blackness and inevitably on the far side of the gulf another and distant world.

He stood then and threw the empty bottle far across the water.

They held their breath and waited and a minute seemed to pass before they heard a tiny splash somewhere out there in the night, perhaps only imagining it.

13

Jericho

Home from the sea free as birds.

❈

Joe was overjoyed when he found out they were going to have a child. He sang and danced all his father's songs and dances and insisted they get married that afternoon, as he had been insisting since before they went to Aqaba.

It's too hot today, September is soon enough. This heat is frightful.

Frightful it is and atrocious and terrible and just plain bad. Now just don't move, you shouldn't be moving, just sit quiet there and fan yourself while I make a cup of tea. Frightful, yes.

You know Joe, I'm really beginning to love Jerusalem.

It's a madhouse isn't it, nothing like it, just what the baking priest said. When he gave me his veteran's papers I looked at him and said, you're eighty-five and I'm twenty and how about apparent age? Laughed, he did. No problems like that in such a place, he said. Apparent anything doesn't mean much in our Holy City, everybody's Holy City, that's what he said. Just a minute now.

I remember once I saw a man in Piraeus who looked a lot like you except he was older.

A sailor?

Yes.

How much older?

Fifteen or twenty years.

Seventeen to be exact. That was brother Eamon jumping ship on his way to join the Rumanian army. He got himself killed fighting for the bloody Rumanians, can you imagine. The father told me all about it before it happened. You saw him in 1915. April.

I'm not sure.

That's when it was. None of my brothers ever wrote home after they left but the father knew what they were up to anyway. You can't fool a prophet can you. Here's a good cup now. Rest quiet and we'll be home from the sea free as birds.

Maud laughed, the summer passed in their small apartment in Jerusalem. September came and again she made some excuse for delaying their marriage. Joe continued to make trips to Constantinople and now each time he returned he noticed changes in her mood. She was withdrawn and irritable. But that's just her state, he thought, surely such things happen, only natural that they would.

With winter coming he decided their rooms were too drafty and cold for her to be comfortable. The warm sun of the Jordan valley would be better. He found a little house on the outskirts of Jericho and rented it, a lovely house on a small plot of land, surrounded by flowers and arbors and lemon trees. Proudly he took her down there and was astonished when she first saw it. She didn't even smile.

But don't you like it, Maudie?

No.

You don't?

I hate it. It looks like some child's idea of a doll's house.

Joe couldn't speak, he was terrified. He rushed inside and pretended to be straightening things, not daring to look at her. What was she doing, what was she saying?

When he went out again she was sitting on a bench under a tree, staring vacantly at the ground.

I'm going up to the market, won't be long. Anything special you want.

She shook her head slightly but didn't raise her eyes. Joe hurried out the gate and ran up the path, running faster and faster trying not to think.

Jaysus Joseph and Mary what's happening? Blessed mother of God what is it? Tell me what I've done please God and I'll do anything to make it up. Jaysus anything.

It became worse and worse in Jericho. Maud spent most of the day away from the house, sitting down by the river. Everything he did now seemed to enrage her, but most of all his trips to Constantinople.

I know, Maudie, but I have to make them, you see that. It's our money, there's no other way for me to make us a living.

You're a criminal.

I know you don't like the work but I've got nothing else right now, it's all I can make do with.

Better no money than that kind of money. Guns are for wounding and killing people, nothing else. You're a murderer.

What are you saying now?

In Ireland you shot people. Didn't you shoot people down?

That was different, that was the Black and Tans. You can't imagine the horrible things they were doing. It was a war we were in then only our side was just women and children and poor farmers trying to grow their crops.

Murderer.

Jaysus don't be saying it Maud, it sounds horrible and it's just not so.

Would you ever kill again?

No.

Liar.

The other thing that infuriated her was his fascination with the Sinai Bible. When he had told her about it, in Aqaba, she had laughed and laughed. Haj Harun writing his memoirs and then losing them? Three thousand years of secret Jerusalem history lying somewhere waiting to be found. Treasure maps to all the two dozen Old Cities? The old man convinced he had actually written the original Bible?

It was wonderful, she had loved it. Joe's fanciful version of the manuscript was marvelous and she had said nothing about the last of the Skanderbeg Wallensteins and his forgery. But that had been in Aqaba. Now she reacted very differently.

Are you still dreaming of finding your stupid treasure map?

It's no dream, Maud. I'm going to find it someday.

No you won't you never will because what you're looking for doesn't exist. What exists is chaos seen through a blind man's eyes and an imbecile's brain.

You'll see, Maud, Haj Harun is going to help me look and someday I'll find it.

Someday. Look at yourself right now in that absurd uniform that's big enough for two of you. Well why don't you leave if you're going to, they must be jumping up and down in the Crimea waiting for you to get there and win the war.

Before he left he brought a present to her down by the river and she threw it in the water. She screamed at him to go away, he disgusted her, she never wanted to see him again. Two weeks later when he came back she wouldn't look at him. She wouldn't speak to him. No matter what he said she ignored him.

At night he sat drinking alone in the garden behind the little house, drinking until he fell asleep, drinking until it was time to make another trip for Stern. not understanding any of it, having no way of knowing that Maud's fear of being left again by someone she loved was so desperate it was driving her to leave him instead.

He was away when their son was born toward the end of winter, away in Constantinople smuggling more arms for Stern and Stern's cause. He had to go to the midwife to find out it was a boy. Maud hadn't even left a note.

Joe sat down on the floor and cried. Less than a year had passed since their month together on the shores of the Gulf of Aqaba.

Someday, he promised himself, I *will* find it.

PART THREE

14

Stern

Pillars and fountains and water-
ways, a place where myrrh grew
three thousand years ago and
forever.

⚜

The tent where he was born in the Yemen stood not
far from the ruins of Marib, the ancient capital of the
Queendom of Sheba which had once sent apes and
gold and peacocks, silver and ivory up the Incense
Road to Aqaba, whence they could be transported
farther north to the heights of Jerusalem. As a boy he
played in the ruins of the Temple of the Moon at
Marib among the former pillars and fountains and
waterways where myrrh grew.

One morning he found nothing but sand where the
temple had been. He ran back across the hills to their
tent.

It's gone, he whispered breathlessly to his immensely tall father and his short round grandfather
who were roaming back and forth as usual, talking
and talking as they pretended to watch over their
sheep, the one a former English aristocrat turned
bedouin hakīm who had been the greatest explorer of
his age, the other an unlettered Yemeni Jew and shepherd who had never left the hillside that was his
birthplace.

The temple's gone, repeated the boy. Where did it go?

Where? said his short grandfather.

A mystery, murmured the one. And not only gone but why?

And not only where, added the other, but when?

Right now, answered the little boy. Right where it's supposed to be. It disappeared overnight.

The two old men shook their heads thoughtfully. The sun was already high enough to be felt so they sought the shade of an almond tree to consider the problem. While they took turns asking him questions the boy hopped from one foot to the other.

We must solve this mystery. What's there in place of the temple?

Sand. Nothing.

Ah, nothing but sand, mysterious indeed. Did you stay there overnight?

No.

Were you there at dawn?

No.

Ah. Could it be then it's only happening now?

They both looked at him. He was barely four years old and the question confused him.

What's happening now? he asked.

His father tugged the sleeve of his grandfather.

Is there really a Temple of the Moon, Ya'qub?

There is certainly. Yes yes, I've seen it as long as I can remember.

But not today? asked father.

No not today but I'll see it again, answered his grandfather.

When? In a week, Ya'qub? Two months from now?

More or less then, o former hakīm. Yes assuredly.

And yesterday?

No.

Six months ago?

Yes and no. But in any case one of those times without any doubt whatsoever.

But what are these yesterdays and next weeks of yours, Ya'qub? These two months from now and six months ago? This strange way you have of discussing time? More or less, you say, running days and dates past and future all together as if they were the same.

His father smiled. His grandfather laughed and clasped the small bewildered boy to his chest.

Do I? Yes I do. It must be simply that the Temple of the Moon is always there for me because I know it in every detail, exactly as I've seen it before and will see it again. And as for the sand that may cover it from time to time, well sand is no matter. We live in the desert and sand simply comes and goes.

His father turned to him.

Do you know it in every detail the way your grandfather does?

Yes, whispered the boy.

And you can see it all in your mind's eye even now? Yes.

His father nodded solemnly, his grandfather smiled happily.

Then it must be as your grandfather says. Above the sands or beneath them is no matter. For you, as for him, the temple is always there.

The boy thought he understood and went on to another question.

Well if it's always there now, how long has it always been there? Who built it?

His grandfather pretended to frown. Again he clasped the boy in his arms.

That's history, he said, and I know nothing of such things, how could I? But fortunately for us your father's a learned man who has traveled everywhere and gathered all the knowledge in the world, so probably he has already read the inscriptions on the pillars and can answer those questions precisely. Well, o former hakīm? Who built the Temple of the Moon in Marib and how long ago would you say? Precisely one thousand years ago and forever? Two thousand years ago and forever?

This time it was Ya'qub's turn to tug his father's sleeve and his father's turn to smile.

The people were called Sabaeans, he said, and they built it three thousand years ago and forever.

The small boy gasped at the incomprehensible figure.

Father, will you teach me to read the inscriptions on the pillars?

Yes, but first Ya'qub must tell us when they will reappear. He must teach us about the sand.

Will you do that, grandfather?

Yes yes certainly. When next the wind blows we'll go out together and sniff it and see if the incense is returning once more to the Temple of the Moon in Marib.

The short round man snorted, he laughed. His father, grave and dignified, led the way back to the tent where water was set boiling for coffee. And that night as so often the boy sat up by the fire until what seemed a very late hour, drowsily slipping in and out of sleep, never quite sure whether the wondrous words the two old men ceaselessly passed back and forth in the shadows were from the Zohar this time or the *Thousand and One Nights*, or perhaps written in the stones of the Temple of the Moon where he played, the mysterious myrrh of his childhood, vanishing pillars and fountains and waterways returning with inscriptions to be read one day as surely as gusts in the turning wind, a heady scent to be forgotten no matter how deeply the strands of incense were buried beneath the sands that night and three thousand years ago and forever, as his father spoke of time in the Temple of the Moon after his long decades of wandering, or that night and the yesterday and next week of forever, as his grandfather described it on that remote hillside beyond ancient Marib which had always been his home.

His mother's teachings also flowed when they walked together in the dim cool light of dawn collecting herbs and wild grasses for their salads. Sometimes she made strange sounds out there and gazed at the ground for whole minutes holding her side, her face weary in a way he didn't understand.

What could she tell him after all, a boy of four? She was going that's all, every day the weight was heavier. When she stooped for a blade of grass it pushed her down and when she straightened again she had to press her eyes closed to hold back the pain. The blessing of a child had simply taken more than her body had to give. But he was young and one day he asked her about it when she staggered on the hillside.

What is it, Mother?

The memory of that moment would never leave him. The stiff fingers, the strained face, the tired haunted eyes. She sank to her knees and hid her face. She was crying.

Where does it hurt?

She took his hand and placed it on her heart.

Where? I can't feel anything.

Here is better, she said, putting one of his tiny fingers on a vein in her wrist.

That's your blood. Is that where the pain is?

No, in my heart where you couldn't feel it.

But Father will be able to feel it. Father was a great hakīm. He can cure anyone.

No. The reason you couldn't feel it is because sometimes we have pains that belong to us and no one else.

Now he began to cry and she leaned forward on her knees and kissed his eyes.

Don't do that. It's all right.

But it's not. And Father can make it better, I know he can.

No my son.

But that's not fair.

Oh yes it is, new life for old is always fair.

Whose life? What do you mean?

Whose life doesn't matter. What matters is that if a time ever comes when you have a special pain all your own you must carry it yourself, because other people have theirs too.

Everyone doesn't.

Yes I'm afraid they do.

Grandfather doesn't. He's always laughing.

So it seems. But underneath there's something else.

What?

Your grandmother. She died long ago and he has never stopped missing her.

Well Father certainly doesn't hurt.

Yes, even him. Now he has a place to rest but for many years that wasn't so. And once just before he came to our little corner of the world and your grandfather found him alone in the dust and brought him home to us, there was a terrible time when he was lost.

The little boy shook his head stubbornly.

But that's not true, Father was never lost. He walked from Timbuktu to the Hindu Kush and floated down the Tigris to Baghdad and marched through three dawns and two sunsets out of the Sinai without even noticing he had no food or water. No one has ever done the things he did.

That may be but I didn't mean he was lost in the desert. He was lost here, in his heart, where my pain is now.

The little boy looked at the ground. He had always accepted everything his mother said but it seemed impossible that his smiling grandfather could really be sad inside. And it was even more impossible to believe his father had ever been lost.

And so, she said, we mustn't tell your father about my pain because he has his own burdens from the past. He came here to find peace, he brought us happiness and he deserves it in return.

She put her hands on his shoulders.

Now promise me that.

He was crying again. I promise, he said, but I also want to help. Isn't there something I can do?

Well perhaps one day you can find our home. Your father found a home with us but your grandfather and I don't really belong here.

Why?

Because we're Jews.

Where is our home then?

I don't know but someday you may find it for us.

I will. I promise.

She smiled.

Come then, we have to pick our grasses for dinner. Those two men of ours talk and talk and never stop and they'll be hungry after spending another day settling the affairs of heaven.

When he went to Cairo for Islamic studies he used one of his father's Arabic names. When he went to Safad to study the cabala he used his grandfather's Jewish name. So when the time came for him to acquire his Western education he asked what name he should use.

A Western name, said his father.

But what? asked his grandfather. The two old men took his coffee cup and studied it. I see many Jewish and Arabic names, said Ya'qub, but I can't make out a Western one, perhaps because I don't know what a Western name is. What do you see, o former hakīm?

His father raised the small cup far above their heads

and peered over the rim. *Stern*, he announced after a moment. Yes quite clearly.

That sounds too short, said Ya'qub, isn't there more to it? Doesn't it have an *ibn* or a *ben* something after it?

No that's all there is, said his father.

Very odd, very curious. What does it mean?

Resolute, unyielding.

Unyielding?

In the face of what can't be evaded or escaped.

Ah that's better, said Ya'qub. Certainly there's no reason to evade or escape the marvels of life.

All at once he wrapped his arms around himself and rocked back and forth. He winked at his grandson.

But then, o former hakīm, do I hear an echo of your own character in the coffee cup of your son?

Impossible, answered the old explorer with a smile. Coffee grounds are coffee grounds. They speak for themselves.

Ya'qub laughed happily. Yes yes they do, how could it be otherwise. Well my boy, there you have it. And where do you go now?

Bologna. Paris.

What? Unheard-of places. How do they number the year there? What do they call it?

Nineteen hundred and nine.

Ya'qub poked his father.

Is it true what the boy says?

Of course.

Ya'qub snorted, he laughed.

Of course you say to an old man who's never been anywhere, but it makes no difference you see. These hills will still be here when the boy returns, only the sand will be different. In fact you'll never leave them. Is that so or not?

Perhaps, said Stern, smiling.

The two of you, muttered Ya'qub, you think you can

fool me but you can't. I know what year it is, certainly
I do. More coffee, o former hakīm? We can thank
God your son is halfway between the two of us and
has some of my good shepherd blood in him so he
won't have to be a genie for sixty years, like you were,
before he becomes a man.

The evening before he left his father took him out
walking in the twilight. Too excited at first to realize
his father had something he wanted to say, he talked
and talked about the new century and the new world
it would bring, how eager he was to get to Europe and
get started, to begin, so many possibilities and so
much ahead, so much to do, on and on until at last
he noticed his father's silence and stopped.

What are you thinking?

About Europe. I was wondering whether you'll like
it as much as you think you will.

Of course I will, why wouldn't I, it's all new. Imagine how much there is for me to see.

That's true yet Ya'qub may be right, it may be that
you'll never leave these hills. That was his way, it
wasn't mine, but then I wasn't born in the desert with
its solitude the way he was, or you. I sought it and
perhaps being born to it is different. Surely there's as
much to see in the desert as anywhere else but to some
it can also give rise to an abiding loneliness, I have
to remind myself of that. Not all men are meant to
wander alone for forty years as I did. Father Yakouba
for example. He lived quite differently in Timbuktu
and was a very wise man with his flocks of little children and their footprints in the sky, his journeys of two
thousand miles in an afternoon while sipping Calvados
in a dusty courtyard. As he said, a haj isn't measured
in miles.

I know that, Father.

Yes of course you do. You have the example of the other Ya'qub, your own grandfather. Well do you know what it is you seek then?

To create something.

Yes certainly, that's the only way to begin. And what of money, does it play any part in your plans? What you want?

No none, it means nothing to me, how could it growing up with you and Ya'qub. But that's a strange question. Why do you ask it when you already know the answer?

Because there's a certain matter I should discuss with you and I've never talked about it with anyone, not even Ya'qub.

Stern laughed.

What could possibly be so mysterious you wouldn't talk about it with Ya'qub?

Oh it's not mysterious, quite mundane as a matter of fact. It's just that there never seemed any reason to mention it. You see before I left Constantinople I made certain financial arrangements, real estate and so forth. I thought I might have some use for the property someday but then I became a hakīm and then I retired here, so of course as it turned out I've never had any use for it whatsoever. And if you don't think you'll need the properties, well then I thought I might return them to their former owners. Possessions are a burden and the fewer burdens one has the better when setting out on a haj.

Stern laughed again.

You're not suggesting I begin naked? Strap a bronze sundial to my hip and leap over a garden wall? But you are being mysterious, Father. Could Ya'qub be telling the truth when he says the two of you own most of this part of the world? Two secret co-emperors with me as your only heir? Why do you smile?

At Ya'qub, at his notion of real estate. To him it's all in the mind and this hillside is not only *this* part

of the world, it's the universe as well. You know how
fond he is of pointing out he has never been anywhere
while it took me sixty years to arrive at the same
place. Well he's right about that of course, about this
hillside and what it has always meant to him and what
it eventually came to mean to me. Anyway, the Ottoman Empire wouldn't be much to own these days
would it, rather tattered as empires go. Something
new will have to replace it soon in this new century
you like to talk about.

Stern smiled.

And in any case there was that first lesson the two
of you ever taught me the day I couldn't find the
Temple of the Moon. That the only real empire is the
empire of the mind.

The old explorer also smiled.

I seem to recall some such conversation when you
were a small child. Well what do you think about
these properties I mentioned. Are you interested in
having them?

No.

Why?

Because I don't intend to become a real estate
dealer.

Just so, fine, that's taken care of then. One less
legacy you'll have to worry about from my old century.

All the same I don't think I'll display myself naked
at a diplomatic reception in Cairo the night I sail.

An apocryphal tale, no such thing could ever have
happened in the Victorian era. Now come, we've arranged your escape from the past and it's time to join
Ya'qub for dinner. He has been laboring all day over
his pots preparing a feast and he must be hungry for
talk.

He must be?

Hm. Did I ever tell you about the time I assembled
certain evidence to deduce the cycle of Strongbow's
Comet?

Stern laughed. He knew his father was really as excited as he was, his leaving bringing back all the memories of that night in Cairo seven decades ago when a laughing young genie had given eyes to a blind beggar and himself set forth on his journey.

I don't think so, Father. Could it possibly involve incidents from the lives of Moses and Nebuchadnezzar and Christ and Mohammed? A few lesser known passages from the *Thousand and One Nights*? An obscure reference or two from the Zohar? A frightened Arab in the desert who was alarmed because the sky was unnaturally dark? Who later turned up as an antiquities dealer in Jerusalem? In whose back room you wrote an anthropological study of the Middle East? No, I don't believe you have ever told me about it.

No? That's odd, because it was quite a remarkable affair. Do you think Ya'qub would be interested in hearing about it?

I'm sure he would, he can never get enough of hearing anything. But of course he'll immediately jumble all your facts and rearrange them to his own liking.

Yes he will, an incorrigible habit. Those eternal jokes and riddles and scraps of rhymes he sees everywhere. Well we'll just have to keep our wits about us and take our chances.

In Europe Stern dreamed deeply of his future. He considered composing symphonies or dramas, painting murals and planning boulevards and writing epic cantos. Unarmed and undefeated, he threw himself fearlessly into these projects.

He haunted museums and concert halls and restlessly paced the streets until dawn, when he fell into a chair in some workingmen's café to smoke and drink coffee and fortify himself with cognac, totally immersed for a time in this one great achievement.

In Bologna he ignored his medical lectures and covered canvases with masses of colors. But months later when he examined what he had done he found it lifeless.

In Paris he ignored his law courses to study music. Whole scores of Mozart and Bach were memorized but when the time arrived for him to write down his own musical notations, none came.

He turned at once to marble. He pored over drawings and eventually attempted sketches, only to find his own designs for fountains and colonnades resembled Bernini's.

Poetry and plays came next. Stern provided himself with a stack of paper and a hard straight chair. He boiled coffee and filled the ashtray on the desk with cigarettes. He tore up sheets of paper, boiled more coffee and filled the ashtray again with cigarettes. He went out for a walk and came back to begin again but still there was nothing.

Nothing at all. Nothing was coming from his dreams of creation.

Looking down at the heaped ashtray he was suddenly frightened. What was he going to do in life? What could he do?

He was twenty-one. He had been in Europe three years yet there was no one to talk to now, he had no friends at all, he had been too busy dreaming alone. He had come here with ideals and enthusiasm, what had gone wrong?

He sat up unable to sleep thinking of the hillsides where he had played as a boy, recalling that Ya'qub had said he would never really leave them, remembering his father on their last evening together wondering aloud what it might mean to be born in the desert with its solitude rather than to have sought it as he had done.

He poured cognac and closed his eyes, images tumbling before him.

A blind beggar in Cairo crying out triumphantly, a march the length of the Sinai without food or water, the Arab village at Aqaba, the great divide of the wadis of northern Arabia, an antiquities dealer's shop in Jerusalem, floating down the Tigris into Baghdad, leeches and opium near Aden, a fever after swimming across the Red Sea, the holy sites of Medina and Mecca in disguise.

Disguises. Strongbow striding back and forth for forty years disguised as a poor camel driver or a rich Damascus merchant, a harmless haggler over pimpernel or a collector of sorrel, an obsessed dervish given to trances and an inscrutable hakīm, a huge immobile presence in the desert speaking with his eyes.

Strongbow the genie changing and changing his size and shape.

Ya'qub the shepherd waiting patiently on his hillside.

And finally, a former hakīm gently led home to rest, brought home to peace.

What was it? What was he trying to find in those three lives?

Stern threw his glass at the wall. He picked up the bottle and crashed around the room knocking over chairs and smashing lamps on the floor. He hated Europe, all at once he knew how much he hated it. He couldn't breathe here, he couldn't think, he couldn't hear with his own ears or see with his own eyes, the noise, the crowds pushing in on him, everything cluttered and unclear, so far from the quiet hillsides of his childhood, the stillness of the shifting sands in the Temple of the Moon.

He'd done nothing here but dream futile dreams and fail, dream hopelessly and fail because this wasn't his place. He had been born in the desert, he couldn't live here. The desert was his home and he had to go back to it now, he knew that.

And do what?

Again he saw the three men. Strongbow marching from the Nile to Baghdad. Ya'qub in his tent in the Yemen. The hakīm at dawn deep in the desert sitting with a troubled bedouin, telling him fix his gaze on the flight of a distant eagle and saying *Yes*, they would find the oasis.

Why did they keep returning to him? To tell him what?

An Englishman, a Jew, an Arab. His father and his grandfather relentlessly striding on, patiently going nowhere, his land and his home and heritage.

The vision burst upon him. *A homeland for all the peoples of his heritage.* One nation embracing Arabs and Christians and Jews. A new world and the Fertile Crescent of antiquity reborn in the new century, one great nation stretching majestically from the Nile through Arabia and Palestine and Syria to the foot-hills of Anatolia, watered by the Jordan and the Tigris and the Euphrates as well, by Galilee, a vast nation honoring all of its three and twelve and forty thousand prophets, a splendid nation where the legendary cities would be raised to flourish once more, Memphis of Menes and Ecbatana of Media and Sidon and Alep of the Hittites, Kish and Lagash of Sumer and Zoar of the Edomites, Akkad of Sargon and Tyre of the purple dye and Acre of the Crusaders, Petra of the Nabata-eans and Ctesiphon of the Sassanids and Basra of the Abbasids, sublime Jerusalem and the equally sublime Baghdad of the *Thousand and One Nights*.

Stern was delirious, the vision was overwhelming, far grander than the promise he had made to his mother as a child. He sat down at his desk and began scribbling feverishly, and when he emerged two weeks later he had not only conjured up the memories of a thousand and one ancient tribes and civilizations and fused them together, he had also written the basic laws for the new nation and designed its flag, sketched some of its impressive public buildings and considered its universities and theaters, pondered its national anthem and listed the components of its constitution.

At the age of twenty-one he had arrived at his plan for life.

Quickly then he packed his bags and left Paris. Having decided who he was, nothing remained but to become that man and work toward the common bonds that perhaps had existed in his homeland three thousand years ago, not since.

This new promise was solemn and certain and he knew he would never break it, not even if it turned in time to break him.

15
The Jordan

*From the soft green heights of
Galilee, rich in gentle fields of
grain and kindly memories, a
promised stream plunging down
and down.*

❈

Stern drove back to the Middle East in a ten-horsepower
French automobile, after being trapped briefly in Albania by the outbreak of the first Balkan war. Once
there he converted the automobile into a tractor car
to use in the desert. Clattering and backfiring, the
tractor roared down wadis and rumbled over mountains covering distances that had taken dozens of painful camel marches in his father's day.

But the clouds of sand raised by the tractor attracted the attention of the bedouin. He needed a more
surreptitious means of transport and naturally he
thought of a balloon.

Stern had first experimented with balloons as a boy
by suspending a basket beneath a sack sewn from
tents. Above the basket was a crock holding a camel-
dung fire. The hot air filled the sack and sent him
bumping down a hillside.

Later he increased the heat of the fire many times
by burning oil sludge from outcroppings in the desert
rock. With this new buoyancy he could lift a larger
sack and sail much higher. Alone as a boy dreaming

on the wind above the Yemen, Stern had learned to read the stars.

Now he built a large balloon with a compact gondola that held a narrow cot, a small writing table and a shaded lamp. The balloon was fed by bottles of hydrogen which he cached in various remote ravines in the desert where he could descend at dawn and remain hidden during the hours of daylight, to sleep and plan the next leg of his trip while keeping secret the passage of his ship.

For Stern was careful to travel only at night. Sometimes he worked at his desk but more often he extinguished his shaded lamp and mused his way silently across the dark sky, invisible to those below when only the stars lit the desert, perhaps suggesting a tiny distant cloud when the moon was waxing through its quarters.

Back and forth he sailed from Aden to the Jordan, from the Dead Sea to Oman, hovering before daybreak to drop gently into a cleft in the rocks to anchor his ship. Stealthily then he made his way on foot down some narrow wadi to a village where he had arranged to meet a nationalist leader, sailing from intrigue to intrigue increasingly suffering from chronic headaches and chronic insomnia and chronic fatigue, celibate and isolated in his balloon, occasionally given to heart palpitations when he drifted too high in the starry night sky, already a victim of the incurable dreams he had known as a boy in the Temple of the Moon.

For as soon as he had his balloon equipped and set out to explore his mission, he discovered his cause had been reduced to a question of smuggling arms and nothing more He had conceived of his great nation as healing the divisions of the past, his own role in helping to found it much like that of a hakīm. But the men he talked to during those first months when he was making contacts could think about nothing but guns. If he raised other subjects they cut him short.

Idiot, yelled a man in Damascus, why do you persist in this foolishness? A constitution? Laws? There's no time for that here, you're not at the university anymore playing with theories. Guns are what we need. When we kill enough Turks and Europeans they'll leave, that's the law, that's our constitution.

But someday, Stern began.

Of course someday. Ten years from now, twenty, thirty, who knows. Someday we may have all the time in the world to talk but not now. Now there's only one thing. Guns, brother. You want to help? Good, bring us guns. You have a balloon and can cross borders at night. Good, get on with it. Guns.

It sickened Stern and he tried to resist it because it was driving him to secret despair. He was appalled to think his splendid vision could so quickly degenerate into nothing more than smuggling arms. But he couldn't argue with those men, he knew what they said was true and if he wanted to play a part it would have to be this.

So he sadly took all the inspired notes and lists and beautiful sketches he had made during those feverish and ecstatic two weeks in Paris, carried them high up above the desert one night and burned them, lit them one by one and dropped their flaming ashes into the blackness, then floated away to the east and early the next morning, the first day of 1914 or 5674 or 1292, depending on the prophet quoted, he delivered his first secret shipment of arms for the sake of a vast peaceful new nation he hoped to help build in the new century.

Stern's most significant act during those early years was also the least known, a brief yet extraordinary encounter that took place accidentally in the desert. To Stern it meant nothing and when he met the same man again after a lapse of eight or nine years, in Smyrna in

1922 when the man saved his life, he didn't even remember having seen him before.

But for the old Arab it was the most important moment in his long life.

The chance meeting occurred in the spring while Haj Harun was on his annual pilgrimage to Mecca, as usual traveling alone far from the customary routes. And as usual at all times of the year, Stern was drifting invisibly above the desert on one of his clandestine missions. At dawn he dropped from the sky to anchor his balloon and found he had nearly landed on a wizened old Arab who had been dozing like a lizard with his head under a rock. At once the barefoot man flung out his arms and prostrated himself.

He appeared both starving and lost. Stern offered him food and water but the Arab refused to raise his face from the dust. At last he did so although nothing could induce him to rise from his knees. In that position he ate and drank sparingly as if performing some ritual.

Seeing the pathetic thinness of the man's legs and the unnatural luster of his eyes, which he took for fever or worse, Stern begged him to accept his water-skins and other supplies. He even offered to float him to the nearest oasis if he was unable to walk, as seemed likely. But the wretched man abjectly refused everything. Instead he asked in the humblest of whispers, his voice trembling, if he might have the honor of knowing his host's name.

Stern told him. The Arab thanked him reverently, whereupon he backed away still on his knees and continued doing so for the rest of the morning until he had crossed the horizon and was out of sight.

Once during the morning Stern happened to glance across the desert in the direction of the retreating Haj Harun who was now a mere dot on the crest of the dunes, still struggling backward on his knees, but Stern didn't really see him and the crazed behavior of the old man made no impression on him. Instead he was busily turning the pages of his notebook planning new routes for smuggling arms.

Initially there were some successes.

In 1914 the kaiser's government was persuaded to pay regular bribes to both the Sherif of Mecca and his chief rival Emir ibn Saud, and Stern ferried German revolutionary orders from Damascus to Jidda. But nothing came of it because the Arabs wouldn't do anything and the English were soon paying them more.

That same winter he arranged a secret meeting near Cairo with an influential English suffragette, a composer of comic operettas who had recently returned from an expedition to the Sudan where she had spent a long afternoon in the privacy of her riverboat cabin photographing a comely young hermaphrodite, a camel breeder currently known as Mohammed but formerly the wife of a tribal sheik.

The sheik had beaten his wife constantly, as the suffragette learned in the course of taking her photographs. Moved by the compassion she always felt for a woman who had suffered the prejudices of the world, she ended the afternoon by making passionate love to Mohammed. But to her great disappointment none of her photographs had turned out.

Stern took her to a Greek artist in Alexandria who was able to render exactly what she had seen, thereby gaining the suffragette's support and propaganda for his cause in her subsequent operettas.

In 1918 Zaghlul was freed from internment and returned to Egypt to demand independence. In 1919 Kemal embarrassed the British by defying the sultan and the Persians resisted their British treaty. Shortly thereafter there were Arab revolts in both Syria and Iraq.

But there were also signs of coming failure in those early years.

In Constantinople the sultan had confiscated modern textbooks because he had learned they contained the subversive formula H_2O, which meant that he, Hamid II, was secretly a cipher and good for nothing.

In 1909 the Turks had massacred twenty-five thousand Armenians in Adana. In 1915, deciding there would no longer be an Armenian question if there were no Armenians, the Turks began marching them into the Syrian desert and murdering them along the way to speed the devastations wrought by starvation and epidemics.

By 1916 legions of spies had descended on Athens only to be surpassed three years later by the even greater hordes of spies congregating in Constantinople, where it was found that certain national representatives on their way to the Versailles peace conference could neither write their names nor recognize them when spoken to.

At a little-known meeting in 1918 between Weizmann and the future Grand Mufti of Jerusalem, the dignified and seemingly innocent Arab revealed his profound capacity for delusion and hate by softly quoting passages from the Protocols of the Elders of Zion.

And worst of all for Stern, the collapse of the Ottoman Empire at the end of the First World War wiped out the investments his father had left him after the former explorer and hakīm, on the eve of Stern's departure for Europe, had performed what he thought was his final act of healing by relieving his son of the burdensome legacy of that Empire he had acquired before Stern was born, an irony immense enough to divide their two centuries forever.

After 1918 Stern never had any money again. He had to sell his balloon and thereafter he became poorer and poorer, continually begging and borrowing from everyone he met in order to live, his income from smuggling, when there was any, always going for more arms because he wouldn't touch it himself.

Yet somehow as he sank deeper and deeper into debt in 1920 and 1921, so deep he knew he would never retrieve himself, he still managed to give the impression he was completely confident in what he was doing, a trait he had learned from observing his father and grandfather perhaps, although with them the confidence had been real.

In any case Stern was so convincing only a few people ever knew the truth, only the three people who were close to him over time.

Sivi, then as before the war.

O'Sullivan Beare a year later in Smyrna when he made his last trip for Stern and broke with him.

And finally Maud a decade after that when the first victims of Smyrna were beginning to fall in that small chance circle of revolving lovers and friends and relatives, all of whom eventually came to discover their lives had once irreparably crossed on a warm September day in that most beautiful of cities on the shores of the Eastern Mediterranean.

Late one cold December afternoon in 1921 O'Sullivan Beare sat slumped in a corner of an Arab coffee shop near Damascus Gate, a glass of wretched Arab cognac empty on the table in front of him. Outside a heavy wind groaned on the rooftops and pushed through the alleys, threatening snow. Two Arabs listlessly played backgammon by the window while a third slept under a newspaper. Night was falling in the street.

Empty as empty out there, thought Joe, not a body stirring and right they are, warm and home with the family where any sane man belongs tonight. Why did the old father back in the Aran Islands have to go

seeing a place like this for me? Bloody trouble, that's
what prophecy is, I could have caught fish like him
and maybe been content with a decent pint by the
fire on bad nights sharing a song and a dance with
the neighbors. Mad Arabs and Jews hustling about, a
soul doesn't need the bloody ups and downs of a
Jerusalem, Jaysus knows.

The door opened and a large hunched man came in
rubbing his hands against the cold. He stamped his
feet and smiled. Joe nodded. Moves softly for a big
man, he thought. Moves as if he had some place better
to go than this dead Arab excuse for a pub and maybe
he has who knows.

Stern pulled back a chair. He ordered two cognacs
and sat down.

You're having us take our lives in our hands with
that item, said Joe, making his fingers into a pistol and
firing once at both their heads. Same business they
use to fill the lamps. Saw them doing it, swear I did,
just before you showed up. Burns better than anything
else, the man said, and is cheaper in the bargain.

Stern laughed.

I thought it might help keep the wind out.

Not likely, be nice if it did. But who'd believe it I
want to know. If anybody at home had said the Holy
Land could be like this I'd have thought they were
waterlogged in the head, been lying out in a bog too
long sleeping one off. Sun and sand and milk and
honey I thought it was, but this is worse than rowing
around my island in a gale. At least then you were
fighting the bloody currents all the time and didn't
have time to worry your mind with things but here
you just sit and wait, you think and then you sit and
wait some more. Bloody wonder how people in this
city just sit and wait.

They take the long view, said Stern with a smile.

Seems they do, that must be it. True religion I
suppose. Jerusalem the city of miracles. The other day

an old Arab I know and myself took a wander in to look at the Dome of the Rock and what's he begin to do but stare and stare at a little chink on one side of the rock. Hello there, I said, is that chink something special? It is, he said, it's the footprint Mohammed's horse made when the Prophet climbed on his horse here and rode off to heaven. I was just remembering how the sparks were flying then, he said, and the horns sounding and the cymbals clanging and thunder and lightning shaking the sky.

Good, I said, that's the job all right, and then a few minutes later we'd moved on and were padding around in the gloom of the Church of the Holy Sepulchre, and the Greek priests were muttering around in their corner waving incense and the Armenian priests were muttering around in their corner waving incense, likewise all the others, everybody's eyes mostly closed, and then shortly after that we're out in the open again trying to get some fresh air up on the hill above Jaffa Gate, and who's there but the same Hassid who was there eight hours earlier when we passed before and he's still not noticing it because *his* eyes are mostly closed too, and he's still facing the Old City more or less oriented in the direction of the Wall but in eight hours he hasn't gotten any closer to it, just rocking and muttering and hasn't moved an inch.

What I'm trying to say is people around here seem to have all the time in the world for that, for waving incense and rocking and muttering and carrying on until twelve hundred years ago or two thousand years ago or whatever it is they're waiting for comes along again and the cymbals clang and the horns sound and everybody climbs on the horse to heaven at last and again, sparks flying and thunder shaking. Weird, that's what it is.

He emptied his glass and choked. Stern ordered two more.

Miserable stuff, said Joe, but it does clean your teeth. You know, Stern, this old article I was just telling you about, the Arab who thinks he was there watching when Mohammed made his move once upon a time, he's something like you in a way. I mean not because he was born both an Arab and a Jew, physical fact, but because he's gotten it into his head he's been living in Jerusalem since before people had such names, since before they were divided into this and that, know what I mean? So thinking the way he does he can play all kinds of tricks with reality the same as you do, pretend it doesn't exist or whatever, only his tastes don't run to politics and that kind of shit.

Joe drank and made a face.

I'm rambling too much, it's this poison seeping into my brain. Anyway there's also this Franciscan I know, the baking priest I call him because he's been spending the last sixty years here baking the same four loaves of bread. I ask him if he thinks he's following in the footsteps of our Savior with all this multiplication and if so shouldn't he be working with five loaves instead of four, and what does he do but put a twinkle in his eye and say No, nothing so grand for me, I wouldn't presume as much as that, I just bake four in order to have the parameters of life. Jaysus, know what I mean? Everybody's daft around here what with holy horses and muttering to themselves and too much incense cutting off the oxygen supply and too much rocking back and forth for sixty years baking heavenly bread. Daft, that's all. Dreaming up crazy impossible things like you. It's in the air or lack of it. No bog gas up here to keep a man in touch with the good slippery muck under his feet.

Stern smiled in a kindly way.

You seem depressed this evening.

Me? Go on you say. Jaysus why would I be down just because I'm in a crazy city twelve hundred years or two thousand miles or four loaves of bread away from home on Christmas Eve? Why?

He gulped the cognac and coughed.

You got one of those awful cigarettes you carry?

Stern gave him one. The first wisps of snow were blowing across the windows, the darkness outside was deeper. Stern watched him fidget nervously with the Victoria Cross, then with his beard.

You know Joe, you've changed a lot in the last year.

Sure I suppose I have, why not, I'm at the changing age. Not so long ago I was a true believer like one of those items you see around here on street corners mumbling over a pile of stones. Sixteen I was at the Dublin post office and then I went into training with an old U.S. cavalry musketoon for three years waiting for the day to come and come it did, calling itself the Black and Tans, so I went on the run in the mountains and it went all right for a while, but do you know what that means being on the run up there?

Joe's voice was rising in anger. Stern watched him.

Being cold and wet every minute of the day and night, that's what, and being alone and alone. Those mountains aren't meant for running, there's nothing but rain and sinking in up to your knee every step you take but I kept running because I had to, ran all night to surprise the bloody Blacks and Tans. You can't run up there but I did, just did is all, there was no other way to be doing what I was doing and do you know where it bloody well got me?

Joe slammed his fist on the table. He was shaking. He grabbed Stern't sleeve and twisted it.

To a vacant lot in Cork that's where, barefoot in rags because the people were starving and some of them were willing to turn a pound by turning informer to keep their children from starving to death. So they informed and the mountains shrank until I had no place to hide and ended up in Cork on the banks of the River Lee listening to shrieking sea gulls, an Easter Monday it was and me exhausted leaning against a ruined tannery wall with nothing to eat in three days, knowing it was all over, the three spires of St Finnbar's up there against the sky and me not smart enough then to ask myself what that Trinity in front of me really meant.

But I'll tell you something else now. While those mountains were shrinking I was growing, I was taking those soggy heaps and putting them inside me and getting bigger, and that abandoned churchyard where I buried the old musketoon in the rain, that mud was consecrated by me and nobody else.

You talk about your kingdom come to be, Stern. Well I fought for mine, I've done that and it threw me out, just kept pushing on me until hope was gone and everything was gone in that vacant lot across from St. Finnbar's beside the River Lee and I had to escape my Ireland as a Poor Clare, Jaysus, me on the run as a nun do you see it. One frightened nun quiet as a mouse on a pilgrimage to the Holy Land, that's what was left of me at the age of twenty.

Joe let go of his sleeve and banged the table.

Bloody motherlands and bloody causes, the hell with them all I say. I never want to see one again.

Stern sat back and waited. There's more, he said after a moment.

What's more? What are you talking about?

This resentment and anger, the way you've changed. It's not really Ireland, you know that. That was over before you got here. It's something that's happened since then.

Joe's eyes softened and all at once his lips began to tremble. He quickly covered his face with his hands but not before Stern saw the tears welling up. Stern reached out and held his arm.

Joe, you don't always have to hide things in front of people, nobody's going to respect you more for that.

Sometimes it's better to let the feelings out. Why don't you tell me about it?

He kept his hands up. The quiet sobbing lasted a minute or two and then he spoke in an unsteady voice.

What's to tell? There was a woman that's all and she left me. You see I just never imagined such a thing could happen, not when you loved someone and they loved you. I thought once you were together like that you just went on loving each other and being together, that's the way it is where I come from. Sure it was dumb of me, sure it was simpleminded not to think it could be another way but I just didn't know. If I wasn't a man in the Dublin post office I damn well became one during those next four years in the mountains, but women, I didn't know anything about women. Nothing. I loved her and I thought she loved me but she just fooled me, just tricked me and did me in like the fool I was.

Stern shook his head sadly.

Don't keep telling yourself that, it only makes you bitter and it might not have been that way at all. It could have been something else altogether. Was she older than you?

Ten years, your age. How'd you know that?

Just a guess. But look Joe, ten years is a long time. Perhaps something happened to her during those ten years that separated you, something she was afraid of, still afraid of, something that had hurt her so much she didn't dare face it again. People cut off love for all kinds of reasons but generally it has to do with them, not with somebody else. So it might have had nothing to do with you at all. Some experience from the past, who knows.

Joe looked up. The anger had returned.

But I trusted her don't you see, I loved her and it never even crossed my mind not to trust her, not once, never, I was too simpleminded for that. I just trusted her and loved her and thought it would go on forever and ever because I loved her, as if that were enough reason for anything to last. Well from now on there's no bloody room in me anymore for believing in things and fooling myself about them lasting forever. The baking priest has been baking the four boundaries of his life for sixty years, laying out his map, and sure you've got to do that, sure you've got to find the four walls of your own chances and I've done that now, they include me and no one else, just me.

But Joe, where will that lead you?

To what I want, being in charge of myself. What do you mean?

Stern spread his hands on the table.

I mean being in charge, what's that?

Nothing going wrong. Nobody throwing me out of my country, because I won't have a country. Nobody leaving me, because I won't be there where they can leave me. Not giving anybody a chance to hurt me ever again.

That can still happen, Joe.

Not if I have the power it can't.

And the glory?

Never mind the sarcasm. As a matter of fact though I don't give a damn about glory, being out of sight is fine with me as long as I have power. Tell me, who's going to be the richest oil merchant in the Middle East when he comes of age?

Nubar Wallenstein, said Stern wearily.

That's him. So what are you doing about it?

Waiting for him to come of age.

The hell with the bloody sarcasm, can't you see I mean what I'm telling you? I'm serious about this. I'm making plans now and before long I'm going to be playing a winning hand in this game they call Jerusalem.

Stern shook his head. He sighed.

You haven't got it right, Joe. You just haven't.

Joe smiled and signaled for two more cognacs. He

took one of Stern's cheap cigarettes and rolled it from one side of his mouth to the other.

Haven't I now, Father? Is that the judgment today from the confessional? Well all I know is I've got it the way it is around here, pretty much the way it is. Maybe not the way the good book says it's supposed to be but still the way it is. So why don't we stop being sentimental on Christmas Eve and get down to talking about guns and money?

He raised his tumbler.

Doesn't bother you does it, Stern? It shouldn't, don't worry about it. Until I find something better to do I'll run guns to your Arab and Jewish and Christian country that doesn't exist and be happy doing it, what do I care that it's never going to exist. And you'll get good value from me, you know that. Just no more shit about somewhere being someplace because it isn't, I don't have a homeland anymore. My last home was in Jericho with a woman who left me.

He grinned.

Cold in Jerusalem wouldn't you say? It seems to be snowing in the land of milk and honey, do you see it now. So here's to your kind of power and mine. Here's to you, Father Stern.

Stern slowly raised his glass.

To you, Joe.

In the spring of 1922 Stern was in Smyrna to meet with his principle contact in Turkey, a wealthy secret Greek activist. The man's chief interest was in seeing Constantinople returned to the Greeks, for which a Greek army was then fighting Kemal and the Turks in the interior. But he had been working with Stern for ten years helping him smuggle arms to nationalist movements in Syria and Iraq, ever since his and Stern's aims had come to coincide during the Balkan wars.

In fact it was Sivi who frequently provided Stern with the money he was always so desperately lacking, the same Sivi who had once befriended Maud and helped her with money after the death of her husband Yanni, his much younger half-brother.

In addition the notorious old man, now seventy, was the undisputed queen of sexual excess in Smyrna, where he always appeared at the opera dressed in flowing red gowns and a large red hat spilling with roses to be plucked off and tossed to his friends when he made his entrance into his box, his ruby rings flashing and a long unlit cigar firmly fixed between his teeth. Because of the reputation of his father as one of the founding statesmen of the modern Greek nation, because of his own eccentric manner and wealth and because of Smyrna's importance as the most international city in the Middle East, he was an extremely effective agent with influential connections in many places, particularly in the numerous Greek communities found everywhere.

He lived alone with his secretary, a young Frenchwoman once educated in a convent but long since seduced by the sensual air of Smyrna society and the salon Sivi ran there. Stern's meeting with him, as usual, was at three o'clock in the morning since Sivi's entertainments ran late. Stern left his hotel ten minutes before that and strolled along the harbor to see that he wasn't being followed. At three he slipped into an alley and walked quickly around to the back door of the villa. He knocked quietly, saw the peephole open and heard the bolt slide. The secretary closed the door gently behind him.

Hello, Theresa.

Hello again. You look tired.

He smiled. Why not, the old sinner will never meet me at a decent hour. How's he been lately?

In bed. His gums.

What about them?

He says they hurt, he won't eat.

Oh that, don't worry about it, it happens every three or four years. He gets it into his head his teeth are falling out and becomes afraid he might have to make a public appearance without his cigar in place. It only lasts a week or two. Have the cook send in soft-boiled eggs.

She laughed. Thank you, doctor. She rapped on the bedroom door and there was a soft thump on the other side. Stern raised his eyebrows.

A rubber ball, she whispered, it means come in. No unnecessary words. It seems opening his mouth to fresh air might hasten the ravaging of his gums. I'll see you before you leave.

Sivi was sitting in bed propped up by an immense pile of red satin pillows. He wore a thick red dressing gown and a swath of red flannel that entirely covered his head and was tied under his chin. The large olive wood logs crackling in the fireplace gave the only light in the room. Stern pulled aside a drape and found all the windows locked and shuttered against the mild spring night. He stripped off his jacket in the oppressive heat and sat down on the edge of the bed. He felt the old man's pulse while Sivi snifled at a pan of steaming water on the night table.

Terminal?

Surprisingly, no. In fact the flesh isn't even cold yet.

Don't joke about it. I may well go within the hour. How can you breathe in here?

I can't, it's one of my difficulties. The oxygen to my head has been cut off. Who did you say you were?

A laborer. I load tobacco on the pier in front of your villa.

The one to the left or the right?

Left.

Excellent. Keep up the good work but watch out for your back. Heavy lifting can damage the back. Is it day or night out?

225

Day.

I thought so. I can feel that unhealthy sunshine creeping along the shutters trying to ooze inside. Winter or summer, did you say?

Winter. It's snowing.

Preposterous, I was sure of it, I've been feverish for hours.

You know when your jaw falls off that flannel sling won't be any help.

Nonsense, all illusions are helpful.

You know something else? In your declining years you're beginning to look more and more like that portrait downstairs of your paternal grandmother.

The old man wagged his head.

I wouldn't mind that particularly, it's an admirable proposition. She was a pious and honorable and hard-working woman as well as the mother of one of the heroes of Greek independence, who was a good friend of Byron by the way, you probably know that. But what you don't know is that the last time I was in Malta, I hired as my valet none other than the grandson of Byron's Venetian gondolier, his favorite pimp and catamite. The grandfather, Tito, led an Albanian regiment in our war and then later was stranded in Malta, destitute, through a series of scandalous misadventures involving his former occupations. What, this intriguing news from a Maltese grandson doesn't interest you? Well tell me what's new in the outside world then. I've been bedridden since the Mahdi took Khartoum.

That phallus you're using as a knocker on the back door is new. It's awful.

Sivi laughed happily and sniffed his pan of steaming water.

It does add a touch, doesn't it. Well naturally there's no reason to hide the general state of affairs around here and anyway, I have a certain reputation to maintain. My father had a son at the age of eighty-four and although that's not my line, virility is in our blood.

Stern handed him a piece of paper and he fixed his pincenez to study the figures.

Ah, my eyesight is deteriorating.

Degenerating.

Damascus this time.

Yes.

When?

By the middle of June if you can do it.

Easily.

And I'd like to set up a meeting here in September.

I don't blame you at all, it's a lovely place to be in September. Who is going to have the pleasure of visiting here and meeting me?

A man who works for me in Palestine.

Fine, guests from the Holy Land are always especially welcome. Is he on your Arab side or your Jewish side?

Neither.

Ah, from a more obscure region of your multiple personality. Druse perhaps?

No.

Armenian?

No.

He can't be Greek, I'd already know him.

He isn't.

Arab Christian?

No.

Not a Turk?

No.

Well we've accounted for the main non-European elements of Smyrna society so he must be some kind of European.

Some kind. Irish.

Sivi reached down beside the bed and brought up a bottle of raki and two glasses.

Doctor, I thought you might prescribe something like this so I had it ready just in case. You are aware how well the Greek army is doing in the interior?

I am.

And precisely when things are going well, along you come introducing a volatile Irish possibility? Do you have any immediate plans for China? Not that it matters, I wouldn't visit either of those outlandish places. I'm staying right here on the beautiful shores of the Aegean until I'm cured.

Your granny, said Stern, raising his glass.

Indeed, intoned Sivi, and quite right too. Not only have I never denied it, I wouldn't have it any other way.

In the autumn of 1929 Stern went down to the Jordan, to a small house on the outskirts of Jericho to meet a man he hadn't seen in several years, an Arab from Amman who was active among the bedouin tribes in the Moabite hills. Although he was a year or two younger than Stern he looked far older. Sitting very still, no bigger than a child, his large dark eyes were flat and opaque in the feeble light thrown by the single candle.

A steady wind rattled the windows and swallowed the sounds of the rivers in the darkness. The Arab spoke in whispers, frequently halting to cover his mouth with a rag. Stern looked away when that happened or rummaged in his papers, pretending not to notice how much worse the man's lungs had become. After settling their arrangements they sat silently over coffee, listening to the wind.

You look tired, the Arab said at last.

It's just that I've been traveling and haven't had much sleep. Won't that wind ever stop?

After midnight. For a few hours. It begins again then.

The Arab's lips smiled weakly but there was no expression in his eyes.

I no longer even cough. It's not far away.

You'll have your own government soon and that's not far away either. Fifteen years you've been working for it, just imagine, and now it's really going to happen.

Stiff, thin, wasted, the tiny figure stared at him through dead eyes, the rag clutched near his mouth.

Before you came. Tonight. I wasn't thinking of Amman. It's strange. Concerns change. I was thinking how we've never known each other. Why?

I suppose it's the nature of our work. We hurry back and forth, meet for an hour, hurry on again. There's never any time to talk about other things.

For fifteen years?

It seems so.

You help us. You help the Jews too. I've known that. Who are you really working for?

Stern wasn't surprised by the question. All evening the man had talked in a disconnected dreamlike way, drifting from topic to topic. He supposed it had something to do with the Arab's illness, his awareness of it.

For us. Our people.

In my hills that means your own tribe. With suspicion, a few neighboring tribes. For you?

All of us, all the Arabs and Jews together.

It's not possible.

But it is.

The man didn't have the strength to shake his head. Jerusalem, he whispered and stopped for lack of breath. A boy, he said after a moment. A garden. A football.

Stern gazed at the wall and tried not to hear the wind. Two months before at the end of the summer a boy had accidentally kicked a football into a garden, nothing at all but the boy was a Jew and the garden an Arab's and it happened in the Old City. A mere football, it was grotesque. The Arab saw the foot of

Zionism on his soil and the boy was stabbed to death on the spot. In Hebron an Arab mob used axes to butcher sixty Jews, including children. In Safad twenty more, including children. Before the riots were over a hundred and thirty Jews dead and a hundred and fifteen Arabs dead, the Jews killed by Arabs and the Arabs killed by the English police, a boy and a football and a garden.

All the Semites? whispered the man. All together? The Armenians are Christians. What has become of them? Where were their Christian brothers during those massacres?

Stern shifted in his chair. Somehow he couldn't bring himself to find the words. What was the point anyway of arguing with a man who would be dead in a week or a month? He rubbed his eyes and didn't say anything, listening to the wind.

The Arab broke the silence by changing the subject again, not really looking for answers or even hearing them, beyond that now, straying from thought to thought as they occurred to him.

The classics. You often quote from them. Why? Did you start out as a scholar too? I did.

Stern stirred. He felt uneasy. It must have been the incessant noise of the wind pushing on his mind.

No. My father was. I guess I have a habit of repeating things he used to say.

Perhaps I've heard of him. I read a lot once. What was his name?

Lost, murmured Stern. Lost. A man of the desert. Many deserts.

But the accent. You have a trace of one.

The Yemen. I grew up there.

Barren hills. Stony soil. Not like the Jordan valley.

No, not like it. Not at all.

Stern slumped lower in his chair. The overpowering wind outside made it impossible for him to keep his thoughts together. He realized he was beginning to talk in the abrupt manner of the dying man across from him. A wind blowing down the valley to the Dead Sea and Aqaba.

For no reason he saw his father striding into Aqaba eighty years ago after marching the length of the Sinai without food or water, unaware he had walked through three dawns and two sunsets until he found a dog yapping at his heels, smiling then when a shepherd boy told him so and asked him whether he was a good genie or a bad genie, as a reward relating to the boy an obscure tale from the *Thousand and One Nights* before striding on, Strongbow the genie, many men in many places, truly a vast and changeable spirit as his grandfather had once said.

What? No. I didn't get this from him. Not like us. No. He became a hakīm in his latter years. First a scholar, then a hakīm.

Better professions, whispered the Arab. Better than ours. Especially the healer. Healer of souls. I would have liked that. But today, you and I. We don't have time. Is that so? Just an excuse we give ourselves?

Stern started to reach for his cigarettes and then remembered. If only the man hadn't mentioned the Armenians. Why did that have to have come up tonight? It always had this effect on him, the memory of the afternoon in a garden in Smyrna, that night on the quay and the Armenian girl soaked in blood whispering *please*, her thin neck and the knife and the crowds and the screams and the shadows, the fires and the smoke and the knife.

His hands were beginning to shake, it was happening all over again. He tried to bury them in his pockets and squeeze his fists closed but it didn't help, the wind outside wouldn't stop .

The hakīm, a huge presence sitting behind a trembling young man at dawn somewhere in the desert half a century ago, telling the frightened man to turn and face the emptiness in all its vastness, to fix his eye on a distant eagle swooping in the first light of day living a thousand years, tracing the journey of the Prophet, the footsteps a man takes from the day of his birth to the day of his death, suggesting the swirls of the Koran shaping and unshaping themselves as waves in the desert and saying *Yes*, the oasis may be small but *yes*, we will find it, *yes*.

The Arab was struggling to get to his feet. Stern jumped up to help him and led him to the door.

It was over. Hurrying back and forth and meeting for an hour, fifteen years gone, leaving again unknown to each other. The man had started as a scholar and would have liked to have ended as a healer but here was his end.

I envy your faith, whispered the man. What you want. I couldn't conceive of it on earth. We won't see each other again. Peace brother.

Peace brother, said Stern as the man limped away in the night toward his river, no more than a hundred yards away but lost now in the blackness, so small and narrow and yet so famous because of events washed by its currents over millennia, and shallow here as well as the earth began to swallow it toward the end of its brief and steeply falling course from the soft green heights of Galilee, rich in gentle fields of grain and kindly memories, a promised stream plunging down and down to the harsh glaring wilderness of the Dead Sea where God's hand had long ago laid lifeless the empty cities of salt.

A few years after that, searching for an explanation of world events, the Arabs in Palestine began to weave the first of their elaborate fantasies around Hitler. One theory was that he was in the pay of the British Secret Service, which was aiding Zionism by having him expel Jews from Europe in order to increase emigration to Palestine.

Or more incredible still, that Hitler himself was a secret Jew whose sole aim in Europe was to undermine the Arabs in Palestine by sending more Jews there.

So Stern's vision of a vast Levantine nation embracing Arabs and Christians and Jews came apart, and the effect of the cascading rumors and swirling events on his dreams might well have been shattering if he hadn't retreated to the memory of a peaceful hillside in the Yemen and begun to take morphine on the eve of his fortieth birthday.

16

Jerusalem
700 B.C.-1932

*The ghostly jogger of the Holy
City surviving and surviving.*

❈

Early one hot July morning in 1932 O'Sullivan Beare
arrived at Haj Harun's barren shop and found the old
man hiding in the back room, cowering deep in the
corner behind the antique Turkish safe. The rust from
his helmet had fallen into his eyes, streaking his face
with tears. He was trembling violently and the look
he gave the Irishman was one of total despair.

Jaysus, said Joe, easy man, get ahold of yourself.
What's going on here?

Haj Harun cringed pathetically and wrapped his
arms around his head as if expecting a blow.

Keep your voice down, he whispered, or they'll get
you too.

Joe nodded gravely. He moved in closer and gripped
the old man by the shoulders to try to stop the pitiful
shaking. He bent over the crouching figure and spoke
in a low voice.

What is it man?

I'm dizzy. You know how I always feel dizzy first
thing in the morning.

Jaysus I do and no wonder. After what you've seen

out there in the last three thousand years anybody would expect you to be dizzy when you suddenly had to take another look at it. A new day is always trouble so that's all right, calm down and give me a whisper of the problem we're facing.

Them. They're still out there.

Are they now. Where exactly?

In the front room. How did you manage to get around them?

Sneaking on my tiptoes along the wall, a mere shadow of myself. How many did you say there were?

At least a dozen.

Bad odds. Armed?

Only daggers. They left their lances back at the barracks.

Well there's that at least. What sort of cutthroats?

Charioteers, the worst kind. They'll cut a man down without thinking twice about it.

O'Sullivan Beare whistled softly.

Bloody bastards all right. Which conquering army are they from then?

The Babylonian, but I don't think any of them are regular Babylonian troops except perhaps the sergeant. He may be, he's arrogant enough.

Irregulars are they? Working for loot like the Black and Tans? There's no meaner bunch.

Yes they're mercenaries, barbarians, by the looks of them hired horsemen from the Persian steppes. Medes, I'd say from their accents.

Medes, are they? Now there's a scruffy lot. When did they break in?

Last night when I was grinding my teeth and trying to fall asleep. They took me by surprise and I didn't have a chance to defend myself. They threw me in here and they've been out front ever since drinking and gambling over their spoils and bragging about the atrocities they've committed. I'm exhausted, I haven't had any sleep at all. They brought a sack of raw liver with them and they've been gorging themselves on it.

Do you say so. Why this particular article of meat?

To arouse their lust. The Medes have always believed the liver was the seat of sexual desire. Now they're talking about loin pie and they say they won't leave until I hand them over.

After them are they. Bad, very bad. Hand what over?

The boy prostitutes.

Ah.

They're terribly confused. They think this is a barbershop.

Jaysus they are confused.

Not so loud. It's true, barbershops in Jerusalem used to be a place to procure boys but wasn't that a long time ago?

More or less I'd say but the important thing now is for me to send them packing.

You'll have to be careful. You can't count on Medes to listen to reason.

I'm not and I won't. Just keep under cover here.

O'Sullivan Beare marched to the door between the two rooms and snapped to attention. He saluted smartly.

Sergeant, emergency orders from headquarters. All liberty's canceled, charioteers to return to barracks immediately. Carnage on the southern flank, the Egyptians have just launched a surprise attack. What? That's right, the squadrons are grouping already. To your lances man. Double-time it.

Tell them you're Prester John, whispered Haj Harun urgently from behind the Turkish safe.

No need to, whispered Joe over his shoulder, they're going anyway.

What about the drunken one who passed out in the doorway across the alley?

The sergeant's giving him some bloody sound kicks, that's what. They're leaving, it's safe to come out now.

Haj Harun crept out of the corner and tiptoed timidly over to peek into the front room. He tiptoed to the front door and peered up and down the alley.

Gone, thank God. Do you think the streets are safe?

They are. I saw that whole rabble of an army racing out through Jaffa Gate on my way over here.

Haj Harun sighed and his face brightened.

Wonderful, what a relief, let's take a walk. I need some fresh air, last night was a nightmare. I've always detested the Babylonians.

With reason I'd say. Well which route will we be taking today among the many?

The bazaar perhaps? All at once I'm thirsty.

The bazaar, you're right. So am I.

They passed down several alleys, made a turn and entered the bazaar. Haj Harun's mood had changed abruptly with his release from captivity. Now he was robust and smiling and talkative, exuberantly waving his arms as he pointed out the sights.

Hundreds of sweating shoppers jostled each other and squeezed in front of the open shops where hawkers cried out their wares. Haj Harun absentmindedly picked up a handful of juicy fresh figs from a stand and pressed half of them into O'Sullivan Beare's hand. Peeling and munching, their mouths dripping, they made their way slowly through the dense crowds, edging around loaded donkeys and pushcarts, putting their heads together and shouting to be heard above the noise.

See that shop that sells loquats? yelled Haj Harun. A very grand place in its day, the best cabaret in Jerusalem. Run by a former grand vizier of the Ottoman Empire who introduced the cabaret acts and led the applause at the end. Curious how a man of his former importance could be reduced to such a shabby role in life.

Curious, yes.

What?

Always thought so, shouted Joe.

And this corner here was where I was fined for public cheiromania in Hellenistic times.

What's that?

The man on the corner now? It's hard to say. Either he's had too much hashish or he's gone into a religious ecstasy.

No, I mean that offense the Greeks pinned on you.

Oh that, shouted Haj Harun with a laugh. An obsession with the hand but not what you're thinking. Palmistry without a license was the problem, I used to be quite a good palmist. See that old building there? I was in jail there once.

They stepped up off the cobblestones into a fruit juice stand and Joe ordered two large glasses. Together they stood sipping their pomegranate juice and gazing at the building, Haj Harun beaming and laughing as he reminisced.

That was during the great evil eye epidemic we had here. I don't suppose you've ever heard of it?

It strikes me that I haven't. When was that?

Early in the Assyrian era. For some reason everyone in the city was suddenly terrified of the evil eye. People imagined they saw it everywhere and no one dared go outside. The streets were empty, the shops closed, all commerce stopped. Jerusalem without commerce? Impossible. The city was dying and I knew I had to act.

Joe wiped the sweat off his face and tried to dry his hands on his wet shirt.

Of course you did. What acts then?

Well first I tried baking bread.

Good, always useful, bread.

Yes I thought that would do it. Sexual organs are known to be one of the best defenses against the evil eye because they fascinate it and divert its attention, thereby keeping it from doing harm. Well I reasoned that if bread were baked in the shape of a phallus and eaten plentifully throughout the city, that would provide a sound internal safeguard people could have confidence in.

Joe wiped his face again. It was terribly hot. In the blur of the cloudless sky he caught a glimpse of himself sneaking around Jerusalem one dark night painting evil eyes on doors. The next morning there would be an Assyrian panic and he would suddenly appear with the miraculous loaves of bread, sell them at an enormous profit and make a fortune. But how was he going to get the baking priest to bake the special shape? Tell him it was the arm and fist of God? No good, the arm of Allah was too common an expression here. The ancient Franciscan would think he had succumbed to the heathens and refuse to fire his oven.

A total failure, laughed Haj Harun. Bread was too subtle. People needed a visible safeguard, not a digestible one, so I went around painting phalluses on walls. That helped a little, at least people began coming outside again. When they did I harangued them, urging them to paint phalluses of their own to reassure themselves and they did that, covering lamps and bowls and every other article they owned, even weaving them into their cloaks and wearing specially carved rings and bracelets and necklaces and pendants. Soon Jerusalem was a city of ten million phalluses. Of course you have to remember all this happened back in the days when I still had influence here and people not only listened to me but believed what I said.

Joe tried to pull his shirt away from his chest and let a little air in but he couldn't, it was glued there.

Are you remembering? asked Haj Harun.

I am. Keenly.

Yes. Well for the next stage of my plan I needed the assistance of menstruating women.

I see. Why this unusual convolution?

Because at that time menstruation was a very powerful agent. It was effective against hail and bad weather in general and could destroy vermin in crops, not to mention withering cucumbers and cracking nutshells.

Very good.

I thought so but then it turned out I couldn't persuade any women to expose their private parts on the street when they were menstruating. Home on their farms at night to help their own crops, of course they'd do it then, but not in Jerusalem in public even though it could have assured the safety of the city. I argued and argued with them in the squares but they remained adamant, claiming it would damage their reputations. Can you imagine? People being as vain as that when the whole city was endangered by a crisis? I tell you, people can be selfish.

True.

And ignore the public welfare.

Very true.

Even to the point of thinking only about themselves while everything around them is going to ruin.

Very very true.

Haj Harun laughed.

Well that was the case then, so obviously there was only one thing to do. One final dramatic act was needed to break the impasse, to enlist the entire citizenry in the fight against the danger we were facing. Unquestionably I had to take an extreme religious position against the evil eye, no matter how unpopular and flamboyant it might appear to be, and through personal example show the people what was necessary to save us. There was simply no alternative. I had to do it and I did.

Of course you did. What was it?

Haj Harun grinned at the building across the way.

I took off my loincloth and went striding boldly through the streets and every time I came upon an evil eye I whipped up my cloak and gave it a flash. *Ha.* I flashed and I flashed and each time I did the evil eye's hold over us was weakened and Jerusalem was that much closer to total recovery.

Joe reeled back against the counter of the fruit juice stand and quickly ordered two more glasses of pomegranate juice. His head was spinning and the centuries were making him thirsty, Assyrian centuries, the sight of Haj Harun as a vigorous young man still confident and influential, still respected for his credibility in those far-off days, boldly striding through Jerusalem in 700 B.C. whipping up his cloak to defeat the evil eye at each dramatic new encounter, striking out alone through the streets to do battle with the epidemic that was threatening to lay waste to his Holy City, flamboyant and selfless, shunning vanity and undeterred by any possible damage to his reputation, marching on and doing his duty as he saw it, *Haj Harun the fearless religious flasher of antiquity.*

I got caught, said the old man with a chuckle.

Do you tell me that.

Yes, the Assyrian police picked me up for lascivious behavior or indecent exposure or some other indefensible charge. Anyway they locked me up in that jail over there and said I'd have to stay locked up until I promised to change my ways. But my campaign had been largely successful by then and the great evil eye epidemic was nearly over. They freed me before long.

A personal triumph, said Joe.

I thought so but of course I didn't get any particular credit for it.

Why?

Commerce. As soon as they got their commerce back

they forgot about my religious sacrifice. That happens around here.

I see.

They left the fruit juice stand and once more began pushing their way through the din of the bazaar.

You know, shouted Haj Harun, sometimes it seems I was an old man early in life and had little later to unlearn. When I walk here there are memories and more memories on every side. Did you know Caesar used geese as watchdogs?

Quack, I did not, shouted Joe, but the bustling and shoving may be loosening my brains.

Or that when the Egyptians held the city they had a custom of shaving off their eyebrows when a pet cat died? The cats were then embalmed and sent home to be buried in Bubastis.

Cat city you say? Bubbling my brains quite possibly, it must be this infernal heat. I seem to feel the need for some powerful sobering tonic. Or as you said once, *Time is.*

Haj Harun laughed.

The memories it brings back, that's why I like walking here.

But how do you manage to keep up with them? shouted Joe. These changing nonstop smells of time I mean?

By keeping on the move.

That sounds like what I used to do in the mountains of the old country. But County Cork's a place, or at least it was then. What does it mean in terms of millennia, keeping on the run?

Well take the Roman siege for example, shouted Haj Harun.

Yes let's do that.

What did you say?

I said what happened during the Roman siege?

Oh. Well the Romans bombarded us for weeks with their catapults and there were monstrous boulders falling everywhere. Most people hid in their cellars and many were killed when their houses came crashing down on them. But not me. I survived.

How?

By staying out in the open. I jogged through the streets. A moving target is always much more difficult to hit than a stationary one.

Right you are, thought Joe, and there you have the answer to it all, right there in that picture of Haj Harun jogging through Jerusalem, jogging around his eternal city. Jaysus yes, Haj Harun the moving target of the Roman Empire and every other empire that ever existed. Cloak flowing, spindly legs churning, bare feet wearing down the cobblestones, around and around for three thousand years outrunning siege machines and conquering armies. Around and around in a circle, defying the arsenals of war that were always being dragged up the mountain to defeat him. Plodding stubbornly up and down the alleys wearing down the cobblestones, puffing and wheezing on the run through the millennia, Haj Harun the ghostly jogger of the Holy City surviving and surviving.

The old man clutched Joe's arm in excitement. He laughed and shouted happily in his ear.

Do you see that tower?

Yes, shouted Joe, there it stands in its suggestive shape and I'm ready for it. Which century are we in?

17

The Bosporus

The other hour needed for life.

✠

In 1933 Stern found himself walking beside the Bosporus in the rain, and to him the colors of that gray October sky were reminiscent of another afternoon there when an enormously tall gaunt man had entered a deserted olive grove and ceremoniously removed all his elegant clothes, thrown them together into the black passing waters and climbed back through the dark grove, barefoot and wearing only a tattered cloak, a hakīm making his way south to the Holy Land and perhaps beyond.

Over half a century ago and now instead of an olive grove there was a hospital for incurables where he had just gone to see his old friend Sivi for the last time, or rather the body that had once been Sivi's, tied to a bed and motionless now, staring blindly at the ceiling, the spirit having finally fled its torment.

Stern walked on. By the railing he saw a woman gazing down at the water, a foreigner dressed in a shabby way, and suddenly he realized what she was thinking. He went over and stood beside her.

Not until after dark I suppose. The wind will be high then and no one will see.

She didn't move.

Do I look that desperate?

No, he lied. But remember there are always other things. Ways to help.

I've done that. I just don't have the strength anymore.

What happened?

A man went mad today after it started to rain.

Who was he?

A man. His name was Sivi.

Stern closed his eyes and saw the smoke and flames of the garden in Smyrna, an afternoon eleven years ago that had brought him and now this woman to a railing beside the Bosporus. He squeezed the iron bar as hard as he could and when he spoke again he had control of his voice.

Well if you've made the decision the only thing you have to worry about now is being sure it's a success. Your friends won't have it any other way for two reasons.

He spoke so matter-of-factly she turned away from the water and looked at him for the first time. He was a large bulky man with hunched shoulders, his nationality difficult to place. Probably she didn't see the weariness in his eyes then, just the outline of his shapeless figure beside her in the rain.

Only two? she said bitterly.

It seems so, but they're enough. The first has to do with the guilt you make them feel. Was there something more they could have done? Of course, so they resent you for reminding them of that by still being alive. Then too you also remind them they've wasted their lives and they resent that. When they have to look at you afterward they have an uncomfortable feeling you're not willing to accept as much moral corruption as they are. They're not exactly aware of it but you'll know the minute they sit down with you. A serious face, there's something they have to say. Welcome you back from the dead? No. It's cowardice

they want to talk about. *It's too easy.* Those are always
their first words.

But it is easy, she whispered.

Of course. Real solutions always are. You just get
up and leave. But most people can't do that and that's
why they talk about your cowardice, because they've
been trying to ignore their own for so long. It makes
them uneasy. *You* make them uneasy.

She laughed harshly.

Is that all they say?

No, often there are special concerns depending on
who they are. A mother worrying about how she
brought up her children is likely to criticize you for
not making it look like an accident. After all, how
would your mother have felt?

Touching.

Yes. Then a businessman is likely to point out you
didn't even have your business affairs in order. When
you commit suicide, in other words, you should be
thinking about everyone but yourself. You're only
losing your life. What about other people?

Dreadful to be that selfish.

Yes. But there are also a few people who never
mention it and go right on with you as if nothing had
happened. It's a way of finding out who's close to you,
I admit, but a dangerous one.

You seem to be quite an expert.

No, just one or two experiences. But don't you want
to hear the other reason why you can't fail? It's
because you'll have learned a life just doesn't matter
much except as a memory, even a great life. In fact
I suspect that explains what Christ did after he was
resurrected.

Christ?

Well we know he spent forty days on the Mount of
Olives seeing his friends, then disappeared. And
during those forty days he must have realized he
couldn't go on doing the same things with the same

people anymore. It was over. They had their memories of him and that's what they needed, not him. In the three years he'd been preaching he'd already changed a good deal and of course he would have gone on changing, everyone always does. But his friends didn't want that.

So what did he do?

Stern tapped his forehead.

Two theories, one for good days and one for bad. The theory for bad days is set in Jerusalem. Have you been there?

Yes.

Then you've seen St Helena's crypt in the Church of the Holy Sepulchre?

Wait, I know what you're going to say. It's the man who paces back and forth at the top of the stairs, isn't it. Staring at the floor and muttering to himself and he's been doing it for two thousand years.

You mean you've already heard my theory?

No, but I saw that man once and somebody told me about him.

Oh, well according to my theory for bad days that man is Christ. What happened was that after his forty days with his friends he fully intended to go to heaven, but first he decided he might take a last look at that spot where he was crucified, that hilltop where the most momentous event in his life had occurred. So he did and he was so stunned by what he saw he never left, and ever since he's been there pacing back and forth talking to himself about what he saw.

What did he see?

Nothing. Absolutely nothing. They'd taken down the three crosses and it was just an empty hilltop. For all anyone could tell, nothing at all had ever happened there.

She shook her head.

That's certainly for bad days. What about good days?

On good days I think he did leave. He saw what he saw all right, but then he decided to do something else anyway. So he clipped his hair or tied it up and shaved his beard or grew a longer one, put on some weight and taught himself to speak directly like other men, then went on to acquire a trade so he could pay his way.

What trade?

Cobbler, say, perhaps even carpentry again although I doubt that. After seeing the emptiness of that hilltop he'd probably have preferred to try something new. Yes, cobbler perhaps.

And where did he go?

Oh he didn't go anywhere. Theories for good and bad days have to be set in the same place. He stayed in Jerusalem and now that he'd changed his appearance he could come and go as he pleased without being recognized, perhaps disguised as an Armenian or an Arab. Which he still does of course, being immortal and having long since forgotten his former troubles, even the man he used to be. And all because a very beautiful thing happened, a strange and glorious transformation. It took more time than going to heaven, had he done that, but it happened.

What?

Jerusalem moved. Over the centuries it slowly moved north. It picked itself up from Mt Zion and inched its way toward what had once been that empty hilltop outside the walls. Foreign conquerors who thought they were desecrating the place helped by razing the city every so often, and each time they did the city was rebuilt a little closer to the desolate hilltop. Until the hilltop was no longer far away but right beneath the walls, then within the walls, then nearer to the center of the city and at last in its very heart, crowded around with bazaars and playing children and swarms of traders and pious pilgrims all shouting and laughing and rubbing together. No longer a sad little empty hilltop at all you see. No just the opposite. Jerusalem had come to him, the Holy City had embraced him and that's why at last he was able to forget his former sorrows. He no longer had to fear the nothingness of his death.

Well what do you think? said Stern with a smile.

I think it's certainly a theory for good days.

Yes indeed, a happy ending after two thousand years. And not that impossible either. As a matter of fact my own father did much the same thing in the last century.

Did what? Made Jerusalem move?

No that takes more time. I was thinking about leaving the empty hilltop behind by putting on a disguise. And he was relatively famous too, and rather recognizable you would have thought.

But no one knew who he was?

Only the few he chose to tell.

How can you be sure he told *you* the truth?

Stern smiled. He almost had her now.

I see what you mean but I still have to believe him. What he did is too unreal not to be true. No one could forge a life like his.

All the same, forgeries can be enormous.

I know.

Once a man forged the whole Bible.

I know, repeated Stern.

Why do you say that?

Well you're talking about Wallenstein, aren't you? The Albanian hermit who went to the Sinai?

She stared at him.

How did you know that?

Stern's smile broadened. At last he'd found what he was looking for.

Well isn't that who you mean? The Trappist who found the original Bible and was so appalled by its chaos he decided to forge his own? Then went back to Albania where he survived to the age of one hundred and four in a dungeon beneath his castle, in a totally black and soundless cell, the only place he could live now that he was God? Cared for all that time by the love of Sophia the Unspoken, later when I met her to become Sophia the Bearer of Secrets? Who was overwhelmed when Wallenstein finally died in 1906?

But that's not true.

What?

That Wallenstein died in 1906.

Yes it is.

It can't be. I was there then.

Then you must be Maud, and you escaped to Greece when Catherine had a seizure and all his veins burst, a death willed on him by his own mother Sophia, or so the old woman always believed. She told me the whole fantastic story when I was trapped there during the first Balkan war. Told me everything, it seemed she just couldn't bear the burden of keeping it all a secret anymore. A strange mixture of brilliance and superstition, that woman. She actually believed Catherine's madness had come about because Wallenstein himself was an angel, literally, not a saint but a divine angel who couldn't have a human child because he was superhuman. Well maybe he did have a touch of something considering the scope of his forgery.

Maud stared at him in utter disbelief.

Twenty-seven years ago, she whispered.

Yes.

But can any of it be true?

It's all true and there's more, much more. The baby you had for example. Sophia named him Nubar, a family name, it seems she was of Armenian descent originally. She brought him up with as much love as she had had hatred for Catherine and was able to give him a fortune through her early manipulations in the oil market. He's extremely influential although very few people have ever even heard of him. Now what do you think of that?

Nothing. I can't think anything about it. It's all some kind of magic.

Not at all, said Stern, laughing and taking her by the arm, leading her up the street away from the water.

They talked late that night and many others and slowly she pulled away from despair as eventually it all came out, the horror of her first marriage and the loneliness of her second when she felt she had been abandoned again by someone she loved, the hidden fear from her childhood growing malignantly then until a time came when she could bear it no longer and she ran away from Joe, the great love of her life, the one thing she had always wanted in the world, a magical dream come true in Jerusalem and she had left it.

Every act futile and bitter then. More years when she was terrified at growing old. Trying to find Sivi again, some link with the past, surprised to learn he was also living in Istanbul, tracing him with difficulty and shocked when she found him at last, so vastly different from the elegant and worldly man she had known at the time of the First World War. Pathetically alone now, working as a common laborer in a hospital for incurables.

And the strange muddled story about his former secretary that obsessed him, that he repeated over and over, how Theresa had gone to a place called Ein Karem in Palestine, there to suffer some kind of terrible self-inflicted penance in an Arab leper colony.

It was inexplicable. How could people change so much?

Stern shook his head. It wasn't time to speak, her memory of standing beside the water was too recent.

Sivi? Yes he had known him once, anyone who had ever spent any time in Smyrna had known Sivi. Yes and Theresa too. He nodded for her to go on.

Kind and gentle Sivi, totally broken when she found him, grave and sad and bewildered, living in a small squalid room near the Bosporus, so confused he often forgot to feed himself.

She had decided to devote herself to caring for him, it was the best thing she could do. She cleaned for him and washed and cooked, and for a while she felt stronger. Helping Sivi gave life some meaning again. But then that awful rainy afternoon came when she went to pick him up at the hospital after work as she did every day and found him strapped to a bed, beyond the impenetrable barrier of madness, the same afternoon Stern had found her by the water.

And now after forty-three years what did she have?

The memory of one exquisite month long ago on the shores of the Gulf of Aqaba. That and the son she had conceived there.

Would you like to meet him? asked Maud.

Yes very much.

She looked at him shyly.

Please don't laugh. I named him Bernini. The dreams were crumbling but not quite gone. I suppose I hoped someday he would also carve his own beautiful fountains and stairways to somewhere.

Stern smiled.

And why not? It's a good name.

But Maud looked suddenly troubled. She took his hand and said nothing.

In the small apartment above the Bosporus, Stern tried to amuse the boy with stories from his childhood. He described the first clumsy balloon he had built when he was about Bernini's age.

Did you fly?

For a yard or two, depending on how hard I pushed. After that I just went bumping down the hillside.

Why didn't you put wheels on the basket? Then you could have used it as a sailboat and crossed the desert that way.

I could have I suppose, but I didn't. I kept trying to build better balloons and after a while I made one that would fly.

I wouldn't have done that, said the boy distantly. Sailing would have been good enough for me.

They were sitting on the narrow terrace. Maud came out with tea and the boy lay down on his stomach and gazed at the ships plowing up and down the straits. When Stern left, Maud walked to the corner with him.

He's often like that, I don't know how to explain it. He talks for a minute or two about something and then drops it as if he were afraid to say too much, as if by touching certain thoughts he was afraid they would go away. He wouldn't ask you why you wanted to fly for example, nor would he tell you why he would have preferred to sail. Instead he just lay down and watched the boats. I knew his imagination was working and he was thinking about those things, but he wouldn't talk about it with us.

He's young.

But not that young and sometimes it frightens me. His thoughts don't always follow each other, somehow the sequence is wrong. Again it's as if he were leaving things out on purpose. In school he can't get along at all except for drawing.

Stern smiled.

With his name that's fine.

But Maud didn't smile.

No. He used to draw at home and now he doesn't even do that anymore. He just lies on his elbows and gazes at things, especially the boats. And there's something worse, he can't read. Doctors say there's nothing wrong but he can't seem to learn. I mean he's already twelve years old.

She stopped. Stern put his arm around her. He didn't know how to help.

Listen. He's healthy and good-natured and even though he may be a little too much inside himself right now, that's not necessarily bad or wrong. After all he seems happy enough and isn't that the most important thing?

There were tears in her eyes.

I don't know. I just don't know what to do.

Well at least you could share the burden. Why not get in touch with the boy's father? He's still in Jerusalem, near enough.

She moved her feet uneasily.

I couldn't do that. I'm too ashamed of the way I treated him.

But that was twelve years ago, Maud.

I know but I still couldn't bring myself to do it. I was too cruel to him and none of it was his fault. That would take a kind of strength I don't have yet.

Stern looked at the ground. She took his hands and tried to smile.

Well don't worry about it. It'll be all right.

Good, he said in a soft voice. I know it will be.

And now you're going to be away for a while?

He grinned.

It shows that desperately?

A man on his travels, yes.

About a month probably. I'll cable.

Bless you, she whispered, for being who you are.

She went up on her tiptoes and kissed him.

Stern used to tell her how his father had somehow managed to mark his memory as a child with every name and event from his long years of wandering, in

the course of time narrating his entire journey much as
a blind man might have done in the days when there
was no other way for the stages of the past to be
passed from generation to generation, in effect rewriting the haj of his life in indelible ink upon his young
son's mind, swirling stroke around stroke in the complex etching of a spiritual stylus.

Yet strangely in those myriad experiences, those
majestic flowing volumes that together comprised
Strongbow's legendary voyage through the desert,
never once had the old explorer talked about the
gentle Persian girl he had loved so dearly in his youth
for a few weeks, no more, before she was carried off
in an epidemic. Why?

Why should he have? answered Maud. He had
loved her, that's all, what more was there to say?
Besides, when we look back on it there are always
mysteries in someone's life and perhaps the gentle
Persian girl is his.

You may be right, said Stern vaguely, standing and
then sitting down again. But Maud didn't think he
was really talking about the Persian girl and Strongbow. There had to be something else on his mind the
way he was acting, something much more personal.
She waited but he didn't go on.

What else did he never mention? she said after a
moment.

It's very curious, but the Sinai Bible of all things.
Surely he knew about it. Why that one secret held
back?

Why do you think?

Stern shrugged. He said he couldn't imagine why.
He got up again and began roaming around the room.

When did he die? I don't think you've ever told
me that.

August 1914, the very month the nineteenth century
came to an end. You know I remember that prophecy
you said O'Sullivan Beare's father made two months

255

before that, that seventeen of his sons were going to
be killed in the Great War. Well Strongbow must
have had the gift too. He was ninety-five years old
and he'd gone blind by then but his health was good
and his mind was certainly as clear as ever. The main
thing seemed to be simply that he felt he'd lived long
enough. I was there with him in Ya'qub's old tent
during those last days and that's exactly what he said.
It's enough.

Ya'qub had already died?

Yes, but only a few months before, the two of them
inseparable to the end, always talking and talking over
their endless cups of coffee. Anyway, after he said it
was enough he did something that couldn't have been
a coincidence.

Stern frowned and lapsed into silence. He seemed
to drift away.

Well?

I'm sorry, what?

The thing he did, what was it?

Oh. He predicted the hour of his death and went to
sleep to await it.

And never woke up.

That's right.

And what wasn't a coincidence?

Dying like that. It was a story he'd heard long ago
from some bedouin called the Jebeliyeh. Around 1840
a blind mole did the same thing at the foot of Mt
Sinai after talking to a hermit on the mountain. And
of course you know who the hermit was.

Wallenstein.

Yes, Wallenstein. A hermit in 1840 and a blind mole
in 1914. Strongbow was obviously dreaming Wallenstein's dream when he died. Dreaming of the Sinai
Bible.

Once more Stern's voice trailed off and his attention
drifted away. Maud waited as he restlessly crossed the

room to the window and returned and went back to the window again.

And if it was so important to him, you still can't imagine why he never told you about it?

No, said Stern quickly.

A thunderstorm had broken overhead and lightning suddenly lit the room in a violent burst but Stern seemed unaware of it.

No, he repeated. No.

Maud gazed at the floor. She wanted to believe him but she didn't. She knew it wasn't true, there was no way it could be true. And even though she knew the two old men only through Stern, she could picture exactly what had happened. It was as clear to her as if she had been there and seen Ya'qub and Strongbow marching back and forth between their almond trees in one of their interminable rambling discussions.

Ya'qub saying merrily that this was fine, all the things the boy was learning, but then suddenly serious and tugging Strongbow's sleeve and whispering earnestly that one mystery must be excluded from their teachings, at least that, for the boy's sake, one for him to discover alone by himself.

The former hakīm pondering the words and nodding solemnly over this piece of wisdom, the two of them sitting up late that night in their tent trying to decide which mystery it should be among the thousands they shared after all their years of tramping from Timbuktu to Persia, of tracing a hillside in the Yemen and going nowhere.

So Stern was lying to himself. He pretended all his days and nights were taken up with his clandestine cause but it just wasn't so. There was something else more important to him.

Dizzily then she recalled things he had said and all

at once it became obvious. For years he too had been secretly in search of the Sinai Bible.

Wallenstein. Strongbow. O'Sullivan Beare and now Stern.

Where would it ever end?

She didn't want to talk about it but she knew she couldn't just ignore it, so finally she asked the question.

Stern, what made *you* begin looking for the Sinai Bible?

It was late afternoon and he was pouring himself a glass of vodka. His shoulders seemed to twitch and he poured more than he usually did.

Well, when I realized what it meant I had to. What was in it I mean. What's still in it wherever it is.

And what's that, Stern? For you?

Well everything. All my ideas and hopes, what I was really looking for years ago in Paris when I thought of a new nation here, a homeland for Arabs and Christians and Jews alike, you see what I mean don't you? That homeland could have been here in the beginning before people were divided into those names, the Sinai original might show that. And if it does I would have proof, or at least I could prove it to myself even if to no one else.

Prove what? What you've done? What you work for? Your life? What?

Well yes, all those things, everything.

Maud shook her head.

That *damned* book.

Why say that? Think what it could mean if it were found.

Maybe, I don't know anymore. It just makes me angry.

But why does it make you angry? Because of O'Sullivan Beare? Because he wanted to find it so much?

Yes and no. Perhaps it was just that then, now it's something more.

What?

She shrugged wearily.

I'm not sure. The way it obsesses people. The way it sends lives careening off in all directions. Wallenstein in his cave for seven years going mad while the ants eat his eyeballs, Strongbow marching through the desert for forty years never able to sleep in the same place twice, Joe and his wild search for treasures that don't exist, you and your impossible nation. Why are there these mirages that pull men and pull them on and on and on? Why does it have to be the same with all of you? You hear about that damn book and you go crazy. You all do.

She stopped. He took her hand.

But it's not the Sinai Bible that does it, is it?

More vodka?

Maud?

No I know it isn't, of course it's not. But all the same I wish that damn fanatic Wallenstein had never had his insane dream. Why couldn't he have left us alone?

But he hasn't got anything to do with it either. It was there and all he did was find it and live it, or relive it and bring it back to us, all the things we've always wanted. Canaan, just imagine it. The happy land of Canaan three thousand years ago.

It wasn't happy.

It might have been. No one can say until the original is found.

Yes they can. You know it wasn't.

He didn't answer.

Damn it, say you do. Admit it. Say you know.

All right then, I know.

She sighed and began stroking his hand absentmindedly. The anger in her face had drained away.

And yet, she whispered.

Yes that's right, that's always it. And yet. And *yet*.

She picked up the vodka bottle and looked at it.

Christ, she muttered. Oh Christ.

Yes, said Stern with a thin smile. Among others.

Dizzying and more, for although O'Sullivan Beare had the account of the Bible all mixed up, confusing it with the vague stories Haj Harun told him, Stern actually knew where the Sinai original was. He *knew* it had been buried in the Armenian Quarter of Jerusalem.

Yet he had never looked for it there.

Why?

Stern laughed and filled his glass.

You know that's the only part of Sophia's story I've never believed. It would have been too obvious a hiding place for someone as clever and dedicated as Wallenstein. Look at it. He spent twelve years in a basement hole in the Armenian Quarter before he went to the Sinai to do his forgery. Would he have been likely to come back and bury the original in that same basement hole? Ask questions about him and someone would remember, the spot could be found and all of Wallenstein's efforts would have been for nothing. Would Sophia have allowed that considering how much she loved him? She knew what the forgery had cost him, what it eventually cost her too, so she lied to protect him, to protect herself, to keep their suffering from being meaningless.

Stern went on talking, pacing and puffing cigarettes. He poured himself another drink. Maud looked out the window in embarrassment.

Why was he saying all this? There was no reason for Sophia to lie to protect Wallenstein after he'd already protected himself. When he went to Egypt to find parchment he'd traveled as a wealthy Armenian dealer in antiquities. Who knew what other disguises there had been?

The basement hole could have had a large house over it where he passed himself off as someone else. Or a shop where he actually dealt in antiquities. Or a church where he'd gotten himself ordained as a priest, or a monastery where he was posing as a monk. Anything at all. Obviously the manuscript would never be found by asking questions about Wallenstein and his basement hole.

Stern, a little drunk now, began to describe all the places he had looked for the manuscript. At first he thought it must have been hidden in a large city so he went to Cairo and Damascus and Baghdad, into the back alleys at night.

Did anyone have a very old book to sell? A precious book? He was willing to pay a great deal.

Knowing smiles. Levantine language. He was led through shadowy rooms where every sort of living creature was offered for sale, the body in question guaranteed to be as satisfying as the oldest book in the world.

O venerable scholar, added his guide.

Stern fled to the open air. Perhaps a small cave near the Dead Sea? Wallenstein having chosen this secure place as he was limping home from Mt Sinai?

Stern cranked up his tractor car and sped down wadis and across the dunes chasing stray camels, on the lookout for caves. When he spied a bedouin on the horizon he raced over to him and whipped open the steel hatch. Up popped Stern's dusty face, his tanker's goggles staring blankly down at the frightened man.

A very old book? A cave in the vicinity? Even a small one?

Next he favored the idea of a remote oasis, a dot in the desert so small it supported only one family, surely an ingenious hiding place.

The hydrogen valves hissed and his balloon swelled. On the tip of the Sinai peninsula he hovered over a tiny clump of green. The woman and children ran into the tent and the man raised his knife to defend his family against this floating apparition from the *Thousand and One Nights*.

Twenty yards above the ground Stern's head appeared.

Any old books down there?

He changed his mind. It wasn't a place he should be looking for but a person. Wallenstein had found a wandering holy man and fixed the dervish with his eyes, whispering that here was the true holy of holies. The dervish must carry it until he was ready to die and then pass it on to another holy man in a similar way, for this bundle or ark was the manifestation of God on earth carried by secret bearers since the beginning of time and henceforth to the end of time, letting it fall being no less a matter than letting fall the world itself.

Stern went into the deserts and bazaars asking his question.

What sacred object do you carry?

Rags were unwrapped and treasures appeared, slivers of wood and crumpled flowers and thimbles of muddy water, carved matchsticks and cracked glass and smudged slips of paper, a live mouse and an embalmed toad and many other manifestations of God, in fact just about everything except what he sought.

And you? Stern wearily asked once more.

I have no need for graven images, answered a man disdainfully. God is within me. Wait and tomorrow at dawn you will see the one and true God.

Stern spent the night. The next morning the man rose at an early hour, ate a meager breakfast and moved his bowels. He went through the mess and came up with a small smooth stone which he reverently washed and anointed with oil, then swallowed again with a triumphant smile.

Tomorrow at the same time, he said, God will

appear again if you wish to return and worship Him.

And so Stern went on telling more stories and pouring more vodka and lighting more cigarettes, laughing at himself and making Maud laugh until long after midnight.

When he left she went around the room picking up ashtrays and sweeping up the ashes that had fallen everywhere as his hands flew and he talked and talked. In the kitchen she stood holding the empty bottles, gazing down at the sink. All at once she was exhausted.

She understood now why he had never made love to her, why he had probably never made love to anyone, why the sexual encounters in his life could never have been more than that.

Removed, anonymous, quickly over, and Stern alone in the end as in the beginning.

Never with someone who could know him. Never. Too fearful of that.

He had already been tossing for several hours, his sleep torn by the grinding of his teeth. The only rest he ever knew was when he first lay down and now, two hours before dawn, even the tossing was over. His jaw aching, he reached for the blankets thrown off at his feet and lay shivering in the dark.

At last a gray light came in the window. Stern slid open a drawer by his bed and took out the needle. The warmth rolled over him and he fell back on the bed.

I'm slipping beautifully, he thought. Every night a dozen new chapters for the secret lost book he dreamed of finding, exquisitely beautiful episodes, nothing would ever come of them.

Once more he was a boy floating high in the night sky above the ruins of Marib among the breezes and stirring stars, above a distant drifting world, far above the Temple of the Moon suddenly seen in the sands. For minutes it lasted, all the minutes of his childhood in the Yemen with his father and his grandfather, wise and gentle men waiting for him to grasp their mysteries.

I'm slipping beautifully, he thought as the gray in the window faded to whiteness and he slept again under the morphine, the other hour needed for life.

He awoke feeling numb and drowsy and threw cold water over himself. No dreams now, only an empty day, but at least he had survived the harsh coming of the light.

18
Melchizedek
2200 B.C.-1933

Faith never dies, Prester John.

※

On a spring evening in 1933 Haj Harun and O'Sullivan Beare sat on a hillside east of the Old City watching the sunset, the light shifting slowly over the towers and minarets and changing their colors, softly laying shadows along the invisible alleys. After a time the old man sighed and wiped his eyes.

So beautiful, so very beautiful. But there are going to be riots, I know there are. Do you think we should get guns, Prester John? You and me?

Joe shrugged. *You and me*, the old man really meant it. He actually believed the two of them could do something.

Ever since Smyrna I've been worrying about it, Haj Harun went on. Does it have to be the way it was up there? They had their lovely city too and all kinds of people living in it and look what happened. I just can't understand why the people of Jerusalem are doing this to each other. And it's not as if we were facing the Romans or the Crusaders, it's the people inside the walls who are doing it. I'm frightened. Will we have to get guns? Will we?

Joe shook his head.

No, no guns, they won't get us anywhere. I tried

that when I was young and it's a useless interim game. Use guns and you're no better than the Black and Tans and that's not good enough.

But what do we do then? What can we do?

Joe picked up a rock and scaled it out over the hillside toward the valley separating them from the city.

Jaysus I don't know. I talked with the baking priest about it and he doesn't know either. Just nods and goes back to baking his loaves in the four shapes. Doesn't dance anymore either, which is a bad sign. But these troubles in the city can't be all that new to you and Jaysus that's what makes me wonder. How have you been putting up with it all these years?

Putting up with what?

What the bloody people have been doing to you. Throwing stones at you and knocking the teeth out of your head and clawing you with their fingernails and stealing what little you have, beating you and insulting you and calling you names, all those things. If that had happened to me someplace I'd have left it long ago.

I can't leave. You don't seem to understand.

No I don't and I wonder if I ever will. Look, Smyrna was bad all right but there's something else that's been on my mind since then, worries me and worries me and just won't go away. All this time I've been looking for the Sinai Bible and now I'm beginning to wonder. It has to do with that, you see, with a promise I made myself then. Jaysus I'm just plain confused. Can I ask you a question?

Haj Harun reached out and took his hand. The lights were going on in the Old City and in the hills. Joe looked up and saw that the old man's eyes were shining.

Prester John?

Yes all right, well it's just this. I loved a woman once and she left me but you see I've learned I'll never

love another one. It seems that's it for me and what's
a soul to do then? What's a soul to do?

Simply go on loving her.

So I seem to be doing but what's the sense of it?
Where does it lead?

The frail hand tightened on his and then was gone.
Haj Harun knelt in front of him and held him by the
shoulders, his face serious.

You're still young, Prester John. Don't you see it
leads nowhere? It's an end in itself.

But that's a hopeless way to do things.

No. As yet you have little faith but a time will come.

Faith are you saying? I was born with faith but it's
been going these years not coming, going and going
until it's gone now.

No, that can't happen.

But it did all right, she took it.

No, she gives it, she never takes it.

Oh Jaysus man, there you go again talking about
Jerusalem. This is a woman I'm referring to, a flesh
and blood woman.

I see.

Well then?

Faith never dies, Prester John. If you love a woman
you'll find her someday. In my time I've seen many
temples built on that mountain across the valley and
although they've all fallen to dust one still remains
and will always remain, the temple of the first king the
city ever had. Yes I'm frightened when I think of
Smyrna and what it may mean for tomorrow, but I
also know that Melchizedek's City of Peace can never
die because when that gentle King of Salem reigned
on that mountain so long ago, long before Abraham
came to seek him out and receive his blessing and
father the sons called Ishmael and Isaac in this land,
long before then Melchizedek had already dreamed
his gentle dream, my dream, and in so doing given
it life forever, without father, without mother, without

descent, having neither beginning of days nor end of life.

Who's that you're talking about now? You or Melchizedek?

Haj Harun smiled shyly.

We're the same person.

Go on with you, you're all mixed up.

Haj Harun laughed.

Do you think so? Come let's go back, she's waiting for us.

They started down the hillside, Joe stumbling and falling in the darkness, Haj Harun floating lightly along the rough path that he had followed innumerable times.

Bloody eternal city, thought Joe, looking up at the walls rising above them. Bloody marvel how he keeps it running, lurking up there on the Mount of Olives at sundown disguised as a broken-down Arab. Keeping watch he is, guarding the approaches, a former antiquities dealer for sure, old Melchizedek the first and last king spinning his city through the ages with no end in sight. Riots and mayhem to come, fearful of Smyrna but still trying to take the long view, as Stern once said.

Madness all right, that's what this place is, daft time spinning out of control, not meant for a sober Christian who just wants to make do with three squares a day and no heavy lifting and maybe a fortune on the side. But all the same who'd have thought a poor boy from the Aran Islands would one day be consulting in the shadows of Salem with the very same king who was handing out blessings here long before these bloody Arabs and Jews even existed with their bloody troubles?

19

Athens

*Life rich and full in the wine of
faraway places.*

❈

When Maud returned to live in Athens, Stern often
came to visit her in the small house by the sea. A
cable would arrive from somewhere and a few morn-
ings later she would be standing on the pier in Piraeus
waiting to meet his ship, Stern all at once leaning
over the rail above her shouting and waving, rushing
out to hug her in the clamor of travelers and banging
gangways, his arms overflowing with the presents he
had brought, masses of brightly colored paper tied
with dozens of ribbons for Bernini to unravel.

Back at the little house by the sea Bernini sat on the
floor working his way through the pile of parcels,
holding up each new wonder as he uncovered it,
amulets and charms and picture books, an Arab cloak
and Arab headgear, a model of the Great Pyramid
made of building blocks complete with secret tunnels
and a treasure chamber.

Bernini clapped his hands, Maud laughed, Stern
bounded into the kitchen reeling off the dishes he was
going to make for dinner that night, lamb in Arab
pastes and fish in French sauces, delicate pastries and
vegetables touched by heady spices and aspics of the
rainbow. She helped him find the pots and pans and
sat in a corner while he chopped and sniffed and

tasted, dashing a drop here and a pinch there and frowning judiciously, all the while carrying on a headlong account of scenes and anecdotes from Damascus and Egypt and Baghdad, exhilarating to Maud in the routine of her otherwise quiet life.

Toward the middle of the afternoon he opened the champagne and caviar and later they lit candles in the narrow garden to be near the sound of the waves as they savored his marvelous dishes, Stern still flooding the table with his stories from everywhere, extravagant costumes and ridiculous gossip and imagined conversations beguiling and raucous by turns, Stern leaping up to act the parts, standing on a chair and swinging his arms and smiling and sneaking along the wall, pointing and making a ludicrous face, tapping his glass, laughing and raising a flower.

Bernini came to say good-night and there was stillness for a while in the spring night of the garden, tender and softly relaxed as they lingered in the silence over their cognac, then gradually the talk swirled again reaching out to embrace forgotten moments, slipping back and forth through the decades in brilliant recollections, spinning its net in ever longer shadows until the whole world seemed to crowd around their circle of candlelight, brought there by Stern.

Sometime after midnight he took out his notebooks to show her his plans neatly arranged and outlined in detail, lists of meetings and supplies and schedules.

By the end of the summer, he said. Unquestionably by the end of the summer. It has to be, that's all.

A point here, another on this page. One two three four.

Orderly in black and white, to be ticked off by his finger from one to twelve. From a hundred to infinity. Foolproof plans. Yes by the end of the summer.

More cigarettes and more bottles uncorked, more

sparkling reminiscences and splendid sentiments in the flickering light as they went on to read poems to each other and quote words that spoke of suffering and grandeur, life rich and full in the wine of faraway places, in time returning through the candlelight under the stars by the sea where they wept and laughed and talked away most of the darkness, holding each other tightly when at the end of the night truly at peace with themselves, the hour so late they couldn't remember blowing out the candles and going inside, Stern snoring lightly on the couch and Maud just as quickly lost in sleep in the bedroom.

The next morning Stern had already left when she awoke but the note said he would be back by late afternoon with the makings of another feast. And so there would be another superb evening under the stars and then the following day they were walking down the pier in Piraeus once more, the brief hectic visit over.

In the summer he came several times and again in the clear mild evenings of autumn, piling the brightly colored packages in front of Bernini and conjuring up the banquets and scenes and memories from everywhere, spinning through the schemes in his notebooks. In his cabin they had a last glass of vodka before the ship sailed, Stern appearing confident and enthusiastic as always, his face flushed with the excitement of a new beginning, perhaps drinking a little more than he had the last time they parted, waving and smiling as the ship pulled away.

This time it was going to happen, whatever it was, by the end of the year. And when he came at Christmas he would say it was going to happen by Easter, and at Easter he would say by the end of the summer.

Always the same with Stern. It was always going to happen but it never did.

She went home and found Bernini playing with his new toys. She asked him if he liked them and he said Yes, very much. She wandered out into the garden thinking of Stern and the presents he brought, the expensive food and champagne.

She knew he had no money. She knew he had probably gone away with almost nothing in his pocket but he always insisted on doing it, on paying for it all himself and everything the best, imported, it was foolish, and taking taxis which was also foolish, she never used them herself.

But Stern did when he was with her, spending his money quickly, all at once, what little he had, he just couldn't be bothered with it because he was too busy living for the poetry of his ideas and the grand schemes that never came to anything. So warmly generous, so impractical and foolish, yet it was also sad in a way for she knew the poverty it represented.

She could never have done that even if she hadn't had the responsibility of Bernini. It just wasn't in her to squander enough for a month in two days and then go without the rest of the time as he did.

She also thought of his notebooks, the pages filled with neat handwriting, always new illusions deep at night when hope burned in the flame of a candle against the darkness. But the candlelight vanished at dawn and for him Easter would never come.

He knew that, yet the beautiful dreams, the unreal promises, were always there. Why? Why did he do it?

Suddenly she laughed. She had stopped in front of a mirror and was absentmindedly straightening her hair. The face in the mirror was wrinkled, the hair was gray. Where had it come from? Who was it?

Not her. She was beautiful and young, she had just been chosen for the Olympic skating team and was going to Europe. Imagine it. Europe.

She laughed again. Bernini looked up from the floor where he was playing.

What's so funny in the mirror?

We are.

Who's we?

Grown-ups, dear.

Bernini smiled.

I know that. I've always known that. That's why I think I'm not going to be one, he said, and went back to building the Great Pyramid.

When the Second World War broke out in Europe, Stern found her a job in Cairo. He was involved in various clandestine work and frequently away from Cairo, but when he returned they were always together. Now the long nights of talk and wine they had known in Athens before the war seemed far in the past when they drove out to the desert and sat silently beside each other under the stars, accepting the solitude, wondering what each new month might bring.

Stren had aged severely in the time she had known him, or perhaps it was just that she always remembered him the way he had appeared that first afternoon by the Bosporus in the rain, hunched and tall and massive beside the railing, his very bulkiness reassuring. Now the bulky shape had gone and his body was terribly wasted. He moved unsteadily with his mouth set in a thin painful line, his speech hesitant, his face ravaged and deeply marked, his hands often trembling.

In fact when Maud first saw him in Cairo, after a separation of nearly a year, she was so alarmed she went to see his doctor. The younger man listened to her and shrugged.

What can I say. At fifty he has the insides of an

eighty-year-old man. And there's his habit, do you know about that?

Of course.

Well then.

Maud looked down at the backs of her hands. She turned them over.

But isn't there something that can be done?

What, go back? No. Change? He could, but it would probably be too late anyway.

Change what, doctor? His name? His face? Where he was born?

Oh I know, said the man wearily. I know.

Maud shook her head. She was angry.

No I don't think you do know. I think you're too young to know about a man like him.

Maybe so. I was young once, I was only fifteen at Smyrna.

She bit her lip and lowered her eyes.

Please forgive me. I didn't know.

No, there's no reason why you should.

Two years passed before their last evening together. They had driven out to the desert near the pyramids. Stern had his bottles with him and Maud took a sip or two from the metal cup. Often she talked to keep him from depression but not that night. She sensed something and waited.

What do you hear from Bernini? he said at last.

He rubbed his forehead.

I mean about him.

He's fine. They say he liked to play baseball.

That's very American.

Yes and the school's just right for him, he'll learn a trade and be able to get along on his own someday. It's best for him to be over there now doing that and you know I appreciate it. But it still bothers me that you had to send him, when you have next to nothing yourself.

No that's unimportant, don't think about it. You would have done the same for someone, it just happened to be easier for me to get the money together.

He drank again.

Do you think you'll be going home, Maud, after the war?

Yes, to be near Bernini, but it will be strange after all this time. My God, thirty-five years. I can't call it home anymore, I don't have a home. And you?

He said nothing.

Stern?

He fumbled for the bottle, spilling what was left in the cup.

Oh I'll keep on here. It'll be very different after the war. The British and French are finished in the Middle East. There'll be big changes. Anything's possible.

Stern?

Yes.

What is it?

He tried to smile but the smile was lost in the darkness. She took the cup from his shaking hand and filled it for him.

When did it happen? she said quietly.

Twenty years ago. At least that's what I tell myself. Probably it was always there. Beginnings generally are. Probably it goes all the way back to the Yemen.

Stern?

No not probably. Why should I be telling you lies now? Why did I ever? Well you know why. It wasn't you I was lying to.

I know.

Always there, always. I was never a match for any of them. Ya'qub and Strongbow and Wallenstein, myself, fathers and sons and holy ghosts, it's confused but there's a reason why I keep thinking of that.

Anyway, I couldn't do it. I couldn't do any of the things they did. They were too much for me. The Yemen and a balloon, it was hopeless. But that other thing was there too. Twenty years ago was there too. It hasn't all been a lie.

What made you think of it tonight?

I don't know. Or rather of course I do. It's because I've never stopped thinking about it. Not a day has gone by. Do you remember me telling you how Strongbow died? Well it won't be that way with me. Not in my sleep.

Stern, we don't know those things.

Maybe not, but I do this time. Tell me, when did you first find out about the morphine?

That doesn't matter.

Tell me anyway, when?

Early on I suppose.

How?

I saw the black case once when you were sleeping over in Istanbul. I woke up one morning when you were still asleep and it was open on the floor beside you.

But you knew before then, didn't you. You didn't have to see the case to know.

I suppose so but what difference does it make?

None. I just wondered. I always tried hard to make it seem otherwise.

You didn't just *try*, Stern. You *did*.

He fell silent, lost somewhere. She waited for him to go on but he didn't.

Stern?

Yes.

You were going to tell me when it happened. What it was.

You mean when I like to think it was. What I've always told myself it was.

Well?

He nodded slowly.

Yes. It was called Smyrna. I'd arranged a meeting there. O'Sullivan Beare was going to meet Sivi for the first time. I haven't told you about Sivi before. He wasn't just what he appeared to be. The two of us worked together for years. From the very beginning in fact. He was a very close friend. The closest I've ever had except for you.

Then that day you saved my life by the Bosporus, the day we met, you had just been to see him?

Yes.

Christ, she whispered, oh what a fool. Christ, why didn't I think of it.

But Stern heard only the first word. Stern was someplace else, hurrying on.

Christ, you say? Yes he was there too. A small dark man younger than you see in the paintings. But the same beard and the same eyes. Carrying a revolver. He shot a man in the head. And the Holy Ghost was there carrying a sword. Weeping, half his body a deep purple. God himself? I didn't see him but he must have been there carrying something. A body or a knife. Everybody was there in that garden.

Stern?

Yes, a garden. Now when was that exactly.

Stern?

There was an animal sound deep in his throat.

Right at the very beginning of the new century, that's when it was. Right after the world of the Strongbows and the Wallensteins had died in the First World War. It couldn't survive the anonymous machine guns, their world, and the faceless tanks and the skies of poison gas that killed brave men and cowards equally, the strong and the weak all the same, the good and the bad together so that it no longer mattered who you were, what you were. Yes their world died and we had to have a new one and we got it, we got our new century in 1918 and Smyrna was its very first act, the prelude to everything.

Stern?

When, you say. Only twenty years ago and forever, and what a garden lay waiting for us then.

20

Smyrna 1922

*Stern picked up the knife, Joe
watched him do it. He watched
him take the little girl by her
hair and pull back her head. He
saw the thin white neck.*

❈

An Ionian colony said to have been the birthplace of
Homer, one of the richest cities in Asia Minor under
both the Romans and the Byzantines, second of the
seven churches addressed in the Book of Revelations
where John also called it rich and said that one day
it would know terrible tribulation, which it did when
Tamerlane destroyed it.

But now early in the twentieth century once again
prosperous with nearly half a million Greeks and
Armenians and Jews, Persians and Egyptians and
Turks and Europeans in their various costumes in-
dustriously pursuing trade and love, their beautiful
seaport surpassing all others in the Levant in the
bewildering flow of life's goods.

The Greeks and Jews and Armenians and Turks
still given to living in their separate quarters, but the
quarters having come to overlap in time and the rich
of every race finding their way into the opulent villas
of the European Quarter.

A city known for its fine wine and frankincense, its
carpets and rhubarb and figs and opium, the banks
of the streams thick with oleander and laurel and

jasmine, with almond trees and mimosa. Famous for
its devotion to music, its incessant musicales, particularly in love with the native orchestras that mixed
zithers and mandolins and guitars.

A people renowned for their addiction to cafés and
promenades, their fondness for the whispered dramas
emanating from backstreets and courtyards, the secret
dealings of love and commerce no less than the open
acting of the stage.

Renowned as well for their vast consumption of
wines and their insatiable desire to join more and
more clubs of every description where they could play
cards and gamble and eagerly devour the endless
dizzying tales of pleasure and intrigue, forever de-
lighted by the gossip that whirled an afternoon into
evening and softly spun away the tipsy buzzing hours
of night.

On the summit of the mountain the old Byzantine
fortress with the Turkish Quarter on its slopes, a maze
of alleys roofed by vines where men leisurely sucked
their hookahs beside fountains while professional
letter writers in the shadows composed rampant visions
of love and hate.

From the West chandeliers and crystal, from the
East caravans bringing spices and silks and dyes, bells
jangling on the packs of the loping camels. The narrow
waterfront was two miles long and lined by cafés and
theaters and elegant villas with quiet courtyards.
Strollers always knew when the train from Bournabat
was arriving because the air was suddenly filled with
jasmine, brought in great baskets by the passengers
for their friends in town.

Here Stern came at the beginning of September for
the meeting he had been planning since that spring,
the meeting where O'Sullivan Beare would be introduced to Sivi so the two of them could work directly
together.

On September 9 a creaking Greek caïque drew into

the harbor with several passengers on board, one an elderly wizened Arab and another a small dark young man in a ragged oversized uniform from the Crimean War. The caïque tied up at dawn, a Saturday, and even at that early hour the city seemed strangely subdued. O'Sullivan Beare saw a sign facing him across the quay, its black letters two feet high, a new film that had come to Smyrna.

LE TANGO DE LA MORT.

He nudged Haj Harun and pointed but the old man had already seen it. Without a word he backed away from the railing and pulled up his cloak to look at the great purple birthmark that curved from his face down over his entire body.

O'Sullivan Beare watched him uneasily, never having known the old man to take any notice of his birthmark. Yet now he was gazing at it intensely as if a map could be divined in the contours of its shifting colors.

What is it? whispered Joe. What do you see?

But Haj Harun didn't answer. Instead he straightened his rusting Crusader's helmet and stared sadly at the sky.

Two weeks earlier the Greek army facing the Turks two hundred miles away to the east, fighting for an expanded Greece after the collapse of the Ottoman Empire, had been thoroughly defeated. Yet at the end of August life was still going on as usual in the city. The cafés were crowded, the throngs moved slowly along the quays in the evening promenade. Porters bore loads of raisins and figs down to the docks. The opera house was sold out for the performances of an Italian company.

On September 1 the first wounded Greek soldiers

began to arrive by train, the cars so packed men lay on the roofs. All morning and afternoon the trains kept coming, the slumped bodies on top outlined by the setting sun.

The next day came soldiers less seriously wounded in trucks and handcarts, on mules and camels and horses, in lumbering chariots unchanged since Assyrian times. And then on succeeding days soldiers on foot, dragging each other, silent dusty figures stumbling toward a headland west of the city where their army was to be evacuated.

Lastly the refugees from the interior, Armenians and Greeks shuffling under their burdens. They camped in cemeteries and churchyards and those who couldn't find space camped in the streets, drawing their furniture around them. By September 5 thirty thousand refugees were arriving every day and now those who came were increasingly weary and humble, the very poor who limped with no possessions at all.

Finally the Greeks and Armenians in Smyrna began to understand. They boarded their shops and barricaded their doors. The crowds disappeared, the cafés closed.

The Greek general in command of the city had gone insane. He thought his legs were made of glass and refused to leave his bed lest they break. In any case he had no troops. The garrison had been evacuated along with the army. Kemal's Turkish forces had triumphed absolutely in the interior.

On September 8 the Greek High Commissioner announced that Greek administration of the city would end at ten o'clock that night. The harbor was filled with British and French and Italian and American warships ready to evacuate their nationals.

The advance Turkish cavalry rode into the city the next morning, well-disciplined and orderly, followed by infantry units marching in formation. All that Saturday, the day O'Sullivan Beare and Haj Harun arrived in the city, the Turkish forces kept pouring into Smyrna in their confusing array of uniforms, some wearing American army uniforms captured from the Russians.

Looting began quietly at dusk. Turkish soldiers entered deserted shops and sorted through the wares.

Turkish civilians carried out the first armed robberies. They came down from their quarter and held up Armenians and Greeks on side streets. But when they saw the Italian and Turkish patrols ignoring them they quickly moved to the larger stores, scooping up rolls of satin and stuffing them with watches.

Soon the Turkish soldiers had joined them and by midnight houses were being broken into with crowbars. There were some rapes and some murders but loot was still the primary concern. Murders were mostly done with knives so the Europeans wouldn't be alarmed by excessive rifle fire.

But by the following morning, Sunday, restraint was gone. Gangs of Turks raced through the streets murdering men and carrying off women and sacking Greek and Armenian houses. The horror was so great the Greek Patriarch of Smyrna went to the government house to plead with the Turkish general in command. The general spoke a few words to him and then appeared on a balcony as the Patriarch left, yelling at the mob to treat him as he deserved.

The mob swept up the Patriarch and carried him down the street to the barbershop of a Jew named Ishmael. He was ordered to shave the Patriarch but when that proved too slow they dragged the Patriarch back into the street and tore out his beard with their hands.

They gouged out his eyes. They cut off his ears. They cut off his nose. They cut off his hands. Across the street French soldiers stood guarding a French business concession.

Stern saw two Armenian children sneak out of their

ruined house dressed in their finest clothes. Once in the street they smiled and strolled arm in arm toward the harbor speaking loudly to each other in French.

A refugee woman in black carried her bleeding son on her shoulders, he so large and she bent so low his feet touched the ground.

An elderly Armenian made the mistake of unbarring his steel door to pass a letter to a Turkish officer. He was a wealthy merchant, he said, who had supplied Kemal's armies in the interior. The letter, signed by Kemal himself, guaranteed protection for him and his family.

The officer held the letter upside down. He couldn't read. He tore it up and his men stormed inside.

Stern at last reached Sivi's villa on the harbor. He went to the backdoor and found it hanging on its hinges. In the courtyard the old man lay crumpled on a flower bed, his head covered with blood. His French secretary, Theresa, was kneeling beside him.

It just happened, she said. They broke in, he tried to stop them and they beat him with their rifles. They're still inside, we have to get him out of here.

Stern struggled to pull the old man to his feet and all at once Sivi's eyes flew open. He raised his arm feebly and tried to strike Stern.

Sivi for God's sake, it's me.

I won't have it, he whispered. Get Stern here. We must fight back, call Stern.

His head fell forward onto his chest. The two of them dragged him across the courtyard and out into the alley. Theresa was remarkably calm although rifles were going off all around them. Stern was surprised at her control.

My convent training, she said.

In the alley Stern had to stop for breath. He propped Sivi against a wall and closed his eyes trying to think. A soft Irish voice spoke behind him.

The address checks out but what's this little game

here? Taken to robbing and kidnapping old men then?
Having a go yourself now that the Black and Tans
have set things up to have some Saturday night fun?

He turned and saw O'Sullivan Beare grinning, a
revolver tucked into his belt. With him was an elderly
Arab wearing an antique helmet. The Arab's face
went white but Stern didn't see that.

Help me carry him, we've got to move him to another house.

But before Joe could move, the elderly Arab jumped
forward, his face radiant.

If you will, my lord, allow me to help.

Jaysus, muttered Joe, what next. He can hardly
carry himself.

If you will, my lord, repeated Haj Harun ecstatically,
his eyes fixed on Stern.

Look, said Joe, I'll do the heavy lifting and you
guard us from the rear. We need a reliable warrior
back there to make sure some cutthroat of a Crusader
doesn't try to sneak up on us.

Indeed we do, said Haj Harun, stepping back and
proudly straightening his helmet, his eyes still on
Stern.

Between the two of them they managed to carry
Sivi up through the alleys away from the harbor.
Bodies were everywhere. A girl was hanging from a
lemon tree. They went in through the back of a
deserted house and laid him out on a couch. A trail
of blood ran across the floor to a cupboard. Joe looked
inside and quickly closed it. A corpse was stuffed in
the cupboard, a naked girl, one of her breasts cut off.

Theresa worked on the gashes in Sivi's head. She
seemed to see nothing else. Stern turned to O'Sullivan
Beare.

Where did you get the revolver?

The Black and Tans, where else. As usual they've
got the goods. An officer he must have been, the troops
carry rifles.

What happened to him?

A strange occurrence, I don't deny it. All I did was go up to him and salute and tell him I was reporting in for duty on the Crimean front, and what did he do but take one look at me and do a fast tumble. The medals it must have been, awed by all that brass I guess. Anyway he took such a dive he busted his head on the cobblestones before I could catch him. At least it seemed pretty well busted when I requisitioned his revolver so it wouldn't fall into the hands of some dangerous bloody belligerent.

Stern looked at him in disgust.

Go out front and see if we can reach the harbor. When it gets dark the fires will start.

That they will, general, that they certainly will. Come along, he added to Haj Harun, who stood rigidly in the doorway unable to take his eyes off Stern. At the front of the hall the old man gripped his arm.

What is it? whispered Joe.

But don't you know who he is? Once just before the war I saw him in the desert.

Hold it. Which war would we be talking about? The Mameluke invasion? The Babylonian conquest?

No no, the war that just ended, the one they call the Great War. Of course he doesn't recognize me.

Joe was about to answer that he bloody well knew who he was. He was the bloody fake of an idealist who had been trying to play father confessor to him for the last two years while he was smuggling useless rifles to countries that didn't exist and never would, who had gotten them into this mess in the first place by having them come to Smyrna to meet an ancient Greek queen who was now either deranged or dying. But he couldn't say any of those things and his face was respectful.

Saw him did you? Just before 1914 in the desert? In person and all?

286

Yes I truly did. I was on my annual haj and he deigned to manifest himself from the skies at dawn and speak to me.

Speaking you say? From the skies? Manifesting himself? Well that's an event by any account. And who might he have been then?

Haj Harun's lips quivered. Tears trickled down his cheeks.

God, he whispered in a hushed voice.

Joe nodded gravely.

Oh I see, the very article himself. What did he have to say?

Well I mentioned that I knew God has many names and each one we learn brings us closer to him. So I asked him if he would tell me his name that day and he did. Apparently, although it's been a total failure, he must have found some virtue in my attempt to defend Jerusalem over the last three thousand years.

Good, very good. What name did he give then?

Stern, whispered Haj Harun reverently. It was the moment in my life I will always cherish above all others.

O'Sullivan Beare staggered against the door and hung there.

Stern? Out of the sky? Stern?

Haj Harun nodded dreamily.

God, he whispered. Our most gracious Lord descending gently from the heavens.

Joe crossed himself. Jaysus, what's he talking about now and how did he learn his bloody name really?

They moved from house to house making their way toward the harbor. At last they came out in a side street beside it, or rather Joe did. Haj Harun seemed to have fallen behind. He waited and after a while the old man came creeping around the corner carrying a heavy sword.

What's that?

A Crusader's sword.

It looked like it might be. Just turn up did it?

It was on a wall in one of those houses we went through.

And what will you be doing with it then?

Haj Harun sighed.

Bloodshed is wrong, I detest it. But I remember how the Babylonians and the Romans were and I've been assigned to guard our party, so now as then I'll do my best to defend the innocent.

The fires didn't wait for darkness. Long before sunset whole streets were ablaze. When they got back to the house in the Armenian Quarter smoke already hung heavily over the city.

Well? said Stern.

We can get there, general commandant sir, but why we should want to I don't know. The Black and Tans have half the Irish nation down there beating the shit out of them. A bad lot they are, better not to mix with them unless you're standing at the right end of a cannon loaded with rusty nails. Now I grew up on the sea but I cast the vote of the Aran Islands this time for going straight overland.

We can't with him, whispered Stern, nodding at Sivi.

No problem there, said Joe, smiling and patting his revolver. I'll just find a mule and a cart that happen to be going our way.

But he's Greek, you fool.

So we'll cover him with a blanket. Or are you afraid they might take you for an Armenian? They might do that you know and then where'd you be? No place I guess, as bad off as the Irish nation. Ever seen the Black and Tans working themselves up for a session before? No I imagine you haven't, but I'll tell you this is just the beginning. Wait until night comes, that brings out the best in armed men working over an

unarmed populace. Night, that's the item, not afraid
of it are you? Couldn't be so could it? Not our very
own general in charge of building Middle Eastern
empires?

O'Sullivan Beare grinned and Stern took a step
forward. Boots slapped in the corridor. The door
banged open.

Two Turkish soldiers were pointing rifles at them.
Their eyes went to Theresa kneeling beside the couch.
One of the soldiers pushed Stern and O'Sullivan
Beare against the wall with his bayonet. The other
soldier grabbed Theresa by the hair and forced her
down over Sivi's unconscious body.

Don't move, she said coolly. They'll leave when
they've done what they want.

The soldier by the couch planted a knee in her back
and pulled open his trousers. Suddenly there was an
angry roar. The soldier with the bayonet slumped, his
head nearly severed. The soldier by the couch tried
to stand but Haj Harun was upon him just as quickly.
The sword sliced through his shoulder into his chest.

Something had happened to Haj Harun's birthmark.
In the gloom it had turned a richer and deeper purple,
much darker than O'Sullivan Beare had ever seen it.
Gone were the fainter patches, the varying shades,
the nearly invisible hues. His cloak had fallen to the
floor and he stood in the middle of the room naked
save for his loincloth, the long bloody sword by his
side, his head bowed.

For the Lord Himself, he murmured, shall descend
from heaven with the voice of His archangel Gabriel.

Stern and O'Sullivan Beare were still pressed against
the wall. Sivi lay unconscious on the couch. Theresa
was sprawled across him on her stomach, her skirt
ripped up the back to her waist. All at once she
shuddered and her eyes widened.

What's he talking about?

The two men by the wall came to life.

He thinks he's Gabriel now, whispered Joe. Gabriel revealed the Koran to the Prophet, he added for no reason.

Theresa turned from the Arab to the Irishman and it was as if she were seeing him for the first time, as if she hadn't seen any of them before or the horror around her until that moment. Somewhere inside her a blow shattered the strange calmness Stern had noticed from the beginning. She stared at the Irishman's thin face and long hair and dark searching eyes, especially his beard. The beard from the paintings in the convent of her childhood.

She was on her knees shaking, her arms over her head to protect herself. Her body jerked violently.

Who is that? she screamed and pitched forward on the floor, banging her head up and down on the boards. Stern seized her and she caught sight of Joe standing over her.

Who is that? she screamed again, choking from the blood streaming down her face. Stern slapped her and she fell in a heap, tearing at her chest. He pulled away her hands and held them.

Joe backed away until he was in the far corner. He was trembling and soaked with sweat.

Jaysus, he whispered.

Yes, said Stern quietly, and may it be your first and last time. Now you and the Arab take him, I'll take her. You follow and I'll do the talking.

Most of the alleys were already blocked by collapsed buildings. O'Sullivan Beare slipped on something soft and crashed into the cobblestones. His elbow cracked. He staggered to his feet, the arm hung slack. He couldn't move it. Change sides, he said to Haj Harun. They gripped Sivi under the arms and started off once more.

Did Stern know where he was going? They seemed

to be walking in circles, all the alleys looked the same. Stern tried the gate to a walled garden and pushed his way inside. He put Theresa down. The three men were exhausted.

Five minutes, said Stern.

The Arab went to stand by the gate. O'Sullivan Beare ripped the sleeve off his shirt to make a sling for his useless arm. From beyond the wall came a high-pitched wail.

For the love of God kill me before I burn.

Joe lurched out into the alley, the smoke so thick he could hardly see. The frail cry came again and now he made out the dull yellow of Haj Harun's cloak moving away from him. He followed, stumbling as best he could. The wail was closer. A decrepit old Armenian was feeling his way along a wall, unknowingly walking into the flames. His nose had been cut off, his eyes torn out. Strands of bloody tissue hung from the empty sockets.

Tears of blood. Immovable tears. Joe stopped.

Haj Harun's sword flashed, the old Armenian sank out of sight. Gently Joe took Haj Harun by the arm and led him back to the garden. The Arab was moaning and weeping in despair, his great sword trailing along behind him.

The Romans killed five hundred thousand of us, he whispered, but only the fortunate died right away. There were others, so many others.

Haj Harun wandered around the garden weeping, lost among the ruins. Flames burst overhead, smoke billowed down on them. Joe remembered his numb dangling arm and felt to see if it was still there.

He lay on his back gazing up at the rolling smoke, at nothing. He couldn't breathe anymore, he was sinking into a nightmare of shadows and hazy fiery timbers. Dimly Haj Harun's faded cloak floated across the sky as screams drifted through the nightmare, Sivi screaming he was a Greek from Smyrna, Theresa screaming *Who is that?* Stern was forcing some medicine down her throat and she was vomiting on him, he tried again but he'd already done that before with Sivi and what good did it do, they went on screaming anyway.

It didn't matter, nothing mattered, it must be night now because the smoke was darker and heavier, a thick blanket to sleep under. Already they must have been there for hours, Sivi and Theresa raving and Haj Harun wandering lost through the flowers, fires all around them and all of them strangling in the smoke, even Stern the great general. Stern could go to hell with his dreams, he was no better than anybody else, losing hold like the rest of them.

Field Marshal Stern? Generalissimo Stern? What rank was he taking in his make-believe empire? Noble shit and bloody ideals, as dazed as anybody else in the garden, you could see he'd never been starving and on the run from the Black and Tans.

Smuggling arms for what? Why bother? The Black and Tans would only be back again anyway. If you won today they'd be back tomorrow, they always came back and you couldn't hide forever, not in this world. Better to rest and not worry about it, close your eyes and let it come because it came anyway and there was nothing to stop it, nothing to do about it, coming by itself like the Black and Tans and tomorrow.

A savage pain. He'd slipped and fallen sideways on his broken elbow.

And there it was and Stern hadn't even seen it. Only Haj Harun was awake and guarding them, pathetic in his rusting helmet and tattered yellow cloak, his sword in the air, ready to charge the Turkish soldier who had come in through the gate and was aiming a rifle at his middle.

Why? He'd be dead before he took a step. For what? In the name of what?

Jerusalem of course. His beloved myth of a Jerusalem.

There he was again facing the Babylonians and the Romans and all the other innumerable conquering armies, and conquer they would but he'd still be there defending his Holy City in the flames and smoke, an old man weak from hunger in a ridiculous helmet and threadbare cloak, limping on spindly legs, tottering on visions of Prester John and Sinbad, humiliated and insulted and hopelessly confused, ready to charge once more. As he'd said the first time they ever met, When you're defending Jerusalem you're always on the losing side.

The Turkish soldier was laughing. O'Sullivan Beare shot him in the head.

Then Haj Harun was moving meekly among them calling them children, gathering them up and saying this wasn't the garden where they should rest.

The harbor, chaos. The waterfront two miles long, one hundred feet deep. On one side the Turks, on the other the water.

Five hundred thousand people there and the city burning.

Turks working the peripheries robbing and killing and taking girls. Horses' halters catching fire, the beasts charging through the crowds trampling bodies. The crowds so dense in places the dead remained standing, held up by the living.

Sivi and Theresa delirious, rising to scream, Haj Harun moving back and forth tying bandages and comforting the dying, holding old women and closing the eyes of rigid children in their arms. Stern leaving and returning, searching for an escape.

Now it was night, Sunday night. Flames in the blackness, shrieks in the blackness, hacked arms and legs in the blackness, baggage and old shoes.

A little girl lay beside Joe and he kept turning away from her. Long dark hair and white skin, a black silk dress, her face ripped open. He could see the small white teeth through the hole in her cheek. Eyes shut and lips shut, a wet stain on her chest where she had been stabbed and another below the waist, a black pool between her legs.

The moan was low but every time he turned away it fell on his back with a dreadful weight. How could he even hear it out here? He couldn't, it wasn't there.

A shoe on the cobblestones a yard away. Cheap, worn, the sole rubbed down to nothing, one stiff twisted shoe. How many hundreds of miles had it walked to get here? How many times had it been patched through the years to get here? How many years was that? How many hundreds of miles?

It was pressing on his back, he turned around. The eyes were still shut, the lips still shut. Small white teeth, stains, a black pool between her legs. Eight or nine years old and no one taking care of her. Alone here next to him. Why?

He looked at her shoes. Smooth black leather and new, not worn at all but caked with mud, especially the heels. Mud caked up the heels to her ankles where she had ground them into the earth when the soldiers were on top of her. How many soldiers? How long had it gone on?

Too many, too long. There was nothing anyone could do for her now. She'd be gone in a moment, gone in her black silk dress for Sunday. Sunday? Yes still Sunday.

Can't you hear what she's saying?

Stern's voice. He looked up. Stern was standing over him with a desperate face, exhausted, streaked with grime and blood. The eyes were hollow, he looked at the shoes. Old and not wearing well, he was surprised. Why a cheap pair like that for the great general? Old and not wearing well, Stern's shoes.

What?

Goddamn it, can't you hear what she's saying?

She wasn't saying anything, he knew that. She was just moaning, a soft heavy moan beside him that wouldn't go away. No, not beside him, around him. All around him and louder than the cries and shrieks. Stern was yelling at him again and he yelled back.

Answer me goddamn it.

No I can't hear it, I don't speak bloody Armenian.

Please. That's what she's saying. Where's your revolver?

Lost in the garden.

Take this then.

Stern dropped a knife in front of him and leaned over Theresa, over Sivi. He was fixing something under Sivi's head, a coat probably, it looked like a coat. He was forcing Theresa's mouth open and clamping a piece of wood between her jaws so she wouldn't swallow her tongue or bite it off. Always busy, Stern, always thinking of things to do. Busy bastard.

Where was Haj Harun? Had to keep an eye on the old man or he'd get lost. Always forgetting where he was and wandering off.

Over there, the yellow cloak kneeling beside a shadow. Was that where the new scream was coming from? What was the music? It sounded like music. And who was that man dancing up and down? No shoes at all, that one. Why was he dancing and where was his hair? Dancing and laughing up and down just like that, gone, laughing and dead, no shoes.

Where was the other shoe, the one that had walked hundreds of miles? It was right there a minute ago and now it was gone too. A body had fallen on it.

The soft moan, he turned. The fingers were broken, he hadn't seen that before. The hands were smashed and hanging the wrong way, backward. She must have tried to scratch them and they'd beaten her hands with their rifle butts, crushed them on the stones before stabbing her in the chest, stabbing and doing everything else while she was on her back in her black silk dress and her Sunday shoes.

A pain in his shoulder. Stern had kicked him. Stern was down beside him angry and yelling.

Well?

Well bloody what? Do your own work. I'm no bloody butcher.

Stern's eyes were afraid, he could see that too. He just wasn't the bloody terror he wanted you to think. Tall and strong all right and acting as if he were in charge and giving orders like some great general who'd been through all the wars, Stern the hero who knew what he was doing and had the money to do it and pretended to know all the answers, Stern the visionary who wasn't so much in charge as he wanted you to believe. Staring with those empty eyes, frightened they were too so the bastard might as well hear it again, arrogant and giving orders, a frightened fake of a general without an army, parading his ideals. Well there were none and the bastard could hear it again right to his face. Who did he think he was? Yell it again why not.

No good, Stern. Do it yourself for a change. I'm no butcher. Take your bloody cause of a kingdom come and shove it up your arse. Chase it, dream about it, do whatever you want with it but I'm not there. I'm not working for you or anybody else ever again and I'm not killing again, ever. Hear that, Stern? From now on you and the other fucking generals can do your own bloody killing. Hear it, Stern?

Flames in the sky, someone staggering out of a building, burning. Not a man or a woman now, just a heap burning after walking hundreds of miles to get here, walking all those years just to get here of all places, but then you couldn't see that far really, not here, you couldn't see more than ten yards but of course you didn't have to, here the universe was ten yards wide and there was nothing more to see after that.

Stern picked up the knife, Joe watched him do it. He watched him take the little girl by her hair and pull back her head. He saw the thin white neck.

The wet knife clattered on the stones beside him and this time he didn't look up. This time he didn't want to see Stern's eyes.

Not all the city was burning. Neither the Turkish Quarter nor the Standard Oil enclave was touched by the fire, which the Turks claimed later had been started by the retreating Christian minorities. But the American government argued that the fire was an accident, since the English insurance policies held by American tobacco merchants in Smyrna didn't cover acts of war.

From the quay overloaded little boats carried Greek and Armenian refugees out to the foreign warships that were there to protect and evacuate their nationals, but not authorized to evacuate anyone else lest the Turks be offended. When they came alongside the English warships and threw ropes over the rails, the ropes were cut. Soon the few boats had swamped and sunk.

People were pushed off the quay and drowned. Others jumped in to commit suicide. Still others swam out to the warships.

The English poured scalding water on the swimmers.

The Italians, anchored much farther out, took on board anyone who could swim that far.

The French launches coming into the quay took on board anyone who could say in French, no matter how badly, *I'm French, I lost my papers in the fire.* Soon groups of children were huddled around Armenian teachers on the quay learning this magical phrase.

The captain of an American destroyer turned away children at the quay, shouting *Only Americans*.

A small Armenian girl from the interior heard the first English words of her life while swimming beside the HMS *Iron Duke*.

NO NO NO.

From the decks of the warships the foreign sailors watched the massacre through binoculars and took pictures. The navy bands played late and phonographs were set up on the ships and aimed at the quay. Caruso sang from *Pagliacci* all night across a harbor filled with bloated corpses. An admiral going to dine on another ship was late because a woman's body fouled his propeller.

At night the glow of the fire could be seen fifty miles away. During the day the smoke was a vast mountain range that could be seen two hundred miles away.

While the half-million refugees went on dying on the quay and in the water, American and English freighters went on shipping tobacco out of Smyrna. Other American ships waited to be loaded with figs.

A Japanese freighter arrived in Piraeus packed with refugees, having thrown all its cargo overboard in order to carry more. An American freighter arriving in Piraeus with some refugees was asked to go back for another load, but the captain said his cargo of figs was overdue in New York.

And on the Greek island of Lesbos, the strangest admiral in history was about to launch his fleet.

He had arrived in Smyrna only two weeks before the Turks marched into the city, a Methodist minister from upstate New York who came to work in the YMCA. When the massacre began both his superiors were on vacation so he went to the Italian consul, in the name of the YMCA, and persuaded him to commandeer an Italian freighter in the harbor to carry refugees to Lesbos. He went with the freighter, hop-

ing to bring it back, and in Lesbos found twenty
empty transport ships which had been used to evacuate the Greek army from the mainland. He cabled
Athens that the ships had to be sent at once to
evacuate refugees from Smyrna, signing the cable
ASA JENNINGS, AMERICAN CITIZEN.

The reply came in a few minutes.

WHO OR WHAT IS ASA JENNINGS?

He answered that he was the chairman of the
American Relief Committee in Lesbos, not adding that
he was the only American on the island and that there
was no such thing as a relief committee of any kind.

The next reply was longer in coming. It asked
whether American warships would defend the trans-
ports if the Turks tried to seize them.

It was now September 23, exactly two weeks after
the Turkish army had entered Smyrna. The Turks
had said that all refugees had to be out of Smyrna
by October 1.

Jennings had been sending in code. On that Saturday
afternoon he cabled an ultimatum to Athens. He said,
falsely, that the American navy had guaranteed protection. Falsely, that the Turkish authorities were in
agreement. Lastly, that if the Greek government didn't
release the ships at once he would send the same cable
uncoded, so that Athens would stand accused of
refusing to save Greek and Armenian refugees who
faced death within the week.

He sent the cable at four o'clock in the afternoon
and demanded a reply within two hours. A few
minutes before six it came.

ALL SHIPS IN AEGEAN PLACED UNDER YOUR COMMAND
TO REMOVE REFUGEES FROM SMYRNA.

An unknown man who was the boys' work secretary
of the YMCA in Smyrna had been made the com-
mander of the entire Greek fleet.

Jennings sailed twice and brought back fifty-eight thousand refugees. The English and American fleets also began to evacuate refugees and by October 1 two hundred thousand had been taken away. By the end of the year nearly one million refugees had left Turkey for Greece bringing epidemics of typhus and malaria, trachoma and smallpox.

The estimate of deaths in Smyrna was one hundred thousand.

Or as the American consul in Smyrna said, *The one impression I brought away from there was utter shame in belonging to the human race.*

Or as an American schoolteacher in Smyrna said, *Some people here were guilty of unauthorized acts of humanity.*

Or as Hitler said a few days before his panzer divisions stormed into Poland to begin a war, *Who after all speaks today of the annihilation of the Armenians? The world believes in success alone.*

Stern eventually found them a way out. They set sail at night in a small boat, Sivi and Theresa uneasily asleep in the bunks below, fitfully stirred by their own mutterings, Stern and O'Sullivan Beare slumped on deck against the cabin, Haj Harun in the bow where he could keep a steady lookout on the calm sea.

The few waves rose and fell quietly and only one of the travelers was awake that night and still awake at dawn, untroubled by the dreams that haunted his companions. For unlike them he was going home and his home never changed.

They might weave slaughter in the streets but what was that in the end? The other weaving also never ceased, the weaving of life, and when they burned one city another was raised on the ruins. The mountain only grew higher and towered ever more majestically above the plains and the wastes and the deserts.

Haj Harun looked down at his birthmark. It was faded now and indistinct, once more an obscure tracing of darkness and light and shifting patterns, a map without boundaries. He gazed back at the two men sleeping on the deck. He listened to the agonized sounds from below and shook his head sadly.

Why didn't they understand?

It was so clear.

Why couldn't they see it?

In the early gray light he turned to face east, happy and more. He adjusted his helmet, carefully he straightened his cloak. Any moment now it would appear and he wanted to be ready, to be worthy of that glorious sight.

Solemnly he waited. Proudly he searched the horizon for a glimmer of his Holy City, the worn sturdy walls and the massive gates, the domes to be and the towers and minarets softly radiant and indestructible, eternally golden in the first light of day.

21
Cairo 1942

A gesture. A photograph. To die.

✶

Thus Stern's voyage finally came to an end in the desert not far from Cairo in the first light of another dawn, sitting with Maud after they had talked all night.

There were a few other things after that, he said. Perhaps you'd like to hear them.

No it's all too much. No more anything now.

But it has to be now and anyway, these are good things. After we met that first time in Turkey I went to see Joe in Jerusalem. I told him the real reason why you'd left him in 1921, because you were afraid of losing him. Because you loved him so much and were afraid of losing that love the way you always had before in life.

Don't Stern. It's too long ago.

No listen, he understood that. He said he couldn't go back but he understood it. Then we talked about the Sinai Bible. He'd been searching for it for the last twelve years, right up until 1933, it had become his whole life. Of course I already knew that, what I told him was where to look. In the Armenian Quarter.

So you always knew it was there.

Yes.

Yet in all that time you never looked for it there yourself.

No, I couldn't. I never felt it was mine to find.

Anyway after I talked to him he said he was going to
give up the search and leave Jerusalem.

Why?

It had to be because of what I'd told him about you.
Because time tricks us and he'd never stopped loving
you despite what he said. It wasn't really the Sinai
Bible he wanted, you know that. And all that talk
about money and power and his anger toward me, his
hatred even, especially at Smyrna, that wasn't really
him. Once years ago we discussed it, I remember it
perfectly. It was a Christmas Eve and we were in an
Arab coffee shop in the Old City. It was snowing and
the streets were deserted, before Smyrna when we
were still friends, when he used to come to me for
advice. He brought it up and I talked to him about it
and it was the first time he ever got angry at me. Of
course I didn't have any idea who the woman was
who had left him but I did know he was fooling
himself, and that's why he broke with me after that,
because he knew I knew and it shamed him. So his
resentment grew, that's all, precisely because we had
been close before. He didn't dare trust anyone then,
he went back to being alone in the mountains on the
run. Anyway, after I saw him in 1933 he went out and
gambled away everything he had. He wanted to lose
it. Did you know he'd become very rich?

I'd heard that.

Yes, all those incredible schemes of his. Well he
deliberately lost it all in a poker game with two wild
characters, over a million pounds, but that's another
story. Now listen to this. He went to Ireland to dig up
his old U.S. cavalry musketoon in the abandoned
churchyard where he'd buried it before he became a
Poor Clare. He took it to the vacant lot in Cork where
he'd sat in rags before he'd left the first time. He
picked another Easter Monday to do that and he sat
there all afternoon listening to the sea gulls and
looking at the three spires of St Finnbar's, and at the

end of the afternoon he decided he'd leave again. As he put it in his letter, he felt he had finally come to terms with the Trinity. So he shipped out to America, you'll never guess where.

The Southwest?

Yes you know him all right, he wanted the desert, he was still thinking of that month you'd spent together in the Sinai. It was New Mexico he went to. To an Indian reservation eventually. He passed himself off as a Pueblo and before long became the chief medicine man on the reservation.

Maud smiled.

Joe? A medicine man?

She gazed shyly at the sand.

I don't think I ever mentioned it but he was always fascinated by the idea that I had an Indian grandmother. He used to ask me about her all the time. What she did, what she was like, that kind of thing. I don't know what he imagined but his face was like a little boy's at those times.

Suddenly she looked away. Go on, she said.

Well that's who he is. He sits in a wigwam with a blanket around him staring at the fire and muttering in Gaelic, which they take to be some language of the spirits. He keeps the old musketoon at his feet and claims it was his cannon in his private wars against the white man. Interprets dreams and divines the future. The revered and greatly respected shaman of the Pueblos.

Maud laughed.

Dear Joe. I was so foolish and he was too young to understand. So long ago.

Wait, there's more. He keeps an old book in his lap which he pretends to consult when the Indians ask him questions, but of course he can't read a word of it. He makes up his stories as he goes along and whether they're prophecy or history no one can say because the book's so old, three thousand years old in

304

fact. The tales of a blind man written down by an imbecile.

Maud stared at him and this time Stern also smiled.

It's true. He has it.

But what? How?

Well it seems a few years after he left Jerusalem his Arab friend found it and sent it to him. As to how and why the Arab found it, that must be another story too. But that's where it is now. In 1933 the British Museum bought Wallenstein's forgery from the Soviet government for one hundred thousand pounds, and in 1936 Haj Harun sent the original to a wigwam in New Mexico, where it rests in the lap of the chief medicine man of the Pueblos.

Maud sighed.

Well at last. Dear Joe.

She gazed at the sand lost in the memory of that month on the shores of the Gulf of Aqaba. The most beautiful moments she had known in life and so brief. So long ago.

She looked up. It had been there just on the other side of the Sinai, not so far away really. And the sparkling water and the bursting sunsets, the hot sand beneath their bodies through days without end and the numberless stars over nights without end, love and the all-healing sea, love and the solitude of the desert where the two of them had reached for the fire of the sand, she could feel its heat now when she closed her eyes.

But no, she couldn't feel it, too long ago. Now the sand was cold beneath her fingers. She heard a rattling sound, Stern's bottle against the rim of his cup. She took them from him and filled it for him. She put her arms around him.

It's over, he said simply. Finished. Done.

Don't say that, Stern.

Well not quite, you're right. There are still a couple of things left to do. After the war you'll go to America to be with Bernini and someday you'll see Joe again, of course you will. But as for me I'll never leave that hillside in the Yemen where I was born. Ya'qub was right after all. I'll never leave it.

She hung her head. There was nothing to say. Stern managed to laugh.

Simple in the end, isn't it. After all the struggling and trying to believe, the wanting to believe, two or three things sum it up and say it all. A gesture. A photograph. To die.

Clumsily he lurched to his feet and threw the empty bottle toward the new sun on the horizon, a gesture Joe had once made on the shores of the Gulf of Aqaba long ago against the darkness, this time made against the light. Then he took her camera and framed a picture of her between the Sphinx and the pyramids, clicking the shutter on their love, Maud robust and smiling for him on their final day, their time together ended in the lure of a Holy City, the lure of the desert, a weaving now within the bright somber tapestry of invincible dreams and dying days they had shared over the years with others, a tapestry of lives that had raged through vast secret wars and been struck dumb by equally vast silences, textures harsh and soft in their guise of colors, a cloak of life.

A gesture then, a photograph now, a cloak thread-bare and resplendent from century to century. And the unsuspecting weavers of the cloak, spirits despised and triumphant, threads to the tapestry and names to the sands and seas, souls for recollection in the whispers of love that had come to weave the chaos of events into a whole and the decades into an era.

Love gentle and kind and ferocious, rich and starved and hallucinatory, damned and diseased and saintly. Love, the bewildering varieties of love. That and only that able to recall the lives lost in the spectacle, the hours forgotten in the dream.

Hopes and failures given to time, demons pressed

into quietude, spirits released to memory in the chaotic book of life, a repetitious and contradictory Bible suggesting infinity, a Sinai tapestry of many colors.

And so that evening with a quarter of a grain of morphine steadying his blood Stern walked through the sordid alleys of Cairo to his last meeting, entering the bar and sitting on a stool and beginning to whisper to his contact who couldn't decide whether he was an Arab or a Jew, giving instructions for a secret shipment of arms to somewhere in the name of peace.

Tires screeched outside and there were shouts and curses and drunken laughter. The man beside him glanced nervously at the curtain separating them from the street but Stern didn't turn to look, he went on talking.

The young Australians had fought in the disastrous battle of Crete and survived the fall of the island, survived in the Cretan mountains through the winter starving and cold, planning to escape to Egypt in the spring, which they had done by paddling a rowboat across the Libyan Sea. And now out of the hospital with their wounds healed and false arms and legs in place of lost ones, they were out drinking and fighting and victoriously celebrating life.

Shouts. Men scuffling and yelling in the street. Laughter. *Bloody wogs.* The shabby curtain flying back and something lobbing in through the open door but no one moving in the room. No one knowing what it was except Stern.

Stern hit the man beside him and saw the astonished expression on the man's face as he went crashing backward across the floor, away from the hand grenade slowly sailing through the air.

But to Stern at that moment it wasn't a hand

grenade at all but a no longer distant cloud high above the Temple of the Moon, a drifting memory in the desert of dim pillars and fountains and waterways, mysterious places where myrrh grew, the ruins of his youth.

Blinding light then in the mirror behind the bar, sudden death merging the stars and windstorms of his life with darkness in the failure of his seeking, bright blinding light in the night sky at last and Stern's once vast vision of a homeland for all the peoples of his heritage gone as if he had never lived, shattered as if he had never suffered, his futile devotion ended on a clear Cairo night during the uncertain campaigns of 1942 when the eternal disguise he wore to his last clandestine meeting, his face, was ripped away and thrown against a mirror in the half-light of an Arab bar, there to stare at a now immobile landscape fixed to witness his death forever.

NOBEL PRIZE WINNER

Saul Bellow

Humboldt's Gift

**THE PULITZER
PRIZE-WINNING
#1 BESTSELLER**

"*Bellow's triumph...it actually breathes!*"
CHICAGO TRIBUNE

"*A major artist...a masterly novel—wise,
challenging, and radiant.*"
NEWSWEEK

"*Rowdy, vibrant, trenchant, stimulating, and
funny...the truly best novel of the year.*"
BOSTON GLOBE

AVON

38810/$2.25

HG 4-78

THE BIG BESTSELLERS
ARE AVON BOOKS

A novel of great passion and eloquent rage by
"ONE OF THE BEST LIVING WRITERS."
Playboy

LANCELOT

THE NEW NATIONAL BESTSELLER BY

WALKER PERCY

"A complete, living and breathing novel . . . the best
by an American since HUMBOLDT'S GIFT."
Saturday Review

"Don't miss it . . . a devastating novel."
New York Daily News

*Coming soon from Avon Books, Walker Percy's
beloved comic and romantic novels, THE LAST
GENTLEMAN and LOVE IN THE RUINS.*

 AVON 36582 $2.25